THE CARVED KNIVES SERIES

THE MARAUDERS

THE CARVED KNIVES SERIES

THE MARAUDERS

BOOK II

GARY ERWIN

TATE PUBLISHING
AND ENTERPRISES, LLC

Published by Tate Publishing & Enterprises, LLC
127 E. Trade Center Terrace | Mustang, Oklahoma 73064 USA
1.888.361.9473 | www.tatepublishing.com

Tate Publishing is committed to excellence in the publishing industry. The company reflects the philosophy established by the founders, based on Psalm 68:11,
"The Lord gave the word and great was the company of those who published it."

Book design copyright © 2016 by Tate Publishing, LLC. All rights reserved.
Cover design by Lauren Brown
Interior design by Mary Jean Archival

Published in the United States of America

ISBN: 978-1-68164-510-0
1. Fiction / Action & Adventure
2. Fiction / Fantasy / General
16.01.04

This book is dedicated to the following people and family, to whom I wish to express my heartfelt thanks and appreciation:

My wife Sandra, our daughters, Emily and Natalie, and our son Jake for all that I put them through during the writing of this book.

My sister Debbie, who's proofreading and initial editing skills are so far superior to any I could ever dream of having, and for having to listen to me cry as she showed me so many mistakes and changes.

I would also like to thank my many fans for your support. To you, I say this:

Enjoy your journey through my world.

Contents

Excerpt from the last chapter of book 1:

Cytar stopped when he saw Gondal and signaled to Macelar. Macelar rode on into the camp to alert the leaders of the party's approach. After letting the camp know of the party and the large amounts of meat and plants, Macelar rode out to the edge of camp with the camp leader, Sandole, and signaled them to come in.

Sandole watched as the thirteen riders and many extra loaded horses approached. "I am glad you rode ahead to warn me, Macelar. Had I seen this group approaching the camp without warning, it would have caused a panic."

"We met the Goyets the same way and sent a messenger ahead to the last Dolnii camp. At the Dolnii Gap Camp, someone saw us doing the hunt before coming into that camp. They met us with an armed group as we were butchering, but the leader of their Mountain Camp was with us and he rode out to meet them."

"Why such a large group traveling together?"

"We travel in troubled times, my friend. You should call a meeting so we can bring everyone here up to date. Are there now, or have there been any strangers around lately?"

"Not really strangers. There have been a few traders through, but I knew them all."

"Good, now we must keep a watch for any to appear."

As Cytar led the party into camp, Sandole showed him where to take the horses for unloading. Those who recognized Sandole waved to him as they rode past.

Clartan leaped from his horse and took a deep breath while slapping his chest.

Barthal watched him and grinned at his youthful exuberance. "Very good, Clartan, we have been here all of three seconds, and you have already made me feel like an old man. You must be proud of yourself?"

"Come on, old man, I will help you down," laughed Clartan and held up a hand to Barthal.

"Get out of my way, squirt, before I decide to make you too sore to move." Barthal slowly stepped down and groaned. What he did next surprised Clartan. With lightning speed, Barthal spun and wrapped an arm around Clartan's neck, held him a moment, and said, "Have I told you recently just how much I like you?" Then Barthal ruffled Clartan's hair with his free hand and waited for an answer before letting him go.

"Not today, you haven't."

"Now I have, want to make something of it?"

Clartan threw both arms around Barthal's neck and hugged him as he laughed loudly. "Yes."

Marcina winked at Antana then said, "All right, children, we still have to unload."

Clartan released Barthal and grinned. Barthal jumped to Marcina and, grabbing her up in a giant hug, spun her around. Other than his own daughter, Marcina had always been one of his favorite Scytan girls. He was a little partial to the female children because of his own daughter, though he showered much attention on all of the children when he came into one of the camps to trade. Marcina had always shown herself to be a little more collected in how she went about daily tasks. Yes, he had grown very fond of her during her lifetime.

After the food was all stored, the traveling gear had to be put away, and the horses needed tending.

As Cytar and Marcina walked to the lodge they were to stay in, they caused quite a row with Dac following her and Pixie following him.

"*Cytar!*"

Cytar turned toward the scream and saw Torena racing toward him. Declon walked up from behind Cytar and joined them.

Torena jumped into his arms and almost smothered him with kisses. Then she reached over and grabbed Declon because it had been a little over a year since she had seen him.

Torena was more than a head shorter than Cytar, yet she dominated her two massive brothers. She had tears flowing freely down her face, which did nothing to hide just how pretty she was. Her face had a slight bit more of an oriental appearance than the men's, though she still showed her European linage also.

Cytar turned her to Marcina. One look and Torena knew this was her new sister, even as she recognized her. "Marcina!" she cried before Cytar could speak and hugged the young woman.

"So you are now my sister? I think this is wonderful." Cytar and Declon looked at each other and shook their heads. Torena had done it again; she had realized the truth of matters before they could tell her.

"Guess what he named his daughter," Declon said to her.

Torena looked at Cytar as she thought. Suddenly a smile spread across her face and she squealed, "There is only one name that comes to me, Shalela."

"I guess maybe I have always used that name a lot more than I thought. I just never realized it before."

Marcina held out Shalela for Torena to hold. Torena took the infant and inspected her thoroughly before noticing how closely a horse and a wolf surrounded her. "With this much protection, I see you will never have to worry about anything hurting you," Torena told the child as she touched her little cheek with a finger.

Torena looked from the horse to the wolf and back as she smiled and asked them if she passed their test. Pixie bobbed her head up and down while Dac licked her hand. Midnight poked out her head from the pouch she was in and also licked Torena.

"Another one, well, hello to you too."

"This is Pixie, my horse that refuses to acknowledge that fact, this is Dac, and this is Midnight, Shalela's personal guard."

"Will Pixie be staying with you or the horses?"

"Torena, do you remember Poacoe?" asked Declon.

"Yes, the little fox that used to sleep with Cytar and would follow him everywhere?"

"I think Poacoe's spirit is in this horse. She acts just like little Poacoe did."

"I remember her. No wonder Pixie felt so familiar to me."

Cytar turned to Pixie before asking, "Poacoe, are you in there?"

Pixie shook her head no, causing everyone to laugh.

As a friend brought up a small toddler, Torena took her and handed her to Cytar. "Sayta, meet your Uncle Cytar. This is Sayta, my daughter. I would introduce you to my mate, Ramoar, but he is out fishing right now."

"Hello, little niece of mine. I am glad to meet you."

"You have grown since I last saw you, little one," Declon told Sayta.

"I still do not understand why you ran off last summer. I have missed you. Where did you go?"

"Come, we must put this down and then we can talk more comfortably." Declon took off into the guest lodge.

Torena put her hands on her hips and smiled her knowing smile as she slowly shook her head while staring after him.

As the others followed him into the lodge, Barthal sang out, "Cytar, you have got to figure out how to keep that horse outside."

"I am open to all suggestions, Barthal. No one we have stayed with has had a setup similar to the one in Snow Camp, and you remember how much of a challenge it was there."

"That is the most perplexing horse I have ever seen. Yes, I know and even there you spent half the winter sleeping in the horse shelter."

Declon and Torena looked at each other and both spoke at the same time, "Poacoe."

Cytar asked for someone to go and get Marselac and Jodac to come join them. They arrived with some of Marselac's Gondal family, and Cytar introduced Marselac and Jodac to Torena.

Marselac told her his mother was Maissee whom Torena knew. A messenger was sent to get Maissee and bring her here to meet new relatives. Word was also sent to Delphinia and Densee of new relatives.

Soon everyone came to meet the new relatives. Only Locar and Ramoar were gone to fish. Even Macelar and the other three traders from Gondal had brought their families to meet the new arrivals. Torena was told of Hantiss, Snow Camp, and the Scytan. Eventually, Sabortay walked in, laughing, and said he had wondered what had happened to half of his camp members. He told them that he would appreciate it if everyone would move to the large ceremonial area so that the rest of the camp could join the gathering and hear the news brought by those newly arrived.

Those of the trading party that were not known to the local people were introduced, and Cytar gave his invitation to them to visit the Kychee, just as he had at every camp before. Then Macelar told of the Sarain attacks on the Scytan and the two on the Dolnii. He then warned about the vision Marcina had about the trouble coming even this far and how the attacks always came without warning.

Then all the other news, how Marselac's Scytan family fared, of hearing about Torena and Ramoar mating and her having a daughter, and how the Goyets were getting along. Declon told of the Bodus people living in the small fishing village far north of here, even farther than the Goyet caves.

Cytar told of his long journey and showed his bow and arrows. He told them both Declon and Torena knew how to make them.

Hunts were described, along with fishing in the streams and rivers. Cytar told of how Zodar had actually come to Gondal once long ago. The night was long, but everyone sat and devoured every bit of information. The animals were discussed, and Cytar had to explain about Pixie, followed by some of the others telling of his exploits with the horse in times past.

Antana gave a welcome to all to visit the Dolnii in her name and those of the three leaders she had met with on the journey. She assured them Meadow Camp would honor the invitation also. Then she told them of listening to Cytar and Declon speak of people even farther from her home to the east than Gondal was to the west and how small she felt as she sat listening, then Cytar telling her of the vast lands far to the south. The children sat wide-eyed as they listened to her, and suddenly, she knew how she must have looked. Antana laughed as one wide-eyed young girl said, "Wow, you live so far away."

Nodding to her, Antana said, "Would you like to know something?"

The girl nodded.

Antana pointed to Marcina and said, "She came from the Scytan people, and they live farther away to the east than I did with my Dolnii people. She had to pass through the lands of the Sarain people to get to the lands of my people. You know Torena? She is of the Kychee who are from the other Far-Reaching Waters even farther away to the east. She met the Cheen people and the Kytain people before getting to the lands of the Scytan people. And I had to pass through the lands of the Goyet people before getting here."

All the children looked first at Marcina then at Torena with open mouths. By seeing three different women at one time, each from even farther away, they began to get the smallest idea of just how far *away* really meant. In fact, many of the adults were getting their first real idea of how far some of these people traveled before getting here. They were impressed at how well this young woman was explaining the distances to the children.

Clartan told of meeting Cytar and the fun he had watching Jilantia and Charlene trying to seduce him and how easily he made them look silly. He told of the leopard cubs and watching Cytar introducing the cubs to the horses.

Cytar got Marselac's attention and both stood up and said, "Oh my!" The two men had fun watching everyone trying to figure out why they had said that and why Clartan had suddenly gotten so flustered and turned red.

Antana gave them with a questioning look.

"Come to think of it, Marselac, I do not recall him saying that again after the Summer Trades."

"I do not either, now that you mention it. I guess it was just a boyhood thing." Both were speaking loudly enough for many of the people to hear them, but looking at Antana.

1

Get Ready for the Marauders

Torena ran up to the fire where Cytar was eating. "Cytar, the fishing boats are back. Come meet Ramoar."

Cytar and his family, consisting of his mate, child, horse, and two wolves, all followed Torena through the camp to the piers where boats were docking. The water was pure shimmering beauty illuminated by the late evening sunset.

Ramoar saw his mate and started toward her, at first with eyes only for her, only to become intrigued as he noticed the oddly mixed group she was with. Was that a wolf next to his daughter? How could a horse stand quietly next to a wolf, and why was a horse next to the piers instead of out with the other horses? He stopped just short of his mate as his little daughter put her arm around the wolf.

Torena saw him watching Sayta with her arm around the wolf and laughed. "Welcome home, my love. We have much to tell you and Locar."

Torena was helping Declon with building the bows that he had decided were needed. First, Declon had built a very strong laminated bow for his own use. When it was finished, he gave his other weaker bow to Torena. Then the two of them started building composite bows. Cytar joined them, and soon, many new bows were started.

Building a proper composite bow took a very long time, but working as a team, many bows could be under construction at the same time.

Apopus and Clartan decided to add their help and the camp toolmaker, Dartez, was included to learn the art of becoming a first-class bowyer. His two apprentices were also included.

Barthal and the other traders that had made the trip collected all the bows they had made and brought for trade and set up an archery field where they were training the camp members to use the bows. With the new bows that were coming, the trade bows were better suited for training purposes.

Apopus still preferred the laminate bows because they were so much faster to build. He sat with Dartez and learned the man originally came from farther south past the range of mountains, and then west along the coast. His camp had also been a very small fishing camp, and he wanted to find a camp with a better selection of women to choose from to find a mate. He had found her here.

Apopus showed Dartez his personal laminated bow and explained how it was made. Dartez decided to work on both types to see which he liked better and to learn to make both. Soon, Apopus and his group had several first quality laminated bows ready. The bellies were made using wood rather than horn, but still held incredible power. Declon showed them how to wrap the "finished" bow with leather to increase the power and to help hold it together more firmly.

Laminated bows were much straighter than the composite bows with recurved ends. Declon explained that laminated bows could also be made with recurve ends and that the recurve ends would add more strength to the bows, and that they could also have horn bellies if the bowyer so desired. Apopus still thought the process would take too long. Of course, he did look at the construction time through a trader's perspective, faster meant more profit. Straight was faster than taking the time to steam curves into the ends, and a proper wooden belly was far faster than one made of horn. Clartan tended to like the recurved better, but while working with Apopus, straight was fine.

Cytar stopped more bows from being started when it was found that there were at least three bows for every man, woman, and child in the camp and over two hundred arrows for every bow.

Sandole began to worry about the many caves of the Ghaunt people about five days ride to the southeast. Cytar had shown both his arrow quiver with the different pockets and his spear quiver, complete with atlatl sleeve, to the local leather workers. Quivers for both soon appeared in abundance.

Rahfaul and another young man from the camp had both excelled with the bow and were given the task of taking two bows with full quivers to each of the caves and give some quick instructions on how to use them. They were also to warn all the caves of the possibility of being attacked by the Sarain. They were supplied with many extra arrows to use in the training. The caves could send people to Gondal to get training on how to build quality bows. A few sent here could learn and take the knowledge back to share with all of the caves there.

Snow was on the ground left, from the first storm of the year, but it was melting. Rahfaul and his companion returned with news of a very small cave that had been all but wiped out. There was only one survivor, an older boy, and he had come to one of the network of caves to tell his sorrowful tale. He had been out hunting rabbits and saw the marauders attack the cave. Instead of running to the cave and being killed, he had shown enough thoughtfulness to go for help instead.

The marauders had dressed strangely and spoke with a language he did not know. By the time, the other cave could mount a rescue party, all at the small cave were dead and the marauders were gone. All of the useful items such as—tools, food, and clothing—were gone as well. All of the caves were alerted and would be ready for the marauders next time. Rahfaul also informed Sandole that the bows had been well received.

They made love with a violent fierceness, and Cytar understood Marcina was missing her home. After finishing, he held her and stroked her hair, gently kissed her, and whispered soothing love talk to her. Soon, she relaxed and slept.

Cytar thought of Nickotian and how much he would enjoy getting his hands on that piece of slime again. He would put an end to her night terrors if only he could get hold of the Sarainian.

As the snow cleared, he took Marcina out to some local areas where many birds gathered. He had made a throwing stick for her, and together, they began to collect birds each day. By moving from one hunting location to another, they found many birds to put into the storage bins where they would stay frozen for the entire winter if needed. The hunting also helped Marcina to sleep.

Luckily, the fishermen had brought in enough fish to help carry the camp through the winter. Cytar, however, was not satisfied and led a hunting expedition that also brought in enough meat for an extended winter. Macelar had known of a good location to find late-season plants and his foraging party brought back an enormous quantity of vegetation. The camp would eat well this winter, no matter if the cold held on for a long time.

Plenty of hides had been taken to make into clothing, bedding, and all manner of useful items. Cytar saw someone wearing a shirt of very hard leather and asked what it was.

"Sharkskin," the man told him. The man told him that although extremely tough, shark could be made very pliable; he preferred it to be hard for protection while working with the ropes, nets, and hooks on his boat.

Cytar asked Sandole about the sharkskins and was told that they did indeed make a great, and almost impervious, shield if cured correctly; and even the pliable skins were more durable and resistant to wear than other leather. Sandole was wearing sharkskin foot coverings and showed them proudly. Sandole then showed Cytar vast piles of the skins in storage.

Cytar explained his idea of using the skins to help protect the camp people and Sandole liked it.

In fact, Sandole liked it so well that he held a meeting and had the fishermen try to take more sharks than usual. He knew that taking sharks was very dangerous, but when the fishermen heard Cytar's plans, they decided the danger was worth the effort.

Sleeveless shirts were made to fit over tunics and forearm braces to protect during close-in combat. Even leggings and round shields were made for some people. Only those using knives or clubs could use a shield because the shield took one hand away from weapons usage.

The blizzard had lasted for three weeks and dropped snow on the open steppes to a depth higher than a man's head while sitting on horseback. Anyone trying to travel in this weather was dead by now. No one could remember another winter storm of this intensity.

Once again, training was given in the different forms of combat. People had begun to take the threat seriously after hearing of the cave massacre. This camp was a prime spot for marauders of all kinds, and they had been attacked before. The mountains to the southeast held many marauders. This training would help defend against them as well.

When the weather was too severe to practice outside, the inside of the largest storage and merchant center was used. Gondal was a major trading center with traders coming from all directions and meeting here. The local merchants used the large merchant center for trading business during the summer and storage during the winter. Tables were also set up outside along the front of the building to display their wares.

The local population was learning to keep weapons handy at all times, at the trade tables, cleaning fish, butchering meat, or even to carry them while going to relieve themselves.

Spring finally arrived, with a last-minute snowstorm. Shortly after the snow melted, one of the older boys came running into town and told everyone a group of riders were approaching from the south.

Sandole called to him and asked him to describe the riders.

"I saw no spare horses, all the riders held spears. Oh, and they were spreading out as they came closer."

Sandole turned to Cytar for his opinion. "They sound unsavory to me."

"Me too. Successful traders always have packhorses. Even hunters have them, loaded if the hunt was good or empty if it had failed, but still, there would be spare horses."

Sandole signaled everyone to take cover and be ready for anything.

A ringing yell resounded as the riders burst into camp from several directions, their spears lowered to a lance position. A hail of arrows quickly left their horses without riders. Fourteen dead marauders lay where they had fallen. One of the camp merchants stepped out and told Sandole he recognized several of them. He had been on a trading mission to the south of the mountain range located southeast of Gondal two summers before when these men had ransacked that camp. Afterward, one of the locals there who had survived the assault told him this bunch lived in the mountains there.

Cytar told Sandole that he should take shirts or something from these marauders and hang them on the front of the Merchant Center. The camp members could then point to them and tell visitors about how the camp dealt with marauders here. If other marauders hit, just add to the display. Also, he should set up highly visible practice fields and have a few people out for practice any time strangers were in camp. Word would soon spread about how prepared this camp stayed while waiting to deal with more marauders, such as these. So long as people were seen practicing and keeping weapons close to hand, this would be a camp most marauders would avoid. Just make sure never to let down the camp's readiness. If the camp became complacent, it would quickly become a prime target. Sandole liked the ideas and had items from each marauder collected and displayed.

During the battle, Cytar had caught the finest of the marauders' horses, and he decided to keep it. The others were added to the camp's herd.

Because all of his and Marcina's mares were pregnant, including those he had traded for during the journey, along with Clartan and Antana's horses, he decided to go into the horse training and trading business. To prepare for the increased size of the herd, he would need a larger field just for them. He also knew it would be wise to trade for all the grain and grass he could get to feed them during the winters. He was teaching Marcina,

Antana, and Clartan how to train horses to help keep up with the increased workload.

Once Pixie had her foal, she began to stay with the other horses. He guessed she had either matured enough to decide she would be safe away from him, similar to a child who grows out of being afraid of the dark, or it could be she had realized that from this point on, she would have to be the mother and not the child.

As traders came to the camp, word began to spread about the failed foray attempt. During one day, there were three traders from the group of Ghaunt caves, two traders from different camps to the south, one trader from Goyet, and one man making a journey that had come from far to the southwest.

As Sandole stood watching the trading activity, one of the southern traders stepped up beside him. The trader whispered to Sandole that the southwestern man that claimed to be making a journey and currently standing at a trading table looking over the items on display was in fact a marauder, here to evaluate the chances of an attack.

As the man began to notice armed men staying near and watching him, he became uneasy and soon was seen hurriedly leaving back to the south. It was decided that that band of marauders would choose a different place for their assault.

Word spread about how Gondal was dealing with the marauder problem, and other camps began to emulate them, resulting in more traveling traders suffering attacks, which forced them to begin traveling in armed groups. As time passed, word drifted through that increasing numbers of marauders were moving to other lands where life for them was easier.

During the middle of summer, three horses were stolen. Cytar took Declon and Clartan and went after them. He also took Dac to trail them. Three days later, a camp was spotted just before nightfall. By slipping closer to the camp, they could see the stolen horses along with three others. The camp held five men and a ragged woman.

"I think we should let them fall asleep and slip in and capture them alive. We can take them back to camp to face judgment."

"I like that idea, Declon. It should not—"

Suddenly Dac leaped out of sight and jumped a man that was trying to surprise them. Cytar and Clartan each got off one arrow before the other two men escaped. The woman just fell to her knees and sat there. Cytar ran into camp and checked each of the men there. They were both dead. Clartan ran to the horses to make sure none of them ran off. Declon had gone to help Dac, though by the time he arrived, the man was barely alive. Declon carried him into the camp.

"Please do not hurt me," the woman spoke in Dolnii.

"You are Dolnii?"

"Yes, I am called Galinia, and I was taken from Meadow Camp. I have had to cook and be passed around for all the men to use me. Please help me."

"Do not worry. My brother's mate is Scytan and so is the man out by the horses. His mate is Antana of Mountain camp of the Dolnii. This is my brother coming now."

"I know Antana. Thank you so much. If he is mated to Antana, I know I am safe now. Have you eaten? I will make you some food."

Declon handed his pack to her, saying, "There is food in here if there is not enough in camp." Then he turned and said to his brother, "Cytar, you need to look at the wounds on this man. Dac got rough with him."

Cytar turned to check the man who was mumbling in Sarain. He died before Cytar could do anything for him. Dac had not left much of the man's throat.

Declon looked at the man's injuries and commented, "I get the feeling Dac does not care too much for Sarain people."

"The horses are secured. They left our three and one other one." Clartan stopped when he saw the woman. "I guess that one was hers."

"Clartan, meet Galinia of Meadow Camp, of the Dolnii. She knows Antana. The marauders kidnapped her."

"Then we shall take you to Antana," spoke Clartan in Dolnii. She gave him a grateful smile.

"Do you know who these men were?"

"They were Sarainian, as were the two that escaped, Nickotian and Baytuk. Nickotian is a pig," and she spat.

"Well, we almost got him. Too bad this one ruined it." Clartan moved as if to kick the dead man, but did not. Cytar asked her if she had any injuries. She only had some scrapes and small cuts. Cytar quickly treated them all and made a poultice for a bad bruise.

The bodies were buried, but their shirts and other items were taken. The weapons were of poor quality, but could still be traded. There was little else. *Some successful marauders these were,* thought Cytar.

The little band was seen returning, and many came out to greet them. Cytar gave the shirts to Sandole for the wall and told him two of them had escaped, one of which was Nickotian.

As Antana ran to meet Clartan, she saw Galinia and recognized her. She immediately went to the young woman instead.

"Galinia, how did you get here?"

At seeing and hearing Antana, Galinia's resolve collapsed. She was safe. Antana took her to the woman that was the camp healer.

By the next morning, Galinia was able to talk about what had happened. A large hunting party was just returning to camp and drove the raiders away from Meadow Camp. The reason Galinia referred to the marauders as raiders was because that was what they were called in her home territory. She had been at the river when they rode past escaping. Nickotian had reached down, grabbed her up, and carried her away. Galinia had been beaten and raped repeatedly since then, but she was attractive enough and cooked well enough that they had kept her alive. She saw the men do many terrible things to the helpless people they found. Nine marauders had been killed since she was taken. They had been speaking of finding more recruits when Cytar had arrived.

Galinia looked at Cytar, told him Nickotian had ranted repeatedly about what he would do to that Kychee man, and warned him to be careful. Marcina burst into laughter and told her how she had once thrown him to the ground. "He was all talk and hot air," said Marcina.

"That might be true," Galinia said, "but he was very sneaky."

Cytar asked gently, "Is he was the one that stole the horses?"

"No, that was the one that your wolf killed. Nickotian was very angry about it and said that now Gondal had been warned."

Later, Cytar found the trader from Goyet and asked if a message could be sent to the Dolnii that Galinia had been rescued and was in good shape and staying with Antana. The trader assured him it would be done.

"Cytar, come with me. I will teach you how to really fish."

"Do you mean out in the middle of all that water?"

"Yes, you will love it."

Cytar smiled and winked at his sister. She knew he had grown up, fishing from similar boats, but did not remind Ramoar that they came from a coastal village.

"Well, if you promise to take good care of me out there, I guess we can go. Declon, are you coming too?"

"Not this time, little brother, I have other things to do at the moment."

"Very well, how many of us are going, Ramoar?"

"Just family today, Cytar—you, Locar, and myself."

Cytar gave Marcina a hug and kissed her and Shalela before getting in the boat.

Torena whispered to Locar that Cytar knew what he was doing but would play ignorant to see how Ramoar did things. Locar nodded and smiled.

The boat was quite large but easily handled by the three men. A single mast stood forward of center with a large leather sail for power. There were also oars for when the wind was slack.

Ramoar showed Cytar a harpoon and showed him how to use it and then told him to throw it at the first large fish he saw.

Cytar soon had a mackerel that came up to his waist. When Cytar grinned at Ramoar, he was told that it was all right, but not to waste time with anything smaller. Cytar noticed Locar trying not to laugh and wondered why.

After a while, Cytar saw a shape heading under the boat. It would come out right in front of him. Timing his throw, Cytar soon had a very large shark on his line. Without thinking, Cytar told Locar that when he got it closer, to put a second harpoon into its gills. Locar had already been preparing for that very action.

Cytar braced against the gunnel near the bow and held on. He knew his harpoon was very deep into the shark at the base of the shark's head and was rapidly draining the shark's ability to fight. Soon, he had it at the surface when it turned to run back alongside the boat, giving Locar the perfect chance to hit the gills. His harpoon went in the near gill cover and out the other one. Without gills, the shark could not breathe, and a massive amount of blood was flowing out from the destroyed gills. With

Locar pulling the head up and holding it steady, Ramoar had little trouble putting his harpoon directly into the shark's brain.

It was very hard work for the three men to get the shark into the boat, but they managed. Cytar saw a much smaller shark swim past and added it to the boat as well. Locar decided they had a large-enough load and told Ramoar to head for port. He then turned to Cytar.

"That was a cute joke with the mackerel, but you handled that shark like a professional fisherman."

"Yes, he did," Ramoar stated in a thoughtful manner.

Cytar grinned at Locar and Locar grinned back. "Just like old times, I figure."

"You mean he knows how to fish?"

"Of course. His family lives on water just like this. Have you never listened to Torena tell of it?"

"Uh, yes, hey, I did. And here I was going to show you what to do."

All three men were laughing loudly when they docked. The call had gone out and their families were waiting for them. It took six men to get the large shark off the boat for them.

"Locar, I have been fishing with you for twenty-seven of these fishing seasons. Tell me, how did you get that thing into the boat?"

"I just asked it nicely to step in."

"Step in my…no, do not tell me. Just let me guess."

"All right, I will."

The two old men soon had everyone laughing, but being the experienced fishermen that they were, all noticed the location of the three wounds. There were no meat-ruining body thrusts here. That was good harpoon work, from start to finish.

Locar handed the mackerel to Torena and suggested that they all eat together tonight. Torena smiled at him and left with the fish.

2

The Marauder Camp

The Goyet trader was ready to return home, and because both Marselac and Barthal had done well in their trades, they decided to go with him. They were sure they could make it back to the Dolnii River Camp before snowfall. Jodac had done well training Miss Qing, and both were beginning to fill out. He would be a man by the time his mother saw him again, and Miss Qing would almost be grown.

Galinia decided to travel with them back to her home. She carried her own new bow now, and she would be looking for marauders. Antana had taught her a few tricks that she could try if needed.

Apopus was leaving as well. He had found some other traders interested in going south, and they would be stopping at the Ghaunt cave network along the way. From there, he would drop down to the east/west trail and follow it east to where it entered Marcel's Camp on the coast. He would then follow the trail, as it followed close to the shoreline, north and around to the east, where there were camps along the way to trade and stay with. Sandole warned him that some of the marauders had moved into that area and for him to be watchful always.

"Do not worry, Sandole. I have had Clartan training the men I will be traveling with. We will be ready for any trouble that marauders want to give us."

Marcina and Antana were in tears telling their old friends good-bye. Marselac would be taking messages for both of them to their families and promised to tell glowing tales of Clartan's exploits while sitting around the central fire at Snow Camp. He would also inquire to see if anyone had found the missing "oh my."

"Enough. I keep hearing about this 'oh my,' but I have no idea what you are talking about." Antana had her hands on her hips, causing Rolvalar to hide behind her leg and fearfully peek around and up at her.

Marselac exploded into laughter and took Barthal and Cytar with him. "Antana, this fine mate of yours has always been known throughout the Scytan for saying 'oh my' to almost anything that happened. He seems to have stopped after the battles with the Sarainians, but it is still too good not to tease him with."

Antana let a big grin spread across her face then said, "I do not care. Even if he does have faults, I still love him."

"Oh my" came four echoing replies from the four men. Laughing, she threw her arms around Clartan and gave him a delectably wonderful kiss.

When she let him go, he barely managed to squeeze out a breathless, "O-oh…mmmy."

Declon decided that because of the troubles with Nickotian, he would stay with his family for now. Torena cooked him a great meal to celebrate while Marcina and Antana worked together to make him a fine new parka for the coming winter. They had seen the condition of his old one and knew that his need would be great.

The summer went past uneventfully. Late fall arrived, and everyone began preparing for the first snow.

One of the older boys came running up to Sandole and told him a rider was coming fast from the southeast. Before going to the edge of camp to meet the rider, Sandole called for Thoran to get Sabortay and Cytar.

They were waiting when the rider arrived. He was a Ghaunt trader from the caves to the east and Sandole knew him, and he was so out of breath, it appeared as if that he had run instead of the horse.

"Just...saw...riders—lots of them...riding up fast...from the south. Knew I...had to beat them...and warn you."

Word spread quickly, and everyone was set just as twenty-seven riders reached the camp. Too late, the leader saw he had ridden into a trap. An arrow pierced his chest even as he tried to turn his horse. The volley that followed brought down about half the riders before the others made it into the camp looking for anyone to fight. They were met with lances that caused their horses to rear and struggle.

One marauder leaped from his horse and, standing next to a table, began to fight with Clartan. Suddenly, he screamed and fell as three little spears stabbed his legs. Clartan did not give him time to do anything else but die.

Cytar was using his ivory sword to fight with three men while Declon took on two more. Marcina had her flying spear and began slicing through several arms and legs as the owners fought other camp members.

Cytar sliced through one throat and then gave a second neck a resounding slash that, while killing the owner, also broke Cytar's sword. Releasing the handle, Cytar drew his knife and cut off the right hand of the last marauder that he fought. Cytar then held his knife to the man's throat while scanning the area to see if anyone else needed help.

Declon had used a spear to fight with. The two opponents laughed at him for taking them both on, yet even as they laughed, Declon slashed the tip sideways and ruined the throat of the first marauder. The second glanced at his partner but should not have. As his eyes left Declon's spear, Declon thrust it through the man's heart.

Antana stayed in the background with her bow and brought down two more marauders.

Another man came up to attack Clartan and fell from leg wounds in the same way as his predecessor.

Though Marcina had not killed any of the marauders she hit, they were disabled enough for the camp members they had been attacking to kill them with little trouble.

Sandole looked at her with gratitude. The man he was fighting was beginning to get the best of him when she ruined the man's arm. Sandole quickly thrust his spear into the man's abdomen and ripped it wide open, spilling intestines that tangled the man's feet.

Sabortay had not faired as well as Sandole because a marauder thrust a spear into him just as Marcina disabled the marauder. The newly arrived Ghaunt trader finished the marauder.

As quickly as that, there were no more marauders, except the one being held by Cytar. As the man grew pale from shock and loss of blood, Cytar sat him down and began working on his wrist to stanch the flow. The man was unconscious by the time Cytar finished, and he had two men carry the marauder to the healer's lodge and told them to guard him. Cytar then began checking everyone else for injuries.

Torena stepped out of her lodge doorway with her bow and began calling for Sayta. Sayta, Shalela, and Rolvalar crawled out from under the table by Clartan, each carrying a very small spear with the points covered in blood.

Clartan looked down at the three very small children with more than a little shock. "That was you three under there?"

"Yup," Sayta said and grinned at the two smaller children in her charge.

Marcina and Antana both looked down at their children and then at each other. Both mothers were too stunned to say a word.

Clartan looked at the women and pointed to the wounds on the two dead marauders' legs.

Most injuries were minor, but Sabortay had a bad spear wound in his side. Faleenia, the camp healer, was already working on him so Cytar handled the minor wounds.

After treating all of the wounds in camp, Cytar went to help Faleenia work on Sabortay. Faleenia told Sandole she felt sure Sabortay would recover with no trouble if they could control infection. The shark armor he was wearing had kept the spear from going in too deeply, even though it had hit at a very thin spot in the armor. Word spread rapidly about how the shark armor had saved Sabortay's life.

Two of the marauders' horses were injured too badly to save so they were butchered. The other horses had their wounds treated before joining the camp herd. Cytar liked the looks of the horse the leader had been riding and claimed it as his share of the bounty from the marauders, causing Sandole to laugh at Cytar's ever-expanding herd and tell him that he was getting very wealthy.

Sandole sat listening with Declon and Clartan as Cytar questioned the marauder. The man was still dazed by how easily his hand had been severed by the strange-looking knife, which prompted Cytar to ask if he had never seen a knife with an ivory grip before. Confused and weak, the man forgot about the knife.

"Why did your band raid us? Had you not heard how we deal with marauders?"

"Yes, we heard, but we felt we were good enough fighters to beat you. I guess we were not that good after all."

"Are there others in your band that did not come?"

"No, but it was felt that we had enough without recruiting more. Loot will only go so far, even from a rich camp like this."

"What will your women do now?"

"They will wait for a while then move to other camps."

"You know of more marauding camps?"

"No, not any close to us. There are, however, plenty of regular camps where the women can go and men can be found. There is always someone that is ready to find an easier way to live."

Amused, Cytar chuckled and shook his head as he asked, "Do you call this an easier way to live?"

The man gave a weak smile and answered, "Well, not so much anymore. Lately, everywhere we go, someone is waiting to kill us. Even traders travel in groups now, and let me tell you, some of those traders are fighters. It just is not like the old days. And look at me now, how can a man do anything with only one hand?"

"You could become an honest merchant, I am quite sure you know the value of most things. You could learn to carve or work wood. I used to know a man with one hand missing that was a very good fisherman. He could handle a net with the best of them."

"You make it sound easy."

"Do you have any children?"

"A boy, nine summers, now what is he going to think of me?"

"Have him hunt. Start with small animals. Eat the meat and save the skins, claws, and teeth. You can learn to work the hides. Soon, you will have enough wealth to start trading.

"Leave the drink alone because it will only defeat you now. If you trade for it, make sure you can trade it away for a profit.

"Move to a camp where you do not have to worry about your wealth being stolen. Tell the camp how we keep our members trained at all times to defeat marauders, and they should be grateful for having you be a part of them."

"Are you saying you are going to let me go?"

"I do not know yet, that decision is not up to me. But is there reason for us to continue to worry about you being alive?"

The man laughed. "I am not even sure I can live long enough to get home. There are many predators in the mountains. How am I supposed to fend them off now?"

"How many of those predators are human?"

"There are those in the mountains, always. I have no idea where they live, but they are there to be sure."

Cytar looked at Declon and grinned. Declon laughed and nodded. Clartan perked up and said, "Hey, I am going with you two."

Sandole's mouth dropped open. "Are you...?"

Cytar was still grinning as he nodded to Sandole. "I do not think we could make it back here before spring. The snows are too close."

"Our mates will never let us go alone."

"I know, but just think how surprised any marauders will be if they try to hurt one of them."

The man looked puzzled as the others laughed at the thought of a marauder trying to hurt a woman and getting surprised.

"What is your name?"

"Landar."

"And your family's names?"

"My mate is Baleah and my son is Dorazar."

"About how many people are in your camp right now?"

"Four old men and one old woman, I think about twenty-three other women, and maybe fifteen children."

"How far from there is it to the nearest honest camp large enough for us to take everyone?"

"You want to move over forty people to a camp just before first snow?"

"Well, is there enough food in your camp to feed everyone until spring?"

"I do not know for sure, maybe. We have done a lot of hunting this summer because it was safer than ransacking camps."

"Sandole, how much food do you think you could let us take?"

"I will have to check. I know there is a lot in storage since we thought there would be more traders looking for dried food stores than came through this trading season."

"Did your band come straight here from your camp? How long did it take your band to get here?"

"Yes, it took us about twelve days hard riding to get here. Leading pack horses, I would say at least fifteen days to return."

"Which means we need to go right now. Sandole, too many of our horses had foals this summer. Would it be possible to leave those here and take some of the camp horses that do not have young? We would bring them back in the spring."

"Yes, we can keep your horses for you. Some of them may have to be used for some reason, but they should be fine."

"Clartan, we must go tell the women we are traveling again. It would be best if they stay here, but will they?"

"Cytar, I know this has to be done, but..." Marcina lifted her hands and looked around. Taking hold of her hair and pulling it, she looked back at Cytar. "Very well, I will not spend the winter without you. I will go with you instead."

"Do you wish to leave Shalela with Torena?"

"No, she will still need to be fed."

"Come, we must see how Clartan is faring."

As they walked to Clartan's hearth, Antana looked at Marcina with sad eyes and smiled as she said, "I never dreamed that once I was mated, my home would be the back of a horse."

Declon arrived and told them Torena and her family was coming, as well. That would give them a large enough group to handle most trouble.

Cytar decided that each of them would carry three bows and quivers. That would allow them to keep a bow strung at all times without overstressing any of them. A bow strung for too long would break. They would each take two heavy laminated recurved bows and one composite bow. Each quiver had different types of arrows to use on anything from birds to mammoths.

Ramoar had been an adept student of the bow, and Torena had taught him well. She had also taught him many combat moves. Cytar made little bows for the three children, although the younger two were not given arrows yet. Sayta only got them when she was allowed to practice shooting. Each child also had a small spear to carry in the spear-pocket on its horse. Included would be an atl and spears, plus two throwing spears for each.

Cytar decided to put Shalela on Pixie even though he had to take her little foal. He knew Pixie would take care of Shalela, with the help of the four wolves that would also keep close watch on all of the children.

Cytar rode ahead with Landar and Dac. Declon and Clartan rode out to each side and Ramoar was in the rear. Marcina and Antana rode on each side of the packhorse team, and Torena rode behind it with the children. The other three wolves moved out and away from the group to watch for dangers.

The pack team was tied four in a row with three rows traveling side by side. When the trail became too narrow to allow that many to travel spread out, the three groups of packhorses were tied together into one long line. Two of the packhorses carried the traveling gear, and the rest were loaded with dried foods, including fruits and vegetables.

As the group got closer to the mountains, the land became more rugged. Landar was leading them into a large valley that ran southeast far into the mountain range. He told them the camp was at the far end of the valley right up on the side of the mountain in front of them.

Trees were in the center of the valley, but a wide strip of smooth, clear meadow ran along the side next to the eastern wall. At the start of the second day in the valley, Cytar had noticed a herd of aurochs. He rode back to meet with Clartan and Declon to make note of the herd. The cattle were grazing among the trees and holding close to the watercourse flowing through the valley. The herd hardly noticed the horses, but was nervously watching the wolves. The wolves were kept close in to the riders to help prevent the herd from stampeding away.

The packhorses were fully loaded, but after unloading, it would be easy enough to come back for a hunt if the meat was needed. The end of the meadow was reached late during the following day.

Landar rode forward to lead them into the camp and to greet the women as he entered. Most of the women had come out to meet them thinking they were the returning marauders. Only the fact that they recognized Landar kept them from panicking when they realized it was not their men.

Baleah recognized him and ran to Landar as he dismounted. She gasped and put her hands to her mouth as she noticed his missing hand. Gently, she took his arm and looked up into his eyes with tears flowing from hers. Landar wrapped his other arm around her and hugged her before speaking to the women.

"I am the only man left alive. Simonia said it was prideful counsel, which drove our leader to try taking a camp known for dealing harshly with marauders. She spoke true. Never have I seen such fighting as the people of Gondal displayed. All of you know of my strength, well, this is what is left of me." Landar held up the stub of his right wrist. "Three of us fought together to defeat one man. I got this after my friends died. One man… defeated all three of us."

The women began to cry and wail.

"SILENCE! I have not finished yet! The people of Gondal were not cruel. When I told them of this camp and all of you, they loaded these horses with food to be brought here. In addition, these people with me have come to help us survive the winter. We need to unload the supplies and store them properly. Then I must know what we still need to last until spring. We saw a herd of aurochs out in the valley. If we need more meat, we will get it there."

The women started to murmur among each other.

"We can do this, but only if we work together. These people know how to make this work, but you must trust them."

"Why, they killed my man?"

"Yes, after your man went to Gondal to kill them, but they also came here to help you. They did not have to come here or bring food with them. No one has forced them to come to hunt more food for you. Are you so blinded by your loss that you would rather die than accept their help?"

A very old woman walked up to Landar, put her hand on his good arm, and turned to the women. "Stop this now! You should be ashamed, your men left here to kill these people, yet they still come here to help you. If you do not have your man now, it is only because he was such a fool that he rode against these people. Now get these horses unloaded, and later, we can be introduced to these fine young people. Move, ladies! Time is short to do all that we need to do."

Instantly, the women began to work with the newcomers to store the food. Antana kept the children and wolves out of the way while the women gave the wolves plenty of room and kept an eye on them.

After the food was all stored and an inventory taken of all available stores, it was decided that another nine to ten cattle would bring the camp through the winter in fine shape. The old woman then had some of the women start a communal meal so everyone could eat together in the evening, meet the newcomers, and hear what they had to say.

While the meal was being cooked, the old woman came over, and Landar introduced her as Simonia, the camp's wise woman. She smiled and corrected him, saying she was just very experienced. Another woman approached and said beds should be found for the guests. She was introduced as Mashie and had been mated to the camp leader.

Cytar turned to Simonia and asked, "Has there been any trouble from outside the camp yet?"

Simonia turned a critical eye at Mashie, and Mashie answered, "There is a band somewhere around in the mountains near here, but I am not sure where. I noticed that one of their men was watching the camp from a ridge yesterday. There has been no trouble yet, but I think they are waiting to see if the men return. With our men here, they would not have dared cause trouble, our men could have handled them easily. Now, well, I am afraid we will have them all over us."

"We will keep them out of here if you help us. We need a watch kept so we have a warning if they come. Just make sure none of the women here slip them in on us. You would be surprised how many we can handle if we have the warning."

"That is somewhat reassuring. I will make sure we give you that warning."

"Tomorrow, we need to leave to hunt. We will need most of the women to help us get the meat back here. If we attach a travois to each of the horses, we can move many more of the animals here at one time than if we try to pack the meat on the horses' backs."

"Cytar, how about I take the wolves around the herd and drift it back this way? That would put the herd much closer when you arrive to hunt."

"When do you plan to leave, brother?"

"I think I should grab my gear and the wolves and leave now. You should wait and leave at first light day after tomorrow. That will give me time to get the herd moving without stampeding it. When you find the herd, get out where I can see you so I can clear out from behind them before you hit them."

"Be careful, Declon. I do not want our sister mad at me for letting you go."

"I will be, too, if he gets hurt. Give me a hug before you go big boy, and do not make me mad at our little brother."

"Dec, watch out for two-legged snakes."

"Always."

"Will he be safe out there alone?"

"He will not be alone, Simonia. He will have four wolves with him. With four wolves, he could handle just about anything."

"Well, that one wolf is very big, but the other three are much smaller."

"The big one is named Dac, and he is a male. He is also a summer older than the other three, Mr. Duyi, Moon, and Midnight. But they look to Dac as the pack leader, or maybe the assistant leader after Declon."

Mashie called to Declon, "Your horses are tired. We have a few here. Take my horse and my daughter's horse, and we will ride yours out to the hunt when we come. That way, your horses get to rest." She led him away to where her horses were.

Declon knew the wolves were tired, but he pushed on and only stopped to rest for two hours just before daylight. He knew that even as tired as they were, the wolves would let him know if a threat appeared. He slept well for the two hours.

At daylight, Declon was up and riding again. He kept as far from the herd as possible. To spook them now would be a disaster. He kept a very close watch on the ridgelines, looking for any trouble that might come along.

Later in the day, he was well beyond the herd. He rode down into the trees and found a nice, secluded clearing to camp for the night. The wind was just right to carry his scent as well as that of the wolves and the smoke from his small fire back toward the herd. Although he kept the fire too small to be seen away from his little clearing, he knew the cattle could still smell it. By daylight the next morning, he found that the herd had drifted much farther into the valley toward the main camp. He loaded his packhorse and mounted up. It was time to push the cattle a little.

After catching up with the herd, Declon drifted along just close enough behind, to keep the herd drifting toward the head of the valley, while he watched for Cytar. Shortly after midday, Cytar appeared, and Declon signaled to him and called the wolves to him. He would wait until the herd turned back this way and then hit them from this side.

Landar and Baleah agreed to watch the children while Torena, Marcina, and Antana rode out after the herd with Cytar, Clartan, and Ramoar. Mashie would follow an hour later with a contingent of women and the spare horses to help with the herd. Simonia had the camp children and the women that stayed behind prepare drying fires. The fires would not be lit until they were needed so no wood would be wasted.

3

Estavona's Camp

Cytar rode close to the valley wall to watch for Declon and be in the clear for Declon to see him. The sun had just passed its zenith when the herd was found, and Cytar spotted Declon in the distance.

With one arrow nocked and ready, plus three more held in the fingers of their left hands, Cytar and his band slowly rode close to the herd leaders before releasing the first shots. That left them in fine position to shoot a second arrow each as the remaining cattle turned and ran. The herd suddenly stopped for a moment when the leaders turned back because of the assault from Declon and the wolves. Cytar took advantage of the confusion to lead his party racing up along beside the panicked herd, and each hunter managed to kill a third aurochs before the remaining ones escaped down the valley.

As the herd suddenly rushed toward him, Declon and the wolves hit the ones leading the herd out and caused mass confusion. Declon's arrow brought down a large bull. Dac caught the nose of a large cow and flipped her onto her back. Dac moved to her throat while Moon used her teeth to cut the tendons in both hind legs.

Mr. Duyi caught the nose of her calf and flipped it. He bit that throat while Midnight cut the tendons in both of its hind legs.

The remainder of the herd moved close to the far west wall, away from the wolves, and stampeded past.

Cytar was amazed. In all, nineteen aurochs cattle lay dead on the ground. This camp would not go hungry this winter. Everyone got busy dragging all the cattle close together and field dressing them while waiting for the help and packhorses. Fires were started and butchering began so no meat would be lost while waiting for help.

When the women arrived, Mashie counted the number of animals being handled. She felt that half of the meat should be butchered and dried here and the other half taken back to camp for processing. Mashie had the women take over butchering, so the men could move whole animals to camp to be finished.

By the time the horses were loaded, several entire animals were butchered and on the drying racks. Enough meat was set roasting to feed everyone while they worked. The wolves were enjoying the unlimited supply of fresh scraps.

Cytar took Dac and Midnight back to camp with him. Mr. Duyi and Moon were left at the hunt site. Clartan was also left at the hunt site for security. Cytar wanted some of the men in both locations to handle any trouble that might arise in the form of unwelcome guests, of either the two-legged or four-legged variety.

Ramoar was helping Cytar bring a load back to camp. Declon would bring another load as soon as it was ready to move.

After unloading the horses, Cytar sent Ramoar back out with the horses for another load. Clartan would be at the hunt site at all times while Cytar stayed at the camp. Declon would travel one direction with a pack string, while Ramoar would travel with a second string of horses in the opposite direction.

Antana and Torena stayed at the hunt site also while Marcina came back to the camp to work.

Dac would stay with Marcina, and Midnight stayed close to Cytar. Moon stayed close to Clartan, and Mr. Duyi was with Torena. Pixie stayed close to the children, and Baleah was instructed to watch Pixie for any signs of warning. Marcina made sure she was also close to the children.

Cytar was pleased to see Landar doing his best to handle the fires and meat. It would take time, but Cytar was sure the man would manage to succeed in an honest lifestyle. Cytar also saw that Landar was encouraging his son to learn all he could and to help Landar when needed. Cytar decided to help the boy become a very good hunter.

Simonia could not believe how much meat had been taken. She was glad to see the camp finally get a few good hunters. Before, the men had hunted, but they always returned with two or three animals. For them to return with four was cause for a celebration. Unfortunately, the men had enjoyed celebrating far too much and that meant things never got finished, even when they did get started.

Things were going well. By early evening, all the meat had been butchered, the hides and bones stored, and the drying racks were overflowing. Cytar was very pleased and decided to clean up and grab a plate of food. Midnight had been eating all day and had rested.

He had just finished eating and was still sitting beside a pile of hides between two of the huts when Midnight began to growl. Cytar looked at her and saw where she was looking. Three men were walking into camp. Cytar saw that Dac and Marcina had spotted them also. Even Pixie was watching them. Cytar shot a pebble with his fingers, which hit Declon, who stood behind a horse, out of sight of the men.

Cytar slipped up behind the men and heard them talking.

"The men must be back, look at all this meat."

"I tell you, the men were killed. I heard the story being told."

"Well, these women never killed all this meat."

"Hey you, where are the men?"

Marcina saw Cytar standing right behind them and grinned. "I think that is none of your business."

"What? How dare you speak to me that way? I think you need a lesson in how to speak to men."

Marcina continued to grin wickedly at them and retorted, "Well, I guess I have time to teach you how to show proper respect to a woman."

In shock at such effrontery from a woman, the man drew back his fist and…felt something break!

The other two men spun around, at his cry of pain, and saw Cytar release the broken arm.

"Oh, Cytar, I wanted to break it."

The men looked back at the woman. She was serious. She really did want to hurt them.

As one man went for Cytar, the other made a swing at Marcina. Cytar quickly broke his man's shoulder. Marcina grabbed the wrist of the other man and flipped him, twisting the arm in ways it was never designed to twist, and then, while still holding the wrist, she kicked the elbow, shattering it.

Landar looked at Marcina with a pale face, looked at Baleah, and back to Marcina. "And I thought I came away in bad shape, against Cytar. At least I can still use the rest of my arm. You totally destroyed his arm from one end to the other."

"He needed to learn it is never proper to hit a woman. A man is much stronger and could hurt her badly."

Landar could not help it. Hearing such a speech from such a beautiful woman that had just destroyed a man was more that he could take. After a loud guffaw, he said, "I think I had better go get some help for these fools."

Baleah looked at Marcina in wonder. "How did you do that?"

"I had some excellent training."

"It shows."

Declon walked up and said, "I think they were alone. I could not see anyone else." He was carrying his bow. He faded back out of sight while Cytar began to check the men's arms.

Landar returned with Simonia. Simonia took one look and shook her head. "Those are beyond my abilities."

Cytar asked the man with the broken arm, "Is there a healer at your camp?"

The man nodded.

"How far is your camp from here?"

"Day and a half, or two days maybe.

"Do you have horses, or are you walking?"

"We walked."

Cytar jerked a glance toward Landar. That was too close.

"How big is your camp? How many men?"

"Only twelve men, I think, counting us."

"Is there another camp close by?"

"Towsal's camp, maybe ten days from mine, if going on horseback. Not quite as big or tough as this one used to be."

"I am going to reset your arm, then you are going to show me where your camp is. Do you understand?"

"Why?"

"I will leave the arm broken if you do not. Do you see your friend there?"

The man looked at the one Marcina had dealt with and nodded.

"I will let my mate tend your arm instead of me fixing it."

The man blanched and agreed.

Cytar quickly reset the arm then reset the shoulder as best as he could of the other man he had injured. He knew that the arm of the man with the injured shoulder would always be very limited in its use. Then, after checking the arm of the man Marcina handled, Cytar looked at Simonia and said the only thing they could do would be to remove the arm. Simonia nodded and had them take the man to her lodge.

Cytar decided his band should go in force to the other camp and decide once there what to do with it. The man with the broken arm was named Petraina. Cytar had a water skin full of a painkilling liquid for Petraina who had been mounted on a spare horse.

With seven adults and four wolves, Cytar told the others he thought it would be safe to take the children. There would only be nine to twelve men for them to face. It was agreed, and the band set out.

The marauder's camp was just over the next ridge, but the route to get there meandered along the side of the mountain. It took almost all day to get there, even with the horses. Riding downward, they approached the rear of the camp, and Cytar saw a valley open below them that had to be right next to the valley of Simonia's Camp.

The camp members were quite shocked to find an armed band of warriors inside their own back door. Cytar's band had spread out and sat on their horses with arrows nocked and ready.

Petraina's horse was slightly in front of the others as he called out to Estavona, the camp leader. A man, still looking youngish yet well matured, stepped out and quickly appraised his situation. Never one to make rash decisions, he knew these people were too well armed for his own band to have a chance against.

"What is the meaning of this invasion?"

The man spoke in a language Cytar was unfamiliar with, but Declon answered him with no problem. "Three of your men tried to get a little too familiar with one of our women. We have come to discuss our mutual situation."

"We have a mutual situation?"

"Yes, we are tired of killing marauders, but will continue to do so as long as we are bothered."

Estavona was smart enough not to try to deny being a marauder. "So?"

"Estavona, be very careful with these warriors. See that woman there? Petty tried to hit her, and when she got through with him, they had to cut off his right arm. It was broken all to pieces."

Estavona looked at Petraina with a shocked expression. "A woman did that, to Petty?"

"With her bare hands, Estavona, with just her hands she did that. And, Estavona, the other two women are just as dangerous. In addition, these seven here, they killed nineteen aurochs in one hunt. The camp was still working on the meat when we got there."

Estavona silently mouthed the word *nineteen* as he very slightly shook his head in amazement.

"Another thing, Estavona, they are the ones that killed twenty-six of the men of the camp there and then brought poor Landar home with his hand cut off. Now, they are teaching the women of the camp to fight like they do and use weapons like they do, too. I tell you for sure, the women of that camp will not be messed with without their permission. To try is to lose an arm…or worse."

"There were three of you, Petraina. Where is Dantura?"

"Oh, he is almost as lucky as me. Of course, he will never have much use of his arm once it heals, but at least he still has it. He and I both tangled with that man there. He is the mate of the, uh, woman who breaks things." Petraina weakly smiled.

Estavona had been studying each of the opponents and noticed the bows in the hands of the three children. The older one was aiming a small stick at him with that strange little toy weapon. The smaller two, also, had the little weapons pulled back and aimed at him, but without any little stick in it. He could not help the smile that crept across his face.

"You have three very fierce little warriors there."

Declon laughed and told the others what had been said. All three mothers smiled lovingly at the children.

The presence of the children told Estavona another thing. If these people were so sure of their abilities that they would bring their children with them into this type of situation, he did not want to cross them. He also knew he faced them alone; they had stopped too far away for his men to throw a spear at them.

"I will have my men come out so that you may see them. We must eat and talk. I must admit that I am most impressed."

Suddenly, he heard a growl from his right. He looked that way and saw a large wolf standing in front of one of his men. "Hertalo, what are you doing?"

Declon grinned and called to the wolf, "Dac, sit."

The wolf sat but continued to watch the man.

Declon spoke, first to the young man in the local language, then to the wolf. "You, Hertalo, come here with the wolf. Dac, bring him."

Dac shocked the young man by taking his hand in his teeth and pulling him toward the others. Hertalo was much too frightened to try to get away from the wolf.

Estavona quickly scanned the brush and saw other wolves hidden; he was not sure how many. Children with toy weapons and wolves with real teeth, he realized he wanted to know these people better. Hope suddenly came to him; maybe this was how he would escape the outcast life.

Turning, Estavona called out to the camp for everyone to step out and be seen. "Put away your weapons, for we have guests tonight that I want you to meet. I wish to hear what they have to tell us and find how they can possibly help us. You men do not try to mess with any of these women. Petty tried and one ruined his arm so badly, Petraina says it had to be cut off. The wolves are quite dangerous if you mess with one of them. Also, these people are now under my personal protection. If you try to harm one of them, and they do not kill you, I will."

The camp knew their leader, and if he said he would kill them, he really would.

Estavona turned to Declon and asked, "It is acceptable for Hertalo to go and join the camp, no?"

"Dac, go to Marcina." The wolf walked over to the woman Petraina had indicated earlier. Declon then nodded to Estavona.

Estavona turned to Hertalo and told him to get Rudo and take the guest horses to the small surround and feed them. Turning to Declon, he said, "With your permission, of course."

Declon nodded.

After the two young men led the horses to the surround, Estavona escorted the guests into his camp. He quickly noted that although the guests no longer held their weapons ready for action, they did not remove them either.

"Estavona, do you and your camp speak the Ghaunt language?"

"It is not our first language, but yes. We do much business with the Ghaunt caves." He grinned and continued, "They are too strong for us to attack, so we trade with them and they rob us instead. The prices they charge us, mia."

Declon introduced his party to Estavona and told from where they came.

Estavona rubbed his hands together and called out in Ghaunt, "Stories tonight."

A cheer rose up.

Cytar laughed. People were the same everywhere, even the outcasts. Declon had been trying to teach them the Espanz language ever since the three marauders came into camp and developed a sudden need for medical treatments. Espanz was the language spoken south of these mountains as well as being as common as the Ghaunt language on this side of the range. He was beginning to pick up a little of it here and there. He felt soon he would begin to converse in it.

For now, Cytar let Declon continue to be the spokesman for their group. It had always been this way with them. One would be the spokesman, while the other kept watch. Torena was always alert and watchful. It was seldom that she was needed as the spokesperson, but it had happened.

Estavona knew that his second, Festuno, felt much the same as he did about this lifestyle. It was fun when they were younger, but now it had grown tiring and they both longed for a nice, peaceful life so their children could grow up in safety. He had Festuno join them now to hear what these people had to say.

Declon laid out the agreed-upon plan of moving the camp to be with honest people in the spring. They just had to get through the winter.

Estavona told them that Towsal had been threatening this camp for some time, and Estavona felt that before winter was over, they would raid here.

Cytar asked about their supplies.

"We have enough food for the winter, if it does not last too long."

"How do your men feel about becoming honest?"

"Most would welcome it. We have not fared that well, and now that they have heard the fate of Landar's camp, they realize times are just getting too hard for a group of outcasts to survive for very long."

"How long would it take to move everything over to the other camp? You could then travel out with us next spring."

"But if we are not here, then Towsal will go on to hit the other camp. Of course, he might anyway, after hitting us."

"All the more reason for us to join forces. With nine more men backing us, we could stand off a lot of trouble."

"You get settled and rest tonight. I will hold a council meeting with my camp and discuss it. I will let you know in the morning. Right now, I promised stories. I believe the camp is ready for them."

Shortly after daylight, loading began. The camp had elected to give honesty a try. By the next evening, they arrived at Simonia's Camp. Cytar had referred to it as such during the talks with Estavona and his camp agreed to accept it on a semipermanent basis.

Simonia and Mashie met the returning party. As the new numbers were counted, the two women called a gathering of their camp members to work out arrangements for living quarters.

Simonia chuckled to Cytar, "First, you kill all of our men, then you go and replace them with an entire other camp of the same type of people. You are a strange man, Cytar." She patted his cheek and smiled sweetly, and he knew she truly did appreciate the way he avoided killing when possible.

The storage pits were full and temporary ones added. Supplies from all the temporary storage pits were to be used first. A feast was held to allow everyone a chance to get acquainted. One of the new men had been watching little Torena ever since the day of his arrival at Estavona's camp. Finally, he had to speak to her.

"I know I am supposed to be respectful to you, but would my asking a question be out of line?"

"It depends on how respectful the content of the question is."

"I can understand the fact that your men would beat me to a pulp for being rude, but Petraina said that we should worry more about what you women would do to us. As little as you are, can you really be that dangerous?"

Torena gave an amused laugh. "Stand up. I will try not to hurt you, but I will show you why he said what he did."

Cytar and Declon grinned at each other. Although they knew what this poor fool was in for, they also understood this was good, because it would dampen any ideas the men might have in regards to the women. Declon signaled Estavona to watch.

"Now, try to attack me. Wait! I mean as if you really meant to grab me."

The man lunged, and Torena slapped his hands away, grabbed the front of his tunic, fell backward, and placed her feet into his stomach, throwing him a distance of about her height past her and onto his back. She was on her feet by the time he stopped bouncing.

"Again, this time, I will do something else."

Timed to match his movement toward her, she grabbed his right wrist and put her left hip in front of him easily throwing him again.

"Get up and come again."

The man stood up and shook his head to clear it then shrugged and attacked again. Once more, Torena took his wrist, ducked under his arm, and twisted the wrist causing the man to flip onto his back.

Torena smiled as she looked down at him and asked him, "Are you sure you were really trying to get hold of me?"

The man nodded as he shakily regained his feet.

Torena laughed and dusted him off. "What is your name?"

"Petara."

"Did I answer your question well enough, Petara?"

"I think so, but I didn't get anything broken." His last statement was said with some degree of amazement.

"Well, bones are easily broken if one has the knowledge to do so. It takes more skill sometimes not to break bones. I have both."

"I think you really do. I am sorry to have troubled you."

"You seem to be a nice man, Petara, way down deep inside of you. Come, I will teach you a few moves."

"Really, you would teach me? How do you know you can trust me?"

"I just know it. Besides, I will break you into pieces if you prove me wrong."

Petara's face went white. "I will live up to your expectations."

Torena started teaching him the hip roll that she had used on him. He would stick out his right hand as if to grab her, and she would grab his wrist with her right hand and turn her body so she could place her left hip in front of him as she pulled his wrist.

After he began to learn the move, she told him to try one more time. This time, instead of placing her hip in front of him, she placed her left foot against his right side and gently shoved.

He looked at her foot questioningly and she told him, "Oops, I think I just broke your ribs and shoved them into your lung. See, there are many different moves that can be made from the same start. Try again."

This time as she took his wrist using her left hand, she spun around with her right elbow, coming against his ribs. Petara felt his breath catch and knew she could easily have driven his breath completely from him.

"Remember how I fell backward and used my feet to throw you earlier?"

Petara nodded.

"Just think of the results if I had placed a foot lower into your groin."

Petara involuntarily grabbed his groin and leaned forward at the thought of the pain. Looking around, he saw several of the other men holding their own groins as well.

"We will eat now," and she left to get her food.

Petara looked at his leader. "Did you see that, Estavona? That little thing threw me around like I was a child's doll. You know how well I fight. I will face any man, but I tell you now, I will never try to face her in a real fight."

"Yes, Petara, we have much to learn from these people. But after we learn, we are obligated to use that knowledge to help others, not to harm them."

Petraina said, "Landar tells me he is learning to carve and work leather. He intends to become a peaceful merchant. I think he has given me a lesson in humility, and now I want peace for the rest of my life. Even if I have to fight for it," he chuckled.

Simonia looked up at the sky and said loudly, "We will have snow tomorrow."

The valley held snow up to a man's chest, and all the mountain trails were closed. Much of the camp was under an overhang on the southeast side of the camp, and with the trees on the north side of camp acting as a windscreen, most of the snow was kept away. The temperature was also a little warmer in this protected spot. What little heat from the late-day sun shining into the camp, aided with warming the temperature there. A spring flowed from the rocks at the back of the camp so there was plenty of water all winter.

One thing, which both marauder camps had in common, was that there was plenty of fodder, both grasses and grains, for the horses.

The injuries of both Petty and Dantura had healed. Dantura was beginning to try to be useful, but Petty was sullen and sat around bemoaning his fate in life. To him, fighting had been everything. Never to be able to fight again bothered him greatly, but what troubled him most was how easily a woman had ruined him.

Landar asked Dantura to begin working with him, and they would both learn a useful trade. Dantura appeared to be better at leather working, while Landar was better at carving and also had a natural skill as a trader. By the end of winter, they had decided to run a merchant enterprise similar to the ones in Gondal. Declon was even training them to fight one-handedly in the event that marauders hit them.

Although they tried to persuade him, Petty refused to join them. He was an outlaw, he said, and if he ever found their Merchant Center, he would as soon attack them as anyone else. He found the stores of liquid courage and soon entered into a permanent state of inebriation.

The winter snows had been much heavier than usual, the winter solstice had come and gone three moons past, and the ground had not been seen since the very first snow. Every day, they were glad for the ample supplies that had been laid in before the snowfall.

Towsal's Camp had not prepared so well. They were out of food and the trails were too deep to go out and find more. Towsal knew the closest camp was Estavona's, but would they have any more food than his own? They did have horses, though, and if he killed everyone in Estavona's camp, the horses could be brought back here and eaten. However, Towsal could think of no way to get through the snow to the other camp. The snow was too deep out on the plains, and the mountain trails would be utter suicide. He had to do something though before they were all dead. It was time for a thaw, even a slight one.

4

Towsal's Camp Attacks

Landar picked up some of the tree limbs that he had cut into flat boards and carried them inside. Soon, he came back out, gathered some limbs about as thick as two or three fingers, and took them inside his lodge as well. Cytar asked Declon and Clartan if they knew what Landar was up to. Both said no, but it would be easy enough to go and ask.

The lodges had been well made with rock walls and a pole roof covered over with hides and then tightly tied bundles of grasses packed together to form a warm, watertight seal, and then covered with dirt. Hanging a hide over the opening that could be tied closed during inclement weather, closed the doorway. Inside was room for six family hearths. Hanging hides separated each hearth.

Landar and his family lived in one hearth, and Dantura and his woman Yana lived in the next one. Baleah, Dorazar, and Yana worked with the two men in hopes of building a successful Merchant Center. The four remaining hearths were located in the front of the lodge and would be used as the merchant and storage center.

Both men had worked hard all winter building the skills they needed to overcome their handicaps. Dorazar had spent a lot of time training with Cytar on hunting skills as well as some combat skills. Cytar told him that as he became older, he would be depended on more for defending the Merchant Center and preventing thefts.

Landar found a piece of antler that was curved almost two-thirds of the way back and formed a hook only slightly larger than Landar's left fist. He had studied the antler all winter trying to figure what to do with it. He even carried it with him to community meals.

One morning as Cytar and the other two walked toward Landar's hearth, he stepped out, and the first thing they noticed was the antler fastened to the end of his arm.

"What is this?" Clartan asked.

"My new hand. Like it?"

"How do you use it?"

Landar reached down, caught the point of the hook in a leather skin, and lifted it up to Clartan.

"That is fantastic, Landar."

"Thank you. Now, what brings you three here today?"

Cytar chuckled and glanced at the others. "We saw you working all those flat wood pieces and the round ones and it raised our curiosity."

"That is an easy one. Let me show you."

Landar picked up a round limb with a flat piece inserted into a notch cut into the top. Wooden pins held the flat piece in place. Both ends of the flat piece were pointed. A picture of a small fire and a leg of meat were painted on each end close to the point. He had made a base of rendered aurochs fat and earth, colored differently by using various substances for the paints. The bottom of the round pole was also pointed.

"What…?"

"See, I use the back of my ax to drive this pole into the ground. That is why the bottom is pointed. It will then look like this." Landar held the pole up with the cross piece at the top, as if it were driven into the ground. He watched the men waiting for their reactions.

"And…why?" asked Clartan.

"I will put them along the trail to here. This end points to food and fire this way. The other end points back to the other end of the trail. Traders will see these as they travel along the trail and know to come this way. I will put some on the east/west trail that leads to the coasts, both to the west and to the east. I will put others on the trail to the Ghaunt caves, making sure to put one up at the east/west trail crossing along the way to the Ghaunt caves. In two or three trading seasons, many will know how to find our Merchant Center. We will get wealthy."

Cytar looked at Declon and laughed. "What an ingenious idea. Traders will see those and wonder what they are but will have to follow them, if for no other reason than to find out. Then, they start spreading the word of the trail markers. So simple yet so brilliant."

Landar beamed with pride. "We were all sitting around talking the other night wondering how we could stay here and get anyone to come here to trade. This is what we came up with. What was it that you called them again, trail markers? Humm, trail markers, yes, I like that."

"Dec, come and we will look around a little bit."

Landar followed them back outside; Cytar began to look around at the camp much closer. The protection from the weather here, access in and out, water, even the construction of the structures.

"Landar, how good are the trails through the mountains?"

"Can you see the two peaks back over behind the camp? That is a pass over to the other side of the mountains. It is not too bad in the summer. There is a nice little camp of honest people there. They call it Alba de Casa. They have to travel a long way to get to where they can trade for goods. We are much closer as well as easier to reach, at least in the summer. If they knew a lot of the marauders were no longer in this area, they would come here to trade."

"See the trail leading off to the west? That one is a lot shorter to the coast, but much harder to travel. There is a lot of up-and-down travel over a very dangerous pathway through there. The distance is longer if you follow the river going out through the valley, but very easily traveled and with fresh flowing water all the way. That is where I will place some of my trail markers."

"Are you saying that there is a trail to the Ghaunt caves, and another one that travels to the east and west?"

"Yes, at the mouth of the valley, to get to the Ghaunt caves, there is a trail that goes north and just slightly to the east of our valley. On the west side of these mountains is the Far-Reaching Waters of the West. On the east side of these mountains is another shore. Many people do not know it, but it is the same water. To the south of the mountains is a vast land, but the water is all the way around. I once knew a man that said he sailed in a boat all the way from Gondal around to the west for a while, then south, then east and came north again, and landed at Marcel's Camp close to the edge of these very mountains.

"Actually, if you can get aboard a boat, it is not far from there to the land of the Ital people, but there is also a good trail along the coast. The east/west trail goes from Marcel's Camp, east of us, to the trail that follows north along the coast to Gondal, to the west of us. Then there is the split not too far out of our valley where the trail to the Ghaunt caves turns off to the north."

"Dec, I begin to think Landar has a great idea. Why try to move all of these people when they can stay right here and have an honest trade going. Look, Estavona is coming now."

"Estavona, did you know Landar wants to stay here and open a merchant trading center?"

"No," said Estavona as he too began reassessing the location. After a quick study of all he knew of the area around here, he said, "That may not be such a bad idea. There are a lot of animals to hunt around here, and many more stay in the valley where my camp was, although that camp location left much to be desired. But with the shelter here, this would be great."

"One thing, with more traffic going in and out of the valley, the animals may move away. That is one more concern to worry about," observed Cytar.

Estavona looked closely at the ridge separating the two camps. "Landar, I think that with a lot of effort, we could clear a decent path to my old camp. We could be in the other valley in an hour or two. It would just take a lot of work." Estavona whistled and waved for Festuno, quickly filling him in on the ideas.

"You know," observed Cytar, "with all the extra women in this camp, I think you would soon fill it up with new men. Just make sure they are the kind you want."

Festuno gave Cytar a shining grin.

"There is also another valley to the west of us," attested Landar.

Cytar's eyes sparkled. "How easy is it to get to from here?"

"I can make it there in about an hour on horseback or on foot either."

Festuno was rubbing his hands together now. "When spring thaws, we could have next winter's food stored in a single moon cycle if we get the path finished to the east."

"We should gather the camp for a talk."

Work began on the eastern ridge the next day in spite of the snow. Festuno knew of a very thin section of the ridge and was leading the work on it there. A very smooth path was quickly forming, and Festuno could already see into the old camp. It would not take much longer to break through and have the path completed.

Suddenly, he signaled all work to stop as he peeked down into the old camp. Towsal stood in the middle of the camp looking around as if trying to figure out where everyone had gone. His men were coming out of the lodges empty-handed and shrugging their shoulders. Even though Towsal could not see Festuno, he obviously thought about the camp to the west. A quick signal to his men and they melted back into the mountain trail to head west.

Quickly, Festuno sent everyone to camp for an emergency meeting.

Landar showed the three places the attackers could come off of the mountain. After a little study, traps were set at each one. It was hoped that the attackers would charge from all three spots at the same time. A close check on the trails made Cytar wonder what kind of desperation would send marauders out in such terrible weather conditions. The trails were solid, slick ice. How they could move across these trails without injuries was beyond him. He warned everyone in camp that Towsal's men would be insanely desperate and to take no chances with them.

Many of the camp women had ridden on raids before and could use a spear very well. They had been training throughout the winter and that made them even more dangerous to attackers. The men had also been getting some training. The extra bows that had been brought along on this trip were now in the hands of fourteen selected women. Twenty-one bows would be spitting arrows, eighteen of which would continue to shoot even as the men faced off with the attackers.

Cytar stressed using care to select targets. It would not be helpful to be shooting the men of this camp instead of the attackers.

Water had been poured on the ground from the edge of the trees all the way to the edge of the lodges. Towsal's troops would find it hard to make a run into this camp. A lookout was posted where he could see a portion of the trail up on the mountain from where the attackers would be coming.

The camp was ready.

Towsal stood in the middle of Estavona's camp, but it was totally empty. Everything was gone. From the looks of the camp, they had left before the first snow of the winter. Why would every one of them move out like this? Were they really so afraid of him after all? True, he was here looking for them now and they should have been afraid, but were they really so smart as to know this back then? He could not help but strut a little as he thought of them leaving because of their fear of him.

What about the other camp? From the stories he heard, their men had all been killed and they would be there all alone needing some men to care for them. Towsal had a wolfish grin on his face as he thought of the warm women and good food just waiting for them. Turning, he signaled the men that they were going to the next camp. Though the men grumbled, they knew they could not eat what was not here.

Towsal heard a man slip and fall over the edge. He was already down to eighteen in his assault party. Even the women and children had come because there was just not any food left to eat at his camp. It was pure idiocy to travel these trails, but there was simply no other choice. A short scream and a smacking sound came to him, and he knew a woman had gone down. She must have been killed or knocked unconscious because there was no further sound from her.

Finally, he got a glimpse of the camp and saw smoke coming from the lodges. Good, they were there after all. Just a little farther now, and they would be off of this ice. Just down to that tree and he would split them up into three groups. Another woman went over the edge and screamed all the way down and loudly crashed into the brush at the bottom.

Of all the luck, Towsal was sure the camp had heard that one, but when no one showed, he began to wonder. Where were they, asleep? Well, why not on a day like this? There was not much to do in weather like this, but it seemed to him that there were a lot of tables set up around the camp.

Finally, he could divide his force up. With so few left, it was good that the camp was asleep. He still had sixteen left, seventeen if he counted himself. Two groups of six marauders each, and he made five in the group he led. "Well," he thought to himself, "I am worth any two other men any day in a fight. All I have to do now was give the signal."

At the first yell, Cytar rose up from behind a table and saw the lead attacker on one trail get hit with a log. One was yanked by the foot and swung into sharp spikes on a second trail and another was hit in the face by a large, fast-moving limb with a large knot that hit right where his nose met his forehead. He shot another attacker in the chest.

At his movement, all the defenders began to shoot arrows or throw spears at the attackers. The attackers quickly became hard to hit, for as they reached the ice, they fell down and began sliding everywhere. In spite of being hard to hit, not one attacker ever managed to regain his feet.

As the camp members began to collect the bodies and strip away everything, Petraina made an observation, "It looks like they brought their entire camp. Just look at who all are here, even the younger ones." Even the hardened marauder was slightly pale as he looked over the dead bodies.

It was too cold to bury them so a funeral pyre was made and would be kept burning for days, until there was nothing left but ashes. Everyone was silent as they stood staring into the flames beginning to consume the bodies.

Petara looked at Estavona and said, "A tough bunch of fighters like that, and look how easily we wiped them out. Estavona, I do not ever want to be on a raid again."

Every one of them agreed with his sentiments.

"As soon as the weather permits, we should go to their camp and make sure no one was left behind. If there are any sick or injured people there, we need to see to their well-being."

"I agree with you, Estavona, no one should be left there to suffer."

Hertalo was getting excited. "Can you imagine, when word gets out that three tough bands of outlaws have been wiped out of this part of the land, people will feel free to come here now? What is so funny?" He looked around at everyone laughing.

"Do you realize what you just said?"

"What do you mean, Festuno?"

"You just said *we* were wiped out."

The blank look slowly changed to a grin as he realized his camp was not really wiped out. "Well, you understand what I am trying to say, and we *were* put out of operation anyway. If there are any outlaws left in these mountains, they are probably all way over on the south side."

The next day, Hertalo found a woman who had wandered out of the brush on the mountainside. She had been the last one to fall and had landed in brush instead of on rocks. She was very dazed, cut, and bruised, not to mention starving and freezing; but she was alive. She was only fourteen and very pretty. Hertalo felt it was his duty to attend to her. She seemed pleased with his attentions. Her name was Talola, and she joyfully made the most of the leftover clothing that had been worn by Towsal's camp.

Shortly after Estavona's Camp had joined Simonia's Camp, Hertalo had noticed how Cytar was working with Dorazar, helping him learn to hunt and fight. Hertalo asked if he could work with them also and maybe Rudo could as well. Cytar agreed because he knew these young ones would be the heart of the new camp's future.

Marcina decided Cytar needed to train all of the young camp members. He agreed, and all the younger members were gathered for a talk to find out what skills each one had or wanted to learn. Soon, the older camp members were training the younger ones. Cytar and his group assisted where needed. All the skills needed for a camp to function properly were now being learned. Any older members wanting to learn a new skill joined in the training right beside the young ones. Young people are quick to learn and many times had to help the older ones with the new skills. That helped strengthen the understanding of the younger ones and also formed bonds among the camp people.

This was the second day since the snow had gone, and the men decided it was time to go and check on the remains of Towsal's Camp. Declon and Ramoar would stay and keep order with Festuno, Hertalo, and Petara. Of course, Landar and Dantura were staying as well, though Landar would ride out to the end of the valley with them. He was carrying some of his trail markers. No one even counted Petty any more. Cytar and Estavona took the other men and rode the longer but much easier way that Estavona knew.

The sun had been bright, and much of the water had evaporated or soaked down into the soil, giving excellent footing for the horses. Only two packhorses had been brought to carry tents and food to allow them to travel as rapidly as possible.

As the little band came out of the valley, Estavona found the east/west trail and showed Cytar and Clartan where the trail to the Ghaunt caves split off, turning north. Landar dropped off here and would return to camp after placing his markers for travelers to see. He had made two of the markers that pointed in three directions. He placed the first one at the junction where the north trail split so it pointed east, west, and north.

The men looked at the marker and decided it was going to do its intended job. As they left for the other camp, Landar moved back to the spot where the trail to the valley split off and placed the other three-way marker there. The two markers were within plain sight of each other.

The trail led to a river that turned southwest. Estavona pointed to it. "This river actually comes off the mountain not very far back behind my old camp, but there is no way to follow it from there out to Towsal's Camp."

The river made a bend where it turned southwest, and just below the bend was a natural ford where the east/west trail crossed the river. After crossing the river, Estavona turned south away from the trail.

"Towsal's Camp is about a half day's ride south of here. He located his camp there to prey on traders using this trail. It is getting late, and it would be wise to camp here for the night. That will get us there tomorrow, with plenty of light. Down in this little wash is a good camping site where our fire will not be seen. The trail down to the site is smooth, so if the river rises during the night, we can come back up with no trouble."

The travelers had been riding for about two hours when Cytar spotted a large red deer step out of the trees a good distance ahead. The deer seemed very skittish, often glancing back behind it. Once Cytar knew he was within range of the deer, he decided to go ahead and shoot, because he was sure it was on the verge of bolting. He backed up to a tree for support, noted how the breeze was blowing, drew back his bow, and carefully released the arrow.

The men snorted that he would even try to hit something so far away. They had never seen what a composite bow could really do. The arrow hit the deer in the chest and pierced both lungs. The deer spun and raced away but dropped before reentering the line of trees.

Cytar took a deep sigh of relief before turning to the men. He saw that even Clartan was standing and staring shocked at the distance. Cytar knew the deer was approximately the distance of 210 men standing with their arms outstretched and touching fingertips (or 210 alds).

"I truly do hate shooting at living animals at that range. The chances of a wounded animal rather than a clean kill are far too great. I would not have taken this shot if we had not needed the meat so badly. I am very glad that I did not have to spend the next two days tracking down that deer."

The men were experienced hunters and understood why he was disturbed about shooting over such a long distance. Clartan noticed that Cytar's hands were still shaking slightly as the deer was tied across one packhorse after being field dressed.

Estavona led them into the camp in the middle of the day. An old man stepped out to meet them. Estavona had been in this camp before and knew the old man so he began talking to him. "Greetings, Thomasa. I see you outlasted another winter. I hope Ellsa fared as well."

"Yes, she is too mean and cruel to die before me. I think she lives just to torment me. What brings you here, Estavona?" Thomasa knew Towsal had left here to raid Estavona's Camp. This must mean Towsal came off second best in the two-sided fight. In other words, he lost! Thomasa was not surprised; he had always felt Towsal had greatly underestimated Estavona and his band of men.

"As you fully know, Towsal came to pay us a visit during the winter. Talola has moved in with Hertalo, you remember him. We held the burial rites for the rest of Towsal's band."

"I always did like that sweet little girl, Talola. I am glad she survived. Another one of the youngsters crawled back here with a bad ankle. He said he slipped on the ice and hurt it. Young Cartio, he is close to fourteen now."

"Is anyone else here?"

"No, Towsal took everyone, including two other youngsters I would have liked to see return. There was no food here at all. After he left, I slaughtered one of the oldest horses. I was planning on doing another one tomorrow if Towsal did not return."

"We have fresh meat."

"So I see. Well, get down, and we shall make it edible."

Ellsa stepped out as the men began unpacking. Quickly, she cut a haunch and started it roasting. Cartio came out and also helped unpack, though he was still favoring his foot.

Cytar saw the boy limping and told him to sit down so that Cytar could examine it. He probed and prodded the ankle from every direction and decided it was only a very bad sprain. However, such an injury could, at times, be more painful than a break. Taking the boy inside, Cytar heated a large, high-sided wooden bowl of water and added some of his roots and herbs. When the water was warm enough to suit him, he had the boy place his foot in it and told him to stay there until everyone was inside.

Thomasa told Estavona that the meat pits were still frozen if he wanted to put the meat into one of them. Estavona decided that sounded like a great idea.

Estavona stepped over to greet Ellsa. She looked at him with tears in her eyes and said, "If the sun holds, by tomorrow, I should be able to find us some greens."

Estavona put his arms around her and held her while she cried. "I-I am so glad Towsal did not harm you. Y-you are so much of a better man than he was."

"This camp is terrible, there is no protection from the weather or the wind, the camp is set too far from the water, and the feed pastures for the horses are too hard to get to. I want you and Thomasa to come live with us so we can take care of you. You will also have Simonia to visit with, for that is our home now. Several men are there now that are trying very hard to become honest merchants, and there is a good batch of children of various ages for you to yell at. And for the moment, there are many more women than men. We are in hopes that, as word gets out that we are honest, other honest men that want to find a new mate will feel like joining us."

"What happened?"

"We held a funeral pyre for Towsal and his people. It was much too cold to dig holes."

"Are you and your men so tough now that you could so easily defeat Towsal?"

"Do you see those two men standing over there? They came with two other men, three women, three children and four wolves to escort Landar back to his camp after his band tried to attack Gondal. Landar lost his right hand but was the only one of the marauders to live through the attack. He told them of all the women and children left back at his camp so they brought twelve horses loaded with food to help feed everyone through the winter.

"After they got to the camp, those seven adults went out and drove a herd of aurochs up to the camp and killed nineteen of them, nineteen. They left their children with Landar's woman while they did the hunt. They understand people like a *true* master hunter can understand trail sign and knew that their children would be safe with her.

"When three of my men heard of their men being killed, they went over to the camp and managed to get broken all to pieces. Petty was broken so badly by one of the women, his arm had to be removed. The leader of their little band decided he did not want to have to worry about me all winter and brought his band to my camp. Seven adults, four wolves, and three children showed up. They were so confident of their abilities, they did not even leave their children in the safety of Simonia's Camp.

"When I looked up and saw the children, I knew right then not to oppose them. The oldest girl, three season cycles old, was holding her bow on me with a little stick in it all of that long." Estavona indicated slightly more than the length of his hand and continued, "The younger two held bows also, but they did not have even a stick to put in them. I decided right then I wanted to make friends with them, not fight them. They helped us move our entire camp over with them.

"Then they trained us in fighting techniques I have never seen before. When Towsal hit us, they never even got all the way into camp. Ellsa, when my men saw how quickly and easily Towsal's band died, they—every one of them—swore to me that they were through with ransacking. It is just too dangerous anymore."

"That deer you are cooking, the leader Cytar shot it with his bow from farther away than that big rock on the other side of the river is from here. One shot, and the deer died before it could get back to the trees."

"What is a bow?"

"Cytar, would you show Ellsa your bow and an arrow please?"

Cytar stepped over and held the bow and placed an arrow in it but did not draw it.

"Are you saying that little bitty spear killed this deer from that far away?"

Cytar smiled at her. He had one arrow that had the front half of the tip broken off. He invited her to watch and replaced the good arrow with the broken tipped one as he stepped outside.

Estavona called, "Thomasa, Cartio, come watch this."

Cytar turned to look at Cartio and nodded. Cartio pulled his foot out of the water and came over.

"Cytar, what would happen if you hit that rock over there?"

Cytar chuckled and said, "The same thing that would happen if you hit it with a spear."

In one swift movement, Cytar drew, aimed, and released the arrow. The arrow exploded against the solid rock.

"I never saw a spear hit so hard as to do that." Thomasa was shaking his head.

"Estavona said this deer was farther away than that rock."

Cytar turned and motioned Cartio to go back inside. Cytar quickly followed him inside and wrapped the foot securely, and then told the boy to stay off of it until they left.

Estavona asked Clartan to accompany Ellsa while she gathered greens for the midday meal. The rest of the men went through everything to see if any of it was worth taking back. A pile was made for all of the broken or worn out gear, supplies and tools.

After she returned from gathering greens, Ellsa set aside enough meat to cook for the evening meal and have enough left for a cold breakfast, because there would not be time to cook in the morning. She then started drying the rest.

The last things packed were the hides from the doorways. They were used to cover several of the packs on the horses. Estavona was smiling. They had gained twenty-eight new spare horses, although there were still a couple of rather old ones and a few others, which would need to be culled soon. Cytar saw one fine young mare and traded Estavona for her. He knew he overpaid but was happy to see the look of triumph on Estavona's face. Cytar did not like leaving enemies behind him.

5

Back To Gondal

The band of riders was nearing the north trail split when Cartio called out to Estavona and raced forward. "Estavona, look at this. What do you think it is?"

Most of the men laughed as Cartio rode up to the trail marker.

"Landar will be very proud when we tell him about this." Estavona then explained how hard Landar had worked making the trail markers. When he pointed to the other one, Cartio whooped and rode over to it.

"This one says we could turn this way to find food and fire."

"So be it. We go as it indicates."

Clartan rode ahead of the rest to let the camp know they were returning. After making his announcement to Declon and kissing Antana, he headed back to let Cytar know all was well for them to return. Antana and Marcina grabbed their children and horses and followed him. Dac's pack of wolves followed the women. Declon sat down on the ground and laughed as he watched.

Ellsa shivered as she saw the wolves racing toward them. Cytar rode ahead to speak to Clartan, greet the women, and stop the wolves. Too many of the horses here had not yet met the wolves, and he did not want a stampede. After greeting the pack of women, kids, and wolves, Cytar had Clartan and Antana take the wolves back to camp. Shalela decided she had to ride in front of her father on his horse.

"What about Pixie?" asked Marcina?

"Pict-see," called Shalela and motioned with her hand for Pixie to come. Pixie put her nose on Cytar's shoulder for a moment to greet him then followed along.

Cytar rode next to Ellsa's horse and introduced her to Marcina and Shalela…and Pixie too after she nickered for attention.

"Man-ear," said Shalela.

Cytar looked at Marcina. "Shalela, it was supposed to be a surprise," she said and smiled at the young girl. "Landar's markers worked. We have a new trader here."

Estavona whooped and yelled the news to the rest that the markers had worked."

Cartio was still talking excitedly about the markers that evening after the meal. Landar was beaming with pride.

"Greetings, friends, my name is Tycho," spoke the trader as he started his story. "I am a trader from the little camp named Varnis, of the Ital People. My story is simple. A trader of the Tonopus People and well known to us arrived at my camp from the west just before winter set in. I had just arrived back from my own trading mission. During the winter he spent with us, he told the most marvelous tales of traveling all across the north—from far to the east, in the lands of the Scytan People, to the west, all the way to the Far-Reaching Waters at Gondal."

Clartan started to grin and squirm with excitement. As the tale continued, Marcina and Antana began grinning also. Cytar and his siblings were much better at hiding their emotions.

"His name is Apopus, and he told of wars and renegades, of trading with the people of the Dolnii, the Goyets, the Ghaunts, the Marcels, and of course, the Itals. He brought a new weapon with him and told of a man that he called friend but whose enemies called death. He said this man was named Cytar."

"Hey, that is you!" Cartio cried out. Everyone gave him a dirty look for interrupting the story. Ellsa shushed him.

Tycho looked around the group and asked, "One of you is this Cytar?"

"I am."

"Then you know Apopus."

"Yes, but do go on with your story. Most of the people here have not heard of him."

"Is it true that you fought a great war in the land of the Scytan and mated with their most beautiful woman?"

"Yes, we fought with the Sarain People when they attacked and tried to wipe us out. This is my Marcina." And he pulled her to him. "And Clartan here, also of the Scytan, mated the most beautiful woman of all the Dolnii." Cytar indicated Clartan and Antana.

Tycho beamed with delight. "Yes, he said that as well. And you had running battles with some renegade all over everywhere, from the Scytan lands, clear to Gondal?"

"Yes, his name is Nickotian, and he is of the Sarain, one of the few still alive."

With each exploit, the camp members were becoming more and more amazed. To be hearing of these exploits, not from Cytar or his band, but from a total stranger made them sound even more dramatic.

"You are not of the Scytan People, though, are you?" asked Tycho.

"No, we come from the Kychee People on the shores of the Far-Reaching Waters far to the east."

A gasp went through the crowd. Most were not aware of this fact.

"You said 'we.' Are there others with you?"

"I followed two cycles of seasons after my brother and sister came west. She mated with a man from Gondal. All three are here now, along with her daughter."

"Apopus also said that at Gondal, you wiped out a large band of renegades."

"Actually, there were two attacks against Gondal. He left after the first one. The second attempt was the one made by the original men from this camp. We came here to help those who were left, begin a new life."

Petty staggered up and fell on top of the trader before drunkenly slurring, "Yes an-na wash out fer tha witch there. She t-tr-ripped my a-arm off, shee," while trying to indicate the vacant shoulder with his other hand.

Festuno used a sedative, in the form of a hard fist to the chin, to put Petty to sleep.

Tycho blanched as he looked at the downed one-armed man and up at Marcina.

Marcina smiled and said, "I just taught a ruffian why he should be more respectful of a woman."

Most of the people there laughed and one from the back said, "She sure did that all right."

"You see that little one? She has taught me things about fighting that I never knew before. Understand, I was never afraid to walk anywhere, no matter how rough the place was, but she made me feel like a babe in arms," added Petara.

"She sure did that. She threw him all over the center of camp, and that was just in training."

"You have been training these men to fight better?"

Estavona stepped forward and said, "Let me explain it this way…" He told Tycho the story of their coming after his camp and, later, how they defeated Towsal's Camp.

Then he told how his men came to realize the true futility of living life as marauders and of their desire to start a new, better life. They also understood that as merchants, they would need to know how to protect themselves just as the merchants at Gondal had done.

Tycho continued, "Apopus also told of traveling through this area and being hit by renegades, marauders I believe you call them. There were four other traders with Apopus, and he had taught them how to use the bow and arrows. They killed seven of the marauders long before the marauders could get close enough to strike back, and that caused them to flee."

"That would have been Towsal's band. He is dead now thanks to Cytar." Estavona was speaking generally to everyone.

"How many bands of marauders around here have been totally stopped?" asked Tycho.

"Three from around here," Estavona answered. "I have no idea where the first band that hit Gondal was from, probably from south of these mountains somewhere."

"So do you display the items of the marauders here like they do at Gondal?"

"What?" exclaimed Estavona.

Cytar explained how Gondal was displaying something from each thief that tried to raid Gondal as a deterrent to other bands.

"I am not sure about that. It would really feel weird displaying marauder trophies here. I mean under the circumstances and all." Spoke Landar with evident discomfort.

"How do you think it would feel to be impaled on the end of a marauder's spear, Landar?"

"I see what you mean. Hmmm…"

"When I was wintering in Marcel's Camp a short while back, I saw that they had started to hang up tunics and other items from a small band that tried to hit them," countered Tycho.

"Yes, well, we do have some stuff from Towsal's, but we should ask the survivors if it would bother them first." Estavona turned to the four Towsal survivors. All four thought about it and decided that if it would help prevent more attacks; it should be done.

Cytar got their attention again. "That is part of the deterrent, but not all. You have to have people practicing every day, out where they can be seen, to let spies know you are alert and ready to meet them. The day you get too fat and lazy to practice any more, that is the day you become a target."

Tycho asked if he could travel with Cytar and his band to Gondal and Cytar agreed.

Everyone in camp came out to see them off, resulting in a flood of tears flowing freely, as women said their good-byes to people they had come to love.

As they were mounting up, a new group of four traders rode into camp. "This camp will do well," Cytar thought silently and smiled.

Hertalo and Talola were riding along until they reached the turnoff to the coast trail to post another of the trail markers at that fork. Petara decided to accompany them for safety, but his woman would stay at camp with her children. Petraina was riding with Rudo and Yasmi to go to the Ghaunt caves so as to invite them to come and trade.

Festuno was organizing a hunt over in the next valley to the west. He was leading five of the younger women that had been trained with the bow. It was a new experience for him to be leading a hunting party of women, but he was feeling confident in their abilities. If they were successful, he would send for others to come help with the butchering.

With all the extra horses acquired from the Towsal Camp, there were plenty of spares now and Tycho had traded for two of them. Thomasa wanted the job of caring for the horses just as he had done at his last camp, and Estavona agreed. Declon advised

Festuno to keep the best horses out of sight, or all they would have left would be the older, useless ones.

Festuno informed Declon that the cove in Estavona's Camp was still in good shape. A few of the men were talking of living there, leaving room here for travelers. Now that the pass had been opened, it would only take about a hand and one half of the sun to go from one camp to the other on foot. A watch would be kept at the pass and would send out an alarm if a problem developed. The guards could watch both valleys from there and could give warning of approaching riders or animals that could be hunted. A similar watch would be kept at the west pass, and there was talk of improving that trail as well. From their vantage points, the two guards could see and keep a watch on the mountain trails leading to the camp as well.

All seemed in order to Cytar and his band; this allowed them to leave lighthearted and looking forward to their return to Gondal.

Cytar intended to ride straight north until he hit the river that flowed northwest and follow it all the way to Gondal. As the band was riding out of the valley, three riders were seen coming in. All three were very young and laughing a lot. They did not look prosperous at all.

Cytar took one look at them and, as they neared, called to them. After telling them how safe they would be in the camp, because of how marauders were dealt with there, and of the displays to show for it, the young men snorted and said they did not need protecting.

Torena rode closer and smiled sweetly to them then said, "Little boys, you could not even handle a little woman like me, much less one of those big, mean men in the camp."

No young man of seventeen wants to hear how helpless he is, and for a tiny woman to tell him he is a helpless little boy, was enough to make him very careless.

"Let me tell you something, woman, I was able to whip anyone in camp back home."

"They must have all been very old and helpless." Torena jumped to the ground and motioned the young tough to come on and try.

One of the three was slightly smarter and looked at Cytar. "Are you really going to let him hurt her?"

"I am not worried about her. He is going to find out real fast just how dangerous life can be out here. She eats boys like him for breakfast."

Having a man calling him a boy now was more than his reason could handle. Leaping from his horse, he swung an open hand at her face to slap her.

He was not sure how he got there, but he found that he was on the ground and trying to catch his breath. Oh, he was going to teach her now! Getting up, he kicked out at her and her fist stopped his foot by hitting the shin bone just about the ankle.

He had never felt such pain in his life; he simply could not put any weight on it at all.

"Torena, I think you broke this young buck's leg." Cytar climbed down and checked the leg. "Yep, it is broken. You two take him on into camp and ask the healer to look at it. It will take you about three days to get there."

"What is she, some kind of demon?" asked the smarter one.

"Her, no, not really. When you get there, ask about Petty, the man that had his arm torn completely off by that woman there. And, fellows, they taught the women in the camp how to do the same thing to a man who does not show them enough respect."

"For real, she tore his arm off?" this from the one who had not said anything yet.

"He is still there, but he now stays drunk all the time. Now get going, your friend is in great pain."

Once the young men had ridden away, Tycho's face showed a look of wonder. "Now I know that Apopus was not lying about your fighting abilities. Did it hurt your fist to hit him like that?"

"Not really, I have conditioned my fists to be able to withstand much worse abuse than that."

"I will be seeing Apopus again some day, and I will tell him about this, and also, about the man's arm."

After each day's travel, a short practice session was held. Shalela and Rolvalar were old enough to be given little sticks for their bows, which made them very proud of being so grown up. Tycho was trained right along with the children, the only difference being, that he was allowed real arrows.

Tycho found out very quickly that Shalela was a natural born trader. By the end of the journey to Gondal, she had traded him out of three little necklaces…for three rocks! Even he was shocked at being so gullible.

Clartan spotted a herd of bison and rode over to Cytar to see if they needed to collect any meat before entering Gondal. Cytar had gotten a glimpse of the camp shortly before from the top of a hill. He knew that they would need to send someone on ahead anyway to alert Sandole of their arrival. If they killed more bison than they could carry, they could then ask for help with the meat.

The herd was slowly moving even closer to camp but still grazed behind a hill. Perfect. After getting within bow range, Antana stopped and placed the three children in a side draw right behind a coppice cluster and tied her horse back in the draw with the children. Moon stayed with the children, also to protect them. She stood beside the huge cluster, and could jump behind it if she needed to. The cluster was large enough that no bison could run through it, and was too close to the embankment for any animals to push between.

The wood cut from this cluster showed it to be an obvious favored spot for collecting wood for the camp. It now supplied Antana with wood for a fire. She could light a fire behind the cluster because the wind was blowing from the herd toward her, so the smoke would not spook them. However, it would prevent any bison from swerving around the cluster and harming her or the children. She left enough room to be able to slip between the fire and the trees to avoid any charging animals.

Cytar took Dac and the other wolves around the next hill so the bison would not stampede before everyone was ready. The other hunters slowly rode to the positions they liked and waited for Cytar.

The herd began to turn as they caught the smell of Cytar and the wolves. Cytar yelled and shot a large bull and then a female. Dac and the remainder of his pack took down the calf. Soon the other hunters began shooting. Twenty bison were put down before the rest of the herd moved away.

Ramoar was sent to the camp with the news of twenty dead bison waiting to be butchered and only eleven unloaded horses to pack the meat on.

Antana had two dead bison right beside her so she told Moon to stay with the children and started building more fires around her area before starting on the bison. Cytar began moving the other carcasses nearer to her location. Before long, fires surrounded the dead animals and the work began.

Sandole was glad to see the group and thankful for the large quantity of meat. He told them that although the fishing had been excellent, the hunting had not fared well this spring. If the presence of this herd was any indication, then that problem had been solved.

The women decided to take the children to camp and work on some of the meat and start on the hides. With a string of horses loaded with large pieces of the meat, they set out for camp. After unloading, Ramoar would bring the horses back for another load.

Torena saw the woman with whom she had arranged to keep her lodge clean while she was gone and checked with her to make sure all was in order. Next, she sent word to her brothers that the women would be working out of her lodge and the children would be there. That suited the men because they had stored the extra gear there while they had been gone anyway.

As they worked, Cytar, Declon, and Clartan told Sandole about all that had been going on where they had traveled, and he did the same for them. Tycho was also introduced to him. When told of the trail markers and how well they were working, he got a huge laugh out of the idea.

Tycho received two full bison hides for his share as well as a portion of the meat. The last four hides were given to the camp for their help in butchering and transporting the loads. Even the bones could be taken to camp because of the continuous pack trains moving everything.

Cytar and Declon managed to get twenty-seven predators of various types and sizes while the butchering was going on.

Cytar built a lodge for his family with enough space for Declon also. It was right beside Torena's lodge, and there was an enclosed walkway between the two. Cytar sectioned off separate areas by hanging large hides as interior walls. There was a sleeping area for Marcina and him, one for Declon, one for Shalela, and an extra one for guests or future children. Each sleeping area had a small storage area for extra clothing and other gear. The front doorway opened into a central common room where the hearth fire was kept. There was a covered smoke hole in the roof above the fire pit, which was built up above the walls by a full arm's length to keep the openings above the level of any snow accumulation on the roof.

The walls were of stone and rose above the roof on the two sides to help act as a firebreak between the connected structures. At roof level, a rock ledge was constructed on which to lay the cross poles for support. Just above the completed roof was another ledge to help prevent water from running down the sides of the walls. This ledge was grooved to channel rain down the stone to a drain hole rather than onto the roof. The front side of the roof was higher than the rear and a small ridge ran down the center of the roof from front to back to prevent excess snow from building up too high and crashing through.

Next to Cytar's lodge was another one with the same layout for Clartan and Antana. An enclosed walkway connected those two lodges also. One could enter Torena's lodge and leave through either Cytar's or Clartan's lodge. The spaces between the lodges were enclosed with very thick walls to keep the interior as cool as possible, and each was entered through a small, hide-covered doorway, which also opened into the covered walkway. The areas between the lodges were used for storing anything that needed to be secured or kept cool.

A small, enclosed space was built onto the front of each lodge to store heavy outdoor clothing during the winters. Clartan felt very much at home here since it was constructed so much like Snow Camp.

Cytar also made a table to sit at while working on jewelry, and Marcina used it to prepare food and serve tea. A short piece of log was cut for length with both ends trimmed flat. It was then stood on one end to be used to sit upon while at the table.

Cytar was sitting at his table working on a necklace when Torena, who also had a gift for making jewelry, walked in and asked what Cytar had that she could use for making a piece of jewelry of some type. He took her into the storage space and had her pick up one of the horse pack frames. He grabbed the other two plus his backpack.

Taking them out to the table, he took a bowl and emptied the secret compartment of the pack frame. Another bowl caught the contents of the next frame, then the next. Finally, he emptied the backpack frame into a bowl. One bowl held gemstones of all descriptions, another held teeth and claws, another was full of amber, another held shells, and the last held mother-of-pearl pieces of all sizes and shapes.

While she and Marcina, who had just come in, were getting over their shock, he went back into the storage and brought out two rolled hides. He told Marcina to put the bowls under the table and grinned. First, he showed them the white tiger fur. When Marcina squealed, Antana came running into the room. She screamed, causing Clartan and Declon to come running in from outside. Clartan took one look and said, "I remember those," and grinned.

"Fall festival is coming up, and I think you should make a heavy coat or cape out of that tiger fur because it would look great on you." Cytar handed it to Marcina. Speechless, she rolled up the white fur.

"I will help you make it," offered Antana.

Torena took the tiger's teeth and claws and told Marcina she would make jewelry for her out of them.

Clartan began to rub his hands together as Cytar picked up the other fur and spread it on the table and then poured out the teeth and claws to match this fur. The black fur even caused

Declon to catch his breath. Never had any of them seen such a perfectly pure black fur from a panther.

"This is the fur that Charlene was ready to sell her virtue and mate Cytar for."

"I do not blame her," said Antana as she ran her hand across the fur. "So what should Marcina make out of this one?"

"I have not been able to figure that one out."

Antana looked around the room. "Could we get a very light-colored skin to replace that wall skin with? If so, this would look fantastic hanging in front of the light one. And the teeth and claws could be worked into some type of decoration to bring out the fur's beauty."

"I like that idea, and I can make the decorations." Torena scooped up these as well.

Antana rolled this fur, and Torena put the bowls back on the table. "My dear brother, how on earth did you acquire all of this wealth? Just look at the things in these bowls."

"I killed the animals, polished the shells, and found or traded for the stones."

"You can polish mother-of-pearl? I am impressed. You and I have much work ahead of us, little brother," said Torena, indicating the future jewelry.

"I also have a bundle of various snake skins."

"Weee, belts. I am good at making them," squealed Antana.

Torena took some leather pouches and emptied the bowls' contents into them then placed the pouches into the bowls.

"Little brother, you have enough wealth here that, maybe, even your older brother can find a mate."

"Thank you, Torena, but I will get a mate when I feel like it and not before," stated Declon.

"And while we are waiting, we three women have to spend our time taking care of you."

"So are you that tired of me?"

"You raise your voice to me, and I will throw you to the ground and sit on you."

Ramoar walked in and said, "Are those two at it again. That was what they were doing when I met them."

Everyone laughed then. Torena leaned up against Declon and said, "He knows I would be devastated if anything ever happened to him."

Declon responded by wrapping his arms around her.

"You know, it would be very easy to build another lodge and connect it onto the other side of Torena. A woman would make it a nice, cozy home for you."

"Not you too, little brother."

"Well, you know you are beginning to get a little older now and a nice fat woman would sure help to keep your poor old chilled body warm at night.

Cytar ducked the fist that flew at him along with sputtering, incoherent words, "Fat woman…my…old…"

"Mommy, what is wrong with Uncka Dec?"

"Sweetheart, would it be all right with you for me to bust your father's thick head?" Declon asked the young girl.

"No! Uncka, if you do that I punch you," Shalela said as she held up a tiny fist.

He laughed, picked her up, and squeezed her tightly. She responded by giving him a kiss.

"You see?" asked Ramoar, looking at Clartan as he shrugged and pointed at his mate and her family, "I think the whole family is nuts, even the little one."

Torena patted his arm and kissed him.

6

Cheeville

The women worked on the new outfits for the fall festival with such zeal that the men felt it wise to find projects outside.

Declon was in one of his strange moods. He was looking for a resin that would thicken and then harden after being boiled. He had tried pine sap, and after it cooled, he had a thin liquid that he found would make a terrific solvent but was not close to being what he was looking for.

When Cytar clapped him on the back for such a great find and telling him that Uncle Becarlon would be proud of him, Declon growled and said, "Whoopee." Clartan looked at him, puzzled, and Cytar explained that when Declon started to experiment and was looking for a certain result; he could accidentally discover something different, like a cure for death, and not be happy about it at all. However, he was smart enough not to discard what he did find.

"Why does he want to find something that hardens?"

Declon sat back and sighed. "I want to find an improved coating to put on a new bow after all other work has been completed. I want something that is strong and much more water resistant, yet flexible enough to withstand the stresses of being a bow's outer coating, and very durable to make it last much longer. Of course, a cure for death might be a nice consolation prize."

"Wow, that would be great, about the coating for bows, but why are you so frantic?"

"Have you looked closely at Cytar's bow lately?"

Cytar paled and reached for his bow and saw how worn and ragged the leather wrappings were. He knew he could repair the bow and replace the wrappings, but he could never replace the charmed drawings that covered it. Cytar felt shaken to his very core, for that bow had brought him through so much. Slowly, with his mind in turmoil, Cytar walked out of camp cradling his precious bow in his arms.

"You better follow him and let him see you doing it, but do not get too close. He will not be noticing dangers in that state of mind."

Clartan nodded and grabbed his own bow along with his quiver before calling to Moon and following after Cytar. Dac caught up with Cytar and walked beside him.

The women literally flowed out of the house in their excitement to show their new jewelry to the men.

"Where is Cytar?" asked Marcina.

"In his black mind," Declon said, looking at Torena.

"Oh. He has not had one of those since before we left Kychee."

"What is this black-mind?"

"When something disturbs him deeply enough, he shuts out everything else while he deals with that one thought."

"But what could possibly be upsetting him so much?"

"His bow is sick apparently," answered Ramoar.

Antana snickered. "His bow is sick?"

"Think about it, Antana. What all have you seen him do with that bow?" asked Marcina.

"Yikes, now I understand."

Marcina was looking concerned. "Can it be repaired?"

Declon said with a serious tone, "Yes, we could make it good as new again. However, the paintings on it are very special charms, applied by the bowyer that built the bow. The charms cannot be saved. He would almost as soon burn the bow in a ceremony as to use it without those charms."

Tears began to stream down the cheeks of all three women.

"How soon?" asked Torena?

"Next spring probably," Declon answered.

Torena stood straight. "I may not know the exact charms used on the bow, but you know I have spent a lot of time learning many such magic studies, and from many more different cultures than that bowyer did, I will wager. Therefore, by next spring, Cytar gets a new *Torena* bow. Now we must finish what we are working on because I must start that bow immediately if I want to finish it by then. Dec, will you find me the wood and other materials for it please?"

The Fall Festival was starting and everyone from the camp began gathering.

Antana was wearing a yellow tunic with an X-pattern stitching of sinew, dyed a very dark red, following around all of the edges. A scene of bison on grass was embroidered across the chest area, using various colored stitching.

Her necklace was made of pieces of pink mother-of-pearl, each separated by small white pearls.

Torena wore a tunic of pale green, with slightly darker green fringe along the sleeves and around her hips. Much shorter fringe lined the bottom hem.

Small, delicate shells that looked like raindrops were scattered across the chest area.

Sayta wore an outfit that matched her mother's.

Marcina wore a very dark plain tunic that was almost black. Over the tunic was a heavy coat that covered her to her knees. The design allowed it to be worn open or closed, and it was made from the fur of the snow tiger. A matching hood hung down in the back with a soft wolverine fur inner lining, which was dark gray with very light stripes. Wolverine fur was used because of its property of preventing ice from forming from her breath. Although she was not wearing it tonight, there was an inner liner for the coat made from reindeer fur that could be worn with the fur turned away from her skin for added warmth.

Around her neck hung a necklace made from the tiger's teeth. At the center were four front teeth bracketed on each side by a large canine tooth that hung well below the smaller teeth. Two of the sharp-pointed side teeth came next to separate the next two large canine fangs. Separating each of the center teeth was a small mother-of-pearl teardrop containing a bright red garnet set into its center.

An earbob with a large claw hung from each ear and a bracelet of claws was around her wrist.

Shalela wore a tunic that matched her mother's, but her coat and jewelry were made from a wildcat to match her size.

They were dazzling to look at, and everyone did.

The men were with them, but no one noticed whether or not they wore anything at all.

The snow was deep outside, and the children were bored. Even though the adults were trying to work on projects, the children were just too distracting.

In desperation, Cytar agreed to tell them a story if they would take a nap after he finished.

"Not one of your short-short stories, Uncle Cytar." Sayta knew that he would sometimes tease them and say something silly like, "The pet mouse got away. The end."

Cytar chuckled and agreed.

"This is a story of when Uncle Dec was just a boy."

"I bet it turns out to be something he did and tells them I did it," laughed Declon.

"This was way, far back, long ago, even before the ice came."

"Hey!" grinned Declon.

The children giggled. "Uncka Dec is not that old, Papa."

"Well, it was long ago anyway. He wanted a new tunic and knew that he had to get an animal to skin first.

"He thought very hard about what would the best way to catch an animal. Well, finally, he decided to get a rope and tie it in a tree with a loop hanging down like a rabbit snare. With a rabbit snare, you have to bend over a small tree and tie the rope to the end and then use a slip knot to hold the tree over so when the rabbit puts its head in the loop and pulls, the tree is released and swings back up and hangs the rabbit. He did not know that much about snaring a rabbit yet and probably still does not."

Giggling children looked at Uncle Dec. He wrinkled his nose at them.

"So Uncle Dec found a piece of rope and tied a loop in one end. While holding on to the opposite end, he then started to climb into a tree. Down the trail, someone spooked a small deer, and it ran right under Uncle Dec and caught its head in the loop.

"When the deer pulled on the rope, it pulled Uncle Dec out of the tree, and he landed on the deer's back just like it was a horse. He held on to the rope and rode the deer, all the while screaming, and the deer was screaming too."

Everyone looked at Declon and burst into laughter. "I remember that," said Torena. "It is one of my first memories."

"What happened?" asked a wide-eyed Sayta.

"Well, the deer threw him off and stepped on him, and he died."

"Oh, poor Uncka Dec," said a teary-eyed little Shalela as she put her hand against his face.

"No, silly, see he is not dead. Uncle Cytar, tell the truth," laughed Sayta.

"Oh," giggled Shalela.

"All right, he was riding that deer, and it was twisting and bucking, trying to throw him off, until our Uncle Zestoan ran up and hit it in the head with an axe. The deer fell dead, and there was Uncle Dec, still sitting on top of it. Our mother ran over, picked him up, and held him while the deer was skinned and butchered. Uncle Dec got to keep the skin because he had caught it. Our mother made his new tunic from it."

Rolvalar looked at Declon and said in wonder, "How did she pick him up?"

"I was not much bigger than you at the time," chuckled Declon.

"How big were you, Papa?" asked Shalela.

"I was not born yet."

Sayta's mouth flew open, and she looked at him in shock. "Then how did you know what happened?"

"Just like you do now, I was told the story. Someday you, too, will now be able to tell your children about how Uncle Dec once rode a deer."

All three children jumped on Declon, smothering him with hugs and kisses.

Some of the snow had melted and everyone was able to get outside and visit each other. When the three women looked for the three little ones, they were found in a huddle with several of the camp's other children of similar ages. The moms walked past to get an idea of what the group was up to and heard Sayta telling the story of her uncle riding on a deer.

That evening, as the family sat together, Cytar told them that he had decided to go ahead and build another lodge next to Torena's, with another storeroom in between. If Declon ever mated, he could have the lodge, but in the meantime, it would be left open on the inside and used as a workshop for all of them. There would be a table like this one to sit at and work, and he was also going to build a higher one to stand at and work. The taller one would be built strong enough to withstand heavy loads or hard pounding. That would also give them another storeroom.

Everyone liked the idea and agreed to it. They were able to start collecting the stone the next day and made piles around where the lodge would be built. The weather would have to get better before they could cut the poles. Clartan found a large deposit of flagstone just right for putting in stone floors, and it was also collected. The flooring inside the existing lodges was installed immediately.

Sandole told Ramoar that he had a large number of poles stored just for building usage, and that he would gladly let Cytar use as many of them as he wanted so long as they were replaced next spring. Ramoar told the others of Sandole's offer that evening during the meal.

Currently, they were sharing most of their meals in order to get more of the projects finished. Winter was a time for building, repairing, and replacing. During lulls in the weather when the snow was not too deep, the lodge walls began to rise. It was decided to make the workshop twice the width, side to side, of the other lodges. This would give them room for all to work together, even when the children got old enough to start their own projects. Large poles would have to be used to help support the roof. A supporting wall of stone, midway between the sides and from the back wall to the center of the room, was built to create two sections for different purposes. There would be no room partitions inside other than the half wall.

While designing the workshop, Cytar had wanted an entryway in the back wall but could not think of any way to keep it secured against predators. While going through the poles and wood that Sandole had stored, he found a piece of wood that had been shaved flat on both sides but later discarded. The piece was a little longer than he was tall, between two and three fingers thick, and a little wider than his shoulders. He took the wooden slab back to the site where the workshop would be and sat looking at the slab.

Seeing Cytar studying the wooden slab, Torena came to him and asked, "What are you thinking of doing with that?"

"I am trying to think of a way to use this to make an opening in the back wall that can be secured to keep animals out of the lodges."

He stood the piece on one end and held one edge to let her examine it. As she pulled the opposite edge toward her, both realized the significance of how to use it for the opening. She was the one who thought of using leather straps on one side to attach it to the wall while allowing the other edge to swing open.

The completed building had an aboveground oven built of stone located against the back wall in one of the sections, complete with a stone chimney. The back wall also had a doorway that entered into another small cloak storage entry. Leading outside was the wooden slab, which was mounted to swing inward in case snow was piled against it. More importantly, it could be secured from the inside to help keep predators out. A hide was hung over the inner doorway to help block any cold winds. A cooking fire pit was put in the center of the same section.

Another of the lower tables was built and placed in the cooking area so that food could be prepared, cooked, and eaten without having to leave the workshop, or disrupt projects. Ten more short logs were cut for seating around the lower tables. Torena had a camp carver come in and cut handholds along the top edges to aid in moving the logs.

A second fire pit was created in the work area at the far front corner of the large room for more heat and light when needed. Lamp brackets were built into the walls so that oil lamps could be fitted for lighting. The lodges would be used primarily for sleeping and entertaining guests.

Declon also decided to put a bed in the cooking section of the workshop with hide curtains for privacy. There was plenty of room and he no longer had to sleep in the sleeping area next to his brother's.

Everyone was elated when the roof over the lodge and the storage space were both finished and the floors installed. Now they had the workshop and plenty of room for everyone to work without crowding, plus an entire new storage space.

After the workshop lodge was completed, the entire camp was invited to take a tour through the new structure from one end to the other. The camp tour started at Antana's lodge and ended in the workshop.

The hide drapes across each side of the cloak storage entries were tied open so everyone could see from one end of the covered passageway to the other. The cross drapes were used to help control the heat and airflow through the long hallway. The drape across the inner doorway of each lodge was also tied open to display the living quarters.

Lamps were lit in each living section so everyone could see how it had been decorated. Marcina had made sure that the light from several lamps helped to show the decorative black fur mounted on the wall.

Only the outer drapes were left closed to keep out some of the cold.

Sandole marveled at the structure. He felt that the enclosed cloak storage entries were an ingenious idea since it helped stop the heat loss when someone went into or out of the lodge, and he was not the only one to notice the wooden door leading out the back. He decided to start rebuilding the entire camp after this fashion. In many cases, all he needed to do would be to build the covered walkway onto the front of many of the existing lodges and enclose the spaces between. A straight wall along the back would also help with the uniformity.

Only so many lodges could be connected together, though, or it would make it too hard to get into or out of the camp. Cytar showed him how the firebreak walls worked and explained how they would be a tremendous aid in preventing an entire structure from burning if one lodge caught on fire.

After the camp tour, Declon moved into his new sleeping quarters and work began in the new workshop.

With the spring came a new industrious attitude in Gondal. Hunting was not the only thing that needed to be done. Cytar's clan had to replace the poles used during the initial construction, in addition to acquiring many more for the construction that Sandole was starting to rebuild the camp.

Sandole pushed everyone at a hard pace to get the camp structures finished. The camp took on a "T" shaped appearance. The newly expanded Merchant Center and some workshops faced the west in an aesthetically pleasing straight line.

Across from them, facing east, were many of the home lodges, which were aligned the same way. Seven tall men could lay down head to foot between the two rows of what Sandole had started to call *buildings*. There was still one older section of the camp that would need to be entirely rebuilt, instead of just being remodeled. That section would be done later.

Right in the center of the east-facing buildings, a path, running east/west and just as wide as the north/south path, led toward the north end of the boat docks, with space for future buildings on each side of it. On the north side, facing south, was the Kychee Exchange. At least that was what Sandole had named the dwelling occupied by the Kychee families. Sandole felt that naming the different buildings would give the camp more prestige.

Locar, Tay, and Maissee had discussed the poor condition of their old lodges. Theirs were some of the first built in Gondal and had not been constructed all that well in the beginning. They got together with Sandole and Ramoar and decided to build new lodges just like the Kychee exchange. Because they were now related, they wanted to locate them across from the *Exchange*, and facing it. Their building would be like the Exchange, because they wanted to put Rahfaul into a workshop like the setup Declon had. Their old lodges could then be torn down and another Merchant Center could be built at that spot. The old center was getting overcrowded anyway.

Sandole laughed and said he was going to start calling this section of the camp Kychee Village. Rahfaul laughed and said maybe it should be called Cheeville. Sandole liked it and that was how he began referring to it. Macelar was planning another trade mission to the Scytan and could not wait to tell Marselac about Cheeville.

Ramoar told the rest of the family about the plans at the evening meal and everyone loved the idea. Cytar sat back thinking. There would not be room for much else at the end of the path, but they could put up one long building across the end of it.

A stone-paved walkway, with a wide roof above to give some protection from rain, could run from the end of the enclosed walkway of each family building, to the matching end of the one on the front of the new building. Leaving the sides of the walkway open, allowed passage between the buildings and out of camp. The combined family could then use the new building for general gatherings and meals. It would even be large enough for the entire camp to gather in, should they want to.

Adequate space had been left in between the Cheeville buildings and the new structures making up "Merchants' Row" for future new growth to expand.

Gondal had a new face when the first traders arrived from the Ghaunt Caves. Although work was still ongoing in the rear of many buildings, the front sections were all completed and cleaned up. Sandole had insisted that all trash be taken out of camp to a common site for dumping and the "Human Waste Facilities" were placed outside of camp on a stream that traveled far away from the camp before turning to empty into the Far-Reaching Waters.

Although only Torena was Kychee, the camp was now referring to all three as the Kychee women. This little fact particularly amused Antana because she was not even mated to a Kychee man, though they had both been accepted and thought of as family.

The Kychee women watched as the traders rode into camp looking around to be sure they were in the right place. Although they had all been here many times, the camp now looked completely different. Sandole stepped out to greet his old friends and assure them they had indeed come to the right camp…even if Gondal was not their intended destination.

The women followed as Sandole pointed to the different merchant structures and said that the area was now referred to as "Merchant's Row." He then led the gaunt traders into the newest Merchant Center. The men marveled at the new stone floor as well as the covered walkway at the front of the building. Sandole explained what other future construction still waited for its turn and how proud everyone was of their camp's new appearance.

After more talk of the camp, the men started telling Sandole of happenings at the Caves. The news about the new camp to the south of them that had placed markers on the trail drew the attention of the women.

"Last summer, a man and a very young couple came to Gautier's Cave and told us about their camp and how they were looking for traders. When someone said they recognized him as a marauder, he said that, yes, he had been a marauder until a group from Gondal had convinced his entire camp to start a new lifestyle. He also said that two other marauding camps, which had refused to change and ceased to exist. His camp had agreed and now was open for honest business.

"We decided to be very careful just in case but remembered the trader that had come through telling what we thought at the time were just stories, about some people from Gondal getting rid of marauders. The ex-marauder then said they had placed markers on the trail to the camp. Later, some traders came through who had just come from that camp and said it was a very nice little place. We sent someone down to see for ourselves and had to agree that the people there were really quite nice. At least they were nice until a few tough men came into the camp. They left the camp as broken men. That camp was full of the toughest bunch of people you ever saw. They had explained that the ones from Gondal had taught them what tough really means."

Sandole laughed and pointed to the three women. "Well, there stand three of the ones that went there."

"Hoho! The people of that camp sure talked a lot about you three. It seems everyone there was in love with all three of you," said one of the men.

"We feel the same way about all of them," said Marcina.

"And your men, are they here?"

"No, they are hunting, fishing, and cutting wood."

"I was told you always carry weapons in case of marauders, yet I do not see any on you."

"That table is ours," answered Marcina as she indicated the family table. "We keep some of our weapons behind it just in case. Everyone here does. We also have other weapons placed at different locations. Just some friendly words of advice, never try to attack here."

The men gave a hearty laugh and assured her they would not.

Sayta walked up to the men and asked, "Did you know my Uncle Dec rode a deer?" She had finally found someone that had not yet heard the story. Everyone in camp knew the story by heart now.

It was well past midday when Ramoar and Locar returned with a boat loaded with fish, along with all of the other fishing boats, just as Declon and Clartan led in several other men with horses pulling twelve new poles. Cytar soon followed, leading his hunting party with twenty horses loaded with meat and hides. The camp was very busy that night smoking fish and drying meat.

The Cave traders watched in wonder as the camp worked as a unit with very successful results.

Cytar sat looking at his bow. It was so ragged now that it was almost useless. A tear rolled down his cheek as he tried to work up the courage to begin removing the leather wrappings.

All of his family gathered behind him as he held the bow.

"Cytar?" gently spoke Torena.

"Yes."

"We know how much you love that bow, but I have spent a lot of time and hard work on this and maybe it can help your sadness."

Cytar turned, and Torena handed him a new bow and quiver with a special pouch to hold the unstrung bow. It was built in the Kychee style, and when unstrung, the bow tips almost touched in the front of the bow as they curved back in toward the outside edge of the grip. The leather wrappings were colored a deep green. The front of the grip had inlaid mother-of-pearl cut in the shape of a lightning bolt. The front of the leather wrappings held many beautiful drawings, charms of which he could only identify a few. Several different colors had been used to make the drawings.

The entire bow was coated with a very hard, shiny coating. He glanced at Declon and grinned.

Carefully, he strung the bow. Kychee style bows were known for how tricky they were to string.

As he sat holding the bow ready to be used, it seemed to vibrate and sing to him. He could feel an unexplained power pulsing from the bow. Grasping an arrow, he stepped outside. Far out of camp, he saw a large rock. He fitted an arrow with reverence and felt of the pull. This bow would match his old one for strength.

With a quick draw and aim, the arrow shattered against the far distant rock, as the bow settled into his hand as if saying, "We are one."

Cytar worked his mouth, but nothing came out, so he scooped up his sister and held her to him. Torena assured him that if this bow needed repair, it would allow her to be the one to make them.

"It is incredible," came a soft murmur, muffled against her shoulder.

Everyone moved back inside and discussed what to do with the old bow.

"Give me a few days to ask it what its wish is," declared Torena.

"The bow has spoken to me," Torena explained a few days later. "It deserves and also wishes to end through cleansing fire."

The family left the camp, and that night, Cytar said good-bye to his trusty old bow.

Two days later, a blood-covered man staggered into camp. As Cytar treated his wounds, the man told of his hunting party being attacked by marauders. "I have no idea if anyone else survived," he said. "There were eight of us in the hunting party. It seemed that there were about the same number of them, but I cannot be sure. Everything just happened so fast!"

"Tell us what happened," urged Sandole.

"We had killed two deer and were cleaning them when the spears flew into us. One nicked my side, and as I rose up, I was hit on the head by a club or something. I fell into a brush-filled hollow and seemed to remember a sharp pain on my head. I must have passed out because the next thing I remember is them laughing and talking. I managed to crawl out of the brush without being heard and escaped. It took me two days traveling southwest to get here."

"Do you remember where the attack happened?" asked Cytar as he finished treating the wounds.

"I know where he means," declared Sabortay as the man told of the location.

Cytar turned to Sandole and said, "I would like to take Sabortay, Rahfaul, and Tay along with Declon and Clartan to go and see what there is left to find. Sabortay, Rahfaul, and Tay have all been well trained in using a bow, and all are superb in the woods. I will also take two of the wolves and will need enough food to feed us for two moon cycles."

"What about those other two wolves?" inquired Sandole.

"They will stay here to protect our women. Also, you should keep everyone alert in case the marauders decide to attack here while we we're gone."

It did not take long for Cytar to have his party mounted and ready to go marauder hunting.

7

A Marauder Ambush

As Cytar led out his hunting party, Sabortay rode beside him looking worried.

"It will be fine, Sabortay, we can handle them."

"No, it is not that. This just does not feel right. I know the area where we are going. There is good hunting there, but there is no one that lives close to it except us. I cannot understand why a hunting party would be there. It makes no sense. We should know the members of any camp close enough to hunt there, and that man is a stranger to me."

"Do you feel it is a trap?"

"Yes, I do. I also told Sandole of my thoughts about the whole story."

"Good, then the stranger will be watched closely."

"Cytar, what if we circled around behind them and approached at night? Do you think we could see their fire even if it was hidden from the direction of camp?"

"That is a very real possibility and a great idea."

At their next stop to rest, Cytar and Sabortay explained the plans.

"What if they plan to hit us on the way there before we become alert? Is there a spot where they might try that?" asked Declon.

"Two, in fact. I had not thought of that."

Cytar nodded. "I think we should start the circle now. That way, they might start to get nervous wondering where we are, and we can slowly work back this way looking for them. Also, that will put the breeze blowing from them to us, giving Dac and Moon their scent."

Rahfaul looked at the two wolves and asked, "Cytar, is there any particular reason you chose these two wolves, or did it matter?"

"Dac and Mr. Duyi are both male. They get along in camp, but do not work together as well on a hunt as each would with one of the females. Dac and Midnight obey me, or Marcina best. Moon will obey Clartan better than Midnight would have. This way, the two wolves will work well together, or we can split up if needed and feel confident we each have the best wolf with us."

Rahfaul looked thoughtful and nodded. His father and Sabortay agreed.

"Always remember, Rahfaul, if you are in charge of getting something done, choose the helpers with the best qualifications for each part of the job," instructed Cytar.

Sandole caught the injured man trying to leave after the hunting party left. He had Marcina set Midnight to watching the man. Sandole told him that he would be watched until the hunting party returned. If they did not return, then Sandole would know they had been directed into a trap and that would make him very unhappy. He might even be tempted to hand the man over to Marcina and her wolf.

The man blanched as he looked at the wolf. Sandole chuckled and told him that he should really be worried about the woman. She had already torn off the arm of one man.

Going very white at that news, the man looked at her and with a croaking voice said, "That was you?"

Sabortay led them far to the south and east of where the supposed attack occurred before turning back north and then to the west. It would take them an extra day to reach the site, but that pleased Cytar. He wanted the marauders to get nervous, as they would, if they were there waiting.

Sabortay led them through heavy forest to keep them out of sight while traveling. As they neared the tree line, he stopped them. Pointing up to the top of the next hill, he explained, "Up there is where the attack was supposed to have happened. We should move back into the trees and make a cold camp. After dark, we can search for firelight to see if they are waiting for us."

After dark, with no fires to be seen, Cytar and Clartan split apart taking a wolf each and slowly made their way on foot to the next hill where they met up again. Clartan returned for the rest of the party while Cytar waited and looked off to the west for a glimmer of firelight.

As the others arrived, he pointed toward the west and asked Sabortay if he thought that was light from a fire. Sabortay studied it and agreed that it did look like one. Though it was well hidden, it was not hidden well enough.

Sabortay took a stick and drew in the dirt to give the others an idea of how the land lay where the fire had been sighted. Tay added a small, washed-out ravine that he knew of that led up to the fire, which was clear of brush and easy walking.

Moon and Dac would warn each group of danger. Sabortay divided the party into two groups. Clartan and Moon was in the group with Tay. They would separate at a stand of trees on this side of the fire.

It was the darkest part of the night, the hours just before dawn, as the hunting party approached the marauders' camp from two directions.

Cytar counted twelve men, including the guard. After Sabortay used a club and knocked the guard unconscious, everyone drew their bow partway and aimed at different bedrolls, as Cytar called out to the camp to surrender.

As one, the camp leaped up and grabbed weapons. Cytar again told them to surrender and three of them started to throw at his voice. Each wolf took one marauder. Two marauders slipped away and were gone before they could be stopped. The one outlaw still standing dropped her spear and held out her hands as she listened to the two men screaming in pain from the attacking wolves.

Cytar and Clartan called to the wolves and took charge of the two injured marauders. The six marauders on the ground were dead.

As it grew light, Cytar began treating the wounds of the two men, then the head of the guard. Moon had severely chewed on her man, putting deep bite marks along both arms. Dac had done much worse to his man by crushing the right wrist and breaking the left arm with a terrible bite. Cytar recognized him.

"Well, now, look who we have here. The young punk that thought he was tough and took on little Torena."

The young man grew paler as he saw who had treated him.

"It looks like he got over that broken leg she gave him," observed Clartan.

"Yes, but he will never use this wrist again. When we get back to Gondal, I will have to remove the hand. What happened to your two friends?"

The man looked at his wrist as he struggled to find the courage to answer, "They got scared after the camp told them what happens to marauders at that camp and decided to settle down with two women from there."

"But you were too tough to settle down, huh? Now you have a broken arm to match your leg, plus a wrist that you will never be able to use again. Tell me, young fool, has the marauder life been worth the cost?"

Tears came into the man's eyes as he shook his head. "Most of the time I have even gone hungry with this band. They were a dirty, rotten bunch of losers that mainly stole from each other. Then there was our glorious leader, Nickotian, who was the worst of them, and a coward, which makes him even worse. He is one of the ones that escaped."

"Nickotian, did you say?"

"Yes, he and that dull-witted fool second of his, Baytuk."

"We will take you back to camp with us. I am sure Torena will enjoy seeing you again."

"Please do not let her hurt me again. I saw that man Petty, who the other one tore the arm from. Please, I am begging you, I do not want them to hurt me again." He said his name was Romaleo.

Cytar looked up to see the female marauder crying and saw that she looked very young. That would be typical; Nickotian probably cannot recruit adults any more. They would, too easily, see him for what he really is.

Cytar asked for the name of the other man with bites as he began treating him.

"Manu."

"Where do you come from, Manu?"

"Alba de Casa, but you would not know where that is."

"Actually, I do, or the general location anyway. But I heard it was a nice, friendly camp, not a haven for whelping young marauders."

"It is a boring place with nothing for a man to do."

"So you are having fun out here being torn to shreds by wolves instead?"

"Work the fingers on this hand. Is that all you can move them? Good girl, Moon. I think you cut the nerves in this arm. That means your thieving days are over as well, Manu."

Manu lifted his left arm and tried to move the fingers, tears sliding down his cheeks. "No! It cannot be this way. I refuse to be a cripple. If I cannot fight and raid, I might as well die."

"That is how Petty felt about being a cripple. Romaleo can tell you about the shape he is in. There were two other crippled men there, Landar and Dantura. Did you meet them as well while you were there, Romaleo?"

"Yes."

"Tell Manu about them also, tell how they both quickly overcame the loss of their right hands. Tell him how Landar made a hook from an antler to wear on his right arm."

After finishing treating Manu, Cytar moved to the head wound of the guard. "What is your name and where do you come from?"

"I am called Bear, and I come from a small camp far south of the Scytanians."

Cytar finished wrapping Bear's head and said, "There, you will live, until we get back to Gondal, anyway."

The young woman had regained her control and looked defiantly at Cytar when asked her name. "I am Edda, and I am from the Ital people. A man took me by force, so I killed him. Then I had to run away because my camp wanted to punish me for killing him, even though I could only count eleven summers at the time. Now I count sixteen, and I am still alive. What can you do to me that others would not already do, or have not already done? Even our leader started to take me until I put my knife to his throat."

"How about the man that came to Gondal, what was his name?"

"Bert, and he came from Bodus Camp, which is up north of here somewhere. He was not very intelligent."

Declon shrugged his shoulders and shook his head no when Cytar looked at him.

"We will take all of you back to camp."

"Do not expect to frighten me with your talk of mean women. I, too, am a woman and as tough as anyone."

"No, you are not like their women. You are tough, yes, but if they told me to fight you or one of their women, I would gladly choose you, Edda," declared Romaleo before continuing. "Those women literally tear parts off of a man with their bare hands. You'd have to use weapons to really hurt someone."

"You do not think I can beat you using only my hands?"

"In the shape I am in now, yes. Before that wolf got hold of me, no."

"You know me less than I thought."

"I know those women and was given a broken leg to show for it. Later, I found out she was just playing with me."

"Some women are very big and strong. You should know better."

Romaleo tried to laugh but hurt too much. "Did you say big? Edda, wait until you see her, she is smaller than you are. But she broke my leg just above my ankle merely by hitting it with her fist."

Edda sat back, dumbstruck.

Manu grew even paler. "And they are taking us back to let those women have us to...?"

"Either that or let those wolves eat us. If I remember correctly, there are more than just these two wolves. Maybe they will give Edda to the wolves and us to the women." Romaleo lost the contents of his stomach as he mentally grappled with the thought.

"And we are letting them take us?" Manu began to squirm, but the pain in his arms stopped him.

"You see how useless it is, what can we do against them? Only Edda is whole, but how far do you think she would get with these wolves chasing her down."

Clartan brought in the attackers' horses, while Rahfaul went for the hunter's horses.

"We have gained more horses again." Clartan was chuckling.

Tay stripped the dead marauders before they were buried. Laughing, he shook the tunics and said those would go on the side of Cheeville Center after it was built.

Edda looked at Romaleo and asked, "What did he mean by that?"

"I learned of it in Simonia's camp where my leg was busted. They take the tunics, or some other item of the marauders that they kill, and hang them on the sides of their lodges, to warn other marauders to leave them alone. When I asked, Estavona said that Gondal has more displayed than his camp did, or any other camp for that matter."

"But two of those tunics were worn by women."

"Yes, that is true, but they are dead now and no longer have a voice in the decision."

Edda shivered thinking of her tunic hung from a lodge wall.

Sandole brought out Bert to watch as the riders rode into camp. Bert grew pale as he saw four very sick-looking prisoners and six empty horses.

"It was Nickotian again. As usual, he ran and left his followers to delay us long enough for him to escape. His second-in-command, Baytuk, went with him. We got the rest, as usual. At this rate, Nickotian is going to bring us every young fool there is who wants to play 'Great Marauder' games." Cytar was speaking with evident disgust in his voice.

"We held this one until you made it back."

"You mean that stinking wolf held me," spat Bert.

"See, more wolves just like I said," whispered Romaleo to Edda.

Marcina laughed. "I remember you. Torena, over here, Cytar has brought a friend of yours."

Edda looked at the tiny woman that approached and then to Romaleo, whom she noticed was turning green.

"Hello, my friend. Have you come for more lessons?"

"Please, no, I just chose the wrong friends."

"At least you have learned some manners. But look, you have hurt yourself again."

"Yes, this time the wolf did the teaching."

"Oh, too bad, they do not know to be gentle with little boys like I do."

"Yes, that is true," he replied, as he remembered how gentle she was when she broke his leg. At least the leg was usable again once it had healed.

Declon slid from his mount and walked over to Bert. "Bert, I hear you are supposed to be from Bodus Camp."

"Fish Camp actually. It is a very small camp to the northwest of Bodus Camp along the coast. No one has ever heard of it, because it is so small that it does not even have a proper name."

"You may come to wish you were still there."

Declon walked away from Bert and hugged his sister. As Cytar walked toward Marcina, Bert grabbed Sandole's knife and made a lunge at Cytar. Cytar heard his movement and spun around to face him. He grabbed Bert's right wrist with his right hand, put his left hand into Bert's abdomen lifting Bert at his waist, and with a mighty heave, threw him up and over. Cytar retained his grip on Bert's wrist, causing him to stretch out full length before slamming down flat on his back. Then he took the knife out of Bert's hand before releasing the wrist.

Bert could not move. He had lost all breath and hurt too badly to think as he struggled for air.

Edda heard Romaleo exclaim, "Whoa, and I was afraid of the women."

Cytar handed the knife back to Sandole.

Sandole looked at Bert and shook his head. He was as amazed at Cytar's quick action as anyone but refused to show it. Instead, he said, "Some people just seem to be too foolish to learn."

Romaleo blushed as the words hit home with him. He was sure he would die now, even though he wanted another chance so badly. He was realizing that his old friends had been much smarter than him, not just frightened. His thoughts drifted to the young women they had stayed with, and to the one that had wanted him to stay with her. He began to wonder if Landar had a place for another worker with only one hand, and if the woman he remembered would still want him. He wanted so much to find out.

Cytar had the two injured men taken to the healer's lodge. Edda was put into Antana's care and Moon's. Declon and Mr. Duyi took charge of Bert and Bear. Cytar followed the two injured men to treat their wounds.

Cytar stayed at the healing lodge for three days before coming home. Marcina asked how his patients were doing.

"I think I managed to save Romaleo's hand. When I examined it more closely, I saw that the teeth missed the bones. There is tissue damage and his use of the hand will be limited, but there will be some slight control of it. Only time will tell how much."

That evening, the family gathered on the site of the future family center where they cooked and ate together. Sandole, Thoran, and Sabortay joined them. Edda and Bert were there as well. Bear had been given over to Sabortay's charge but was temporarily being guarded by the twins.

Sandole looked at the tunics hanging on the front of the Exchange and laughed.

Tay smiled and told him they would be moved onto the front of the center after it was finished. Sandole felt that would be a grand idea, but some should also be hung from each of the family lodge complexes as well. In fact, if the camp kept acquiring them, he would have them hung on every structure in the camp. Edda still shivered at the thought.

Declon motioned toward Bert and said to Sandole, "I think this one should be hung up tomorrow."

Bert jumped. Thoran raised his eyebrows, but Sandole nodded. "If that is the conclusion you have come to, I will take your word for it."

"Hey now, hold on here. You cannot just kill me like that."

"I am sorry, Bert, but I do not like you, and I know you are pure poison. There is no redeemable value in you that I have found yet," answered Declon without emotion.

"But what about the other three men, and her? Are you going to kill them tomorrow also?"

Edda stopped eating.

"No, the injured men have not healed yet, and she and Bear were taken with them. We will deal with their cases later. But I do not think you can wait that long."

"You are being very cold-blooded about this."

"No more so than you were when you sent me into an ambush."

Bert swung the knife he was eating with at Declon. Declon blocked the arm with his left hand and used the heel of his right hand to break Bert's nose, driving the bone into his brain. Bert fell over dead as Declon remained sitting.

Sandole stared at Bert. "I have never seen a man killed without using a weapon before."

Torena chimed in with her lovely voice, "There are many ways to kill without weapons, other than those of the body. Where we come from, the bandit problem is so bad that we had to learn them or die. One does not always have a weapon at hand when an attack comes."

"What do you do when they shoot one of those arrows at you?"

"I do not like having to catch arrows in flight, the reflexes need to be so quick to be successful. But I have caught them when it was needed."

Edda had started shaking, uncontrollably, when Bert died and could not stop.

Sandole looked at the family. "You are thinking of letting these others go, aren't you."

Cytar had spent most of the time with the injured men and answered, "We are not sure about Manu yet. His attitude is too much like Bert's. Bear is for you to decide."

"Really?" Edda whispered, unbelieving at what she was hearing.

Cytar grinned. "Besides, our cousin thinks this one would make a fine mate, if he can ever work up the courage to ask her, and if she will have him."

Tay gave a loud laugh and clapped a very red-faced Rahfaul on the back.

"Please do not toy with me if you do not mean it. Will you really let me live?"

"Yes, you have shown us the true you, the one you have hidden deep inside." Antana patted Edda on the arm as she spoke.

"You will release Romaleo also?"

Torena laughed. "He was a little thick in the head, and it took two times, but we finally got through to him."

"Maybe if I were to talk with Manu, he would change too."

Manu began threatening to kill everyone in camp, and Sandole hung him.

Romaleo watched Edda and Rahfaul's mating ceremony. He still had trouble picturing such a wild, slightly crazy, young woman meekly being mated. He decided Rahfaul would have his hands full with that one. When a group of traders decided to go to Simonia's Camp, he agreed to lead them to it. Bear was allowed to go with them as well.

As Romaleo was preparing to leave, Torena came up and hugged him. "Now you be a good little boy and do not make me have to come after you again." Then she kissed him on the forehead by poking him sharply in the stomach with a finger to make him bend over for the kiss.

The traders had learned enough about Torena not to tease Romaleo about her calling him a little boy.

Romaleo again thanked Cytar for saving his hand, hugged Antana and Marcina, and said good-bye to Clartan and Declon.

He then turned to say good-bye to Edda, but she threw her arms around his neck. With her arms firmly around his neck, Edda gave him a very hot, passionate kiss.

"What was that for?" gasped Romaleo as she released him.

"To answer those dreams you kept having about what it would be like to do that to me." She smiled and trotted back to her new mate. As much as he liked the kiss, he knew he would never try to get another one from her. He had seen her already training with Torena.

Two traders were also leaving for Goyet, and word of Nickotian's latest defeat was beginning to spread.

When Nickotian heard the story of his latest disaster, he became incensed. The group laughed as they stood looking at him. He knew he would not find anyone in this camp to follow him. Now, the Ghaunts were actively hunting for him, as were the Dolnii, the Goyets, and the Scytanians. He could not go near any of their camps. He had barely escaped from the Goyets. There were so few Sarainians left, it was hard enough just to put together a hunting party. A raiding party was out of the question. All of the outlaw camps south of the Ghaunts had been wiped out. He was beginning to feel trapped.

He and Baytuk headed south to the Bogdanans.

8

The New Prisoners

The second family lodge complex was finished as was the Cheeville Center. Maissee decided to take the workshop and let the newly mated couple have her lodge. She said that at her age, she did not need so much room. Tay and Delphinia finally convinced her to move into their lodge with them instead. They argued that they had more room than they needed because Rahfaul would be living with Edda, and they would be less lonely with her there.

Macelar and his two friends loaded up for their trek to the land of the Scytanians. Marcina sent her love to her mother and father, as did Antana to her parents. Cytar sent a necklace, made by Torena, to Andonala, and a finely carved ivory handled knife, made by Declon, for Hantiss, to say thank you for being family.

Macelar laughed and said he was anxious to tell Marselac all about Cheeville. Declon sent Jodac a collar made of snakeskin for Miss Qing and Cytar sent two new dolls that Marcina had made out of soft leather, with real arms and legs, to Janolia and Lytiss. All of the family sent their love to Marselac, Hantiss, and their families.

There were many new foals, making the horse herd almost too large. Some of the older horses were separated and were being fattened for fall slaughtering. Several others were traded away throughout the summer. Cytar kept his herd behind the Cheeville Center. Sandole kept the camp horses in another meadow. The horses for trade were kept behind the eastern Merchant Center.

The young mares, which came from Whirlwind, Pixie, Fireflight, and Moonbeam, were all sired by Dancer and showed their bloodline. Dancer also sired the foals of the other mares acquired at various times. Cytar's herd held twenty-two horses and foals, even after recently trading away a few. A few more of the current herd still waited in the trade lot.

Cytar had two young boys watching and caring for the herd. They also rode them to keep them exercised. Cytar had taught the boys to use bows for protecting the horses. They were given arrows, which were heavy enough to take down a lion, if needed. He also taught them to use throwing sticks, so they could kill rabbits or other small animals, for their midday meal. A rock fire pit had been built for them out near the edge of the far meadow for cooking. They were never to let anyone look over the horses without Cytar being there.

A trader came from the Ghaunt caves saying that he needed many horses. He was preparing to lead a group of traders on an extended journey with a vast amount of trade goods. He explained how the band of traders would travel east, past the Ital's lands, and turn south through Tonopus. They would continue traveling to distant lands far to the south for trading.

Cytar and Declon both felt called by the distant lands, but they knew that they could not afford to go off on such a journey while Nickotian still roamed the area around Gondal. Instead, they settled for asking the trader to give their greetings to Apopus in Tonopus and Tycho in Varnis.

Ten of the horses that were traded came from Cytar, leaving him feeling much better about the size and quality of his herd.

The twelve remaining horses were of excellent quality, and Cytar decided that in the future he would be very selective in adding new stock to the herd.

The family had built an oven and fire pit in the central area between the lodges and the Center. Logs had been brought in and placed around the fire for seating. A lone tree grew to one side, and Declon placed a short log in front of it so he could lean back against the tree in comfort, which caused Delphinia to start calling him Cozy Dec.

From the corner of his eye, Cytar watched as Shalela led Rolvalar and Sayta over to him. She sat in his lap, gave him a big hug, and kissed his cheek. He wrapped his arms around her but kept talking to the adults, although he saw that Edda was watching the children and winked at her when she glanced at him.

Shalela gave Cytar another kiss as he continued talking. Edda saw Sayta motion to Shalela, who then gave him another much bigger hug. Edda began to grin at the antics of the children as Cytar hugged her back but still kept talking. Rolvalar began making faces and motioning to Shalela. Shalela leaned over next to his ear and whispered, "I love you." Cytar smiled at her and kissed her on the cheek, then started to turn to Edda.

"PAPA!"

Cytar pretended to jump, causing her to squeeze his neck tightly. "Yes, Shalela?"

"I love you!"

"I love you too, sweetie."

She then made a little fist and knocked on his head. "Is anyone at home?"

"Why, I am sorry, Shalela, did you need something?"

"Yes, Papa, I desper-desper…have to have a story."

Edda was shaking from the effort of trying not to laugh, and tears were running down her face. Rahfaul looked at her and started to ask what was wrong, but she put up her hand to stop him and raced to the nearest doorway holding her mouth. A very concerned Rahfaul followed. She made it inside, but everyone still heard her laughing. She soon returned, smiling, and followed by a very red-faced Rahfaul, but he was grinning now as well.

"Do you want to hear about *The Little Old Woman and the—I Will?*"

"I like this one," beamed Torena.

Shalela nodded, and the other two plopped down at his feet. Edda cuddled with Rahfaul and leaned forward while everyone else got quiet, ready to listen as well.

"Long ago, an old woman lived in a hut with her old mate. One day, he had to go hunting for some food and asked if the old woman would be safe, and then left after she told him yes.

"She was sitting outside the front of her hut when she got very, *very*, lonely. She became so lonely that she cried out really loud in a plaintive voice, 'Who is going to come stay all *niiight* with *meee?*' and you know what?" Cytar asked in a soft voice, barely loud enough to be heard by everyone.

"What?" whispered Shalela, her eyes shining with anticipation.

Cytar pointed toward the woods as he continued, "From way back in the woods, she heard a deep, eerie voice answer, very faintly, '*I—wiiill...I—wiiill*,' and she turned to look"—Cytar gave an apprehensive look toward the woods, before continuing—"but she did not see anything." Everyone looked toward the woods as Cytar had.

All three of the children had very large eyes. Edda held her hand over her mouth while Marcina and Antana were both holding their breath.

"After a while, the old woman got hungry and went inside to get some stew. After she came back outside and ate the stew, she called out again, 'Who is going to come stay all *niiight* with *meee*.'

She heard a much louder '*I—wiiill…I—wiiill*,' from the edge of the woods right behind the hut."

Now Delphinia and Densee also held their hands to their mouths.

"The old woman went back inside to build up her fire and wash her bowl before coming back outside. She was so lonely now that she wanted to cry. 'Who is going to come stay all *niiight* with *meee*?' she called again and '*I—wiiill…I—wiiill*,' came from right behind the wood pile!" All eyes fearfully turned to the stack of wood near the fire.

Cytar chuckled to himself, because even Torena was leaning forward and holding her breath. She had heard this story, probably more times than he had.

"The old woman sat until it started to get dark then went inside again and added more wood to her fire. She got a piece of jerky and came back out to her old log to sit on as she chewed the jerky. She took a drink of water to rinse her mouth and then called out again, 'Who is going to come stay all *niiight* with *meee*?'"

Edda's eyes were now as large as the children's.

"This time it came from right beside the hut, '*I—wiiill…I—* GOTCHA!'" he shouted and lunged for Sayta.

Shalela screamed and almost broke his neck. The other two screamed and jumped up, looking around. Edda screamed and jumped so hard she knocked Rahfaul backward, off the log. Antana covered her face. Marcina screamed and hit Cytar. Torena screamed then laughed and said that story got her every time. Pointing at Rahfaul, Declon laughed so hard that he slid off *his* log. Maissee accused Cytar of trying to kill old people, as she smiled and wiped the tears from her eyes. Delphinia and Densee were both giggling and whimpering at the same time. The other men had jumped, and over by the Merchant Row, Sandole and four other men stood staring at them holding their spears.

Cytar had stepped out of the lodge and walked to where he could see the horses. He noticed one of the boys riding hard toward him and pointing to the east trail. Cytar looked, but could not see at what the boy was pointing. He motioned for him to ride toward the center of camp. Spinning around, he ran back into the lodge calling for everyone as he grabbed his bow. He had taken to keeping a bow ready at all times, just as he had done on the trip to Simonia's Camp, and everyone else did the same. Declon had made sure there were enough bows for every camp member to be able to keep one strung at all times.

Cytar saw Sandole in the middle of Merchant Row talking to Thoran and trotted toward them. The boy stopped his horse just as Cytar arrived. Catching the halter, Cytar calmed the horse so the boy could tell them what had upset him.

"We saw a man on the hill. He was staggering and fell down. I did not see him get back up."

"Show us."

Sandole and Thoran grabbed their spears and called for the rest of the camp, before following Cytar to the hill.

The boy stopped just short of the man, then pointed east, and gasped, "Cytar, lions!"

Cytar had an arrow drawn by the time he saw the first lioness. She was trailing the hurt man.

Cytar put an arrow into her neck that dropped her. Two others trotted up to sniff her and then came on.

Cytar stopped the second lion, but the third one dodged his arrow. It did not dodge Declon's arrow, however.

"Leban, you are higher than us. Can you see any other lions?"

"Steady me," said Leban, and he stood on the back of his horse to better scan the area.

"No—wait—yes, just coming out of the trees." At once, he dropped back down to sit on the horse.

"How many more?"

"Whoa, three, four, and there comes a big male."

Cytar looked around him. Clartan, Sabortay, and Tay had arrived with their bows. Rahfaul was running this way with his. Sandole and Thoran both held spears.

"I think we should have brought bows, too, instead of spears."

"It is always best to have spears to back up archers when hunting lions."

Sandole motioned for some of the men to take the injured man back to the healing lodge in camp. Turning to the bowmen, he said, "If we do not kill all of them now, they will be killing our horses tomorrow. I have seen it happen before."

"I have not seen lions around here for many seasons," said Sabortay in puzzlement. "I wonder where they came from."

"Maybe we can get an idea from the man we brought in. Did anyone know him?"

"Too much blood to tell."

"Let them come closer this time." The male stopped at the first dead female, but the other females came on.

"I guess I will take the male. Rahfaul, have you caught your breath, yet?"

"Yes."

"Do your best to make the first shot count. I do not relish the idea of tracking an injured lion."

Everyone affirmed.

"Ready? On three! One, two, three."

Six arrows flew almost as one. A second volley followed and then all the cats were still.

"Leban, have you seen any more of them?"

"None at all."

"Leban, stay here and keep watch. Everyone else, advance, very carefully, now," said Cytar loudly, before slowly walking toward the big cats.

"Declon and I will stand guard while you work on the lions. We Kychee like cat meat, you suit your own tastes."

Torena and the women arrived and took charge of the lions.

"He is Rudolo from Failan's Cave. It will be morning before he wakes up. I think he will survive, but cat scratches are so prone to infection, so we will have to wait and see." Faleenia had worked on Rudolo for a long while and looked tired.

Cytar wanted to take over for her while she rested, but Sandole told him that, right now, he needed to stay ready to respond should more lions or other threats appear.

Guards were set. The lion remains were dragged closer to be more visible, in hopes, that if other lions were around, they might come to investigate the remains. All the horses were pulled in very close to camp.

Rudolo spoke softly as he began his tale, pausing occasionally because of the pain from his injuries. "Calanar and I were on our way to Gondal when we smelled smoke. We went toward it to investigate the source of the fire and saw several people carrying torches, slowly walking toward us. Just as we saw them, a lioness leaped onto Calanar. I could tell by the way she picked him up that he was dead.

"I turned and tried to get away, and almost did, but another lioness must have seen me or caught my scent, because she came for me. I dropped the butt of my spear to brace it on the ground and caught her with the point when she leaped for me, but she slid so far onto it that she was able to swipe me with her claws before she died.

"I managed to get within sight of Gondal before everything went black."

"Where were you when you first saw the people?" asked Sandole.

"We spent the night in Traveler's Cave and the next night at Clearing Camp. It was shortly after leaving Clearing Camp that we smelled the smoke."

Sabortay looked at Sandole. "That puts the people very close to here. Do you think they were driving the lions with fire?"

"Is that possible?"

Sabortay looked at Cytar and Declon. "What do you two think?"

Cytar and Declon looked at each other and at the same time said one word: "Nickotian."

Sabortay had assured Cytar that the twins, Fartez and Fontez, were the best hunters and trackers he had ever seen and were extremely reliable. They knew all of the land around Gondal for quite a distance. They had followed Dartez north when he moved to Gondal. The three had been childhood friends, and the twins decided to keep the trio together. All had found mates here.

Sandole would keep a sharp watch for the marauders at the camp.

Cytar took Fartez, Fontez, Rahfaul, Edda and Marcina, plus Dac and Midnight, to the northeast. They would skirt the southern edge of a range of hills before turning south.

Declon took Tay, Ramoar, Torena, Clartan, Antana, Mr. Duyi, and Moon to the south, along the coast for three days before turning east.

The children were left with Maissee and Delphinia.

The two bands would rejoin at a certain known spot on the trail east of Traveler's Cave.

The twins always worked as a team when on a hunt. They each carried a quiver of arrows and a bow, but they still preferred to carry a spear while tracking, saying they could respond to a predator threat more effectively with the spear, than the bow.

Cytar sent Dac to accompany them with the command "Protect," so he would stay right with them and not roam. They went out ahead of the rest of the party to lead them and scout for tracks or threats. They were to stay within sight and do their best to keep their direction of travel into the breeze, allowing Dac to smell lions, marauders, or anything else that might lie in wait.

Midnight was told to guard the rest of the hunting party, and she constantly moved around the outer fringes of the group as they traveled. The fourth day out was when Fartez found the first tracks.

Declon and Clartan rode ahead of their hunting party, each with a wolf close by him. Mainly, they searched for tracks, because the terrain was very open and easy to travel. As a result, they rapidly covered a long distance and were sure to be well south of Traveler's Cave. With no signs of movement, other than the normal animals, for most of the trek, they reached the agreed upon campsite on the trail to the Ghaunt Caves late on the sixth day of travel, allowing them to arrive before Cytar's party. They would wait here until Cytar arrived, a wait that could easily be two more days, due to the roughness some of the terrain, which Cytar had to travel across.

Close inspection had shown the tracks of humans following those of lions. Burnt-out torches were found along the trail. The twins did a good job of keeping the small band out of sight as they followed the tracks to the ford where they had crossed the river. The twins explained to the others about the trail they had found, and Cytar decided to backtrack then cross the river farther to the east.

After crossing the river, Cytar called a halt to rest and eat. They agreed to press on so as to meet the other group before trying to follow the trail any further. Cytar decided to press hard, and they made the camp late in the evening of the seventh day.

Early the next morning, the twins set out and returned to where they had left the trail. Camp was made that night close to where Cytar had made the initial crossing.

Dawn the next morning found them studying the marauders' tracks. They now knew for sure that the marauders were still within the circle the hunters had made. From this point onward, only Traveler's Hand Speak would be used. Clartan and Moon joined the twins and Dac, in scouting ahead of the hunters.

Although the heavy forest extended far to the north, the sun did not travel past midday before the hunters were able to reach the steppes on the south side of this river. If a rider then rode due south toward the next river, he would spend at least two nights camping on the steppes before reaching the heavy forest starting just this side of that river. To the west, the two rivers came close enough together for their two forests to merge. From there onward, the forest began to thin out until it only grew in patches with large clear areas between. The alternating thick growth and clear grassland ranged for the rest of the way to Gondal.

The twins managed to keep everyone within the trees as they moved forward, even though the tracks, they followed were out in the open grassland. Although they were only covering the northern forest, Cytar was sure the marauders would be in this growth, rather than the southern one. He was assured of this because the Caves-to-Gondal Trail followed the other river and was used so regularly by travelers.

As the hunters neared the area where Rudolo told them he had encountered the lions, the twins decided to scout ahead with the wolf while the others waited. Declon reminded them that there could still be lions left alive. Fartez told Declon that a nice little clearing between two hills was just ahead, complete with a small stream supplying water. This would make a great camp for them while they waited for the twins to return.

Before leaving to search for the marauders, the twins scouted the campsite to be sure no one was camped there. Once they knew it to be safe, they led in the hunters, and then went in search of the marauders.

Cytar was very impressed with the site. A small fire here at night could not be seen from any direction, yet it would be very close to the ridgeline of the hill where a lookout could see well in all directions.

The twins returned during the morning of the second day. They had found the camp and the marauders were nursing their wounded. The hunters moved forward to a site close enough from which to strike at first light before stopping to rest.

Before going in, Cytar made sure to completely surround the camp. There were ten marauders in the camp. Only two were not wounded. The wounds of the others were bandaged, but still in need of a healer. Two were almost dead. The hunters walked into the camp without a fight. The marauders were all children really, the oldest one being only seventeen and the youngest thirteen.

Cytar cursed when one of the young marauders told him that Nickotian and Baytuk had left the day before and had not yet returned. Although Cytar wanted to go after the other two, he first had to know how this bunch had been wounded.

Oda had just finished giving feed and water to Cytar's horses when he noticed Pixie, Whirlwind, and Moonbeam were nervous and staring out into the night. Slipping back to the guard, he told him something was out beyond the camp in the dark, and from the way the horses were acting, he felt sure it was human. The guard sent him to warn everyone, starting with the extra guards staying in the Cheeville Center and Locar, who were the closest.

The camp came alive as quietly as a snake sensing a mouse. The marauders thought they had entered a hornets' nest. Five of the marauders were left dead at the edge of the camp, as the others fled for their own lives, wondering what had gone wrong with their plans.

After the failed attack, Nickotian had become furious, incoherently screaming and fuming at everything. Everyone in his camp had been afraid to even look at him. Each person feared the anger would turn on him or her. The evening before, they had buried one young man, and the way that Nickotian had been acting, they feared more would soon follow.

Cytar decided to take Clartan and the twins, plus Dac and Moon. He was going after Nickotian, and Declon was leading the others back to camp with the remaining marauders.

Marcina and Antana told their men to come home safe. Neither man wanted to leave his luscious mate, but Nickotian had already caused enough trouble and had to be stopped.

When he left, Nickotian had taken six of his camp's horses. He had used the excuse that he was going hunting and he would need the extras for carrying the meat back to camp. Another fact to be considered was that he had a two-day head start.

Cytar took Dancer and Fire-flight, Leaving Marcina to ride back with Torena. Clartan took his horse and Antana's, letting her ride back with Edda. The twins had two very good extra horses they had been using as packhorses. They took the trail food, leaving the return group just enough to get back to camp.

The tracks showed that Nickotian and Baytuk had headed due north and crossed the river. Once across, they had ridden their horses at a full run, often swapping mounts so they would last as long as possible. It was obvious the two had expected the group from Gondal to send someone after them. They had sacrificed the rest of their band to allow them time to make their own successful escape. Clearly, this was a *classic* Nickotian leadership decision.

Cytar knew they could never catch the two, now. Nickotian was running for his life and would kill his horses before he would let them catch up to him. Once again, Cytar turned back to camp without catching the troublemaker.

Declon made the trip to Gondal as easy as possible for the injured, but two died right after arriving. Of the other six, five healed without too much trouble. The last one, a girl of thirteen, was in serious condition and came very close to dying.

Sandole was caught up in a quandary. He had one male prisoner named Krontus, who was seventeen and was from Tonopus. The next oldest said she had just turned fifteen and was from the Bogdanans, a group of camps on the Great River. She was called Barba, knew how to speak Dolnii, and interpreted for the rest.

Her home camp was not that far from the Dolnii's Gap Camp. Two females, Bea and Gina, and two males, Pino and Tamar, were all fourteen and from a single camp of the Ital People. The youngest two, one male, Beezy, and one female, Alala, were both thirteen. They were from a camp to the northeast of Tonopus, but south of the Great River and were called the Plains People.

Sandole found that conversing with them was an intricate session of translation layered upon translation. Krontus could speak with Beezy and Alala. Beezy and Alala could also speak a small amount of the language spoken by Barba, who could also speak a small amount of the language Beezy and Alala used.

Krontus and the four Ital youths could speak a little to each other.

Apopus had taught a good amount of his language to the trading party while they were together. This gave Antana and Marcina the ability to speak, with limitations, to Krontus, and to the two youngest ones to a lesser extent. Declon had learned a bit of the Ital language. It only took about three hand widths of time for Sandole to learn the name, age, and home of each of the young marauders. He also learned that if he moved too quickly or spoke too loudly, several of them would collapse into hysteria, causing further delays.

Some of the Gondal youths had not helped at all. Barba had heard them talking and understood enough to realize they were talking about hanging the marauders. She then told the others. It took two days for Sandole to calm them down enough to again speak with them. Word quickly spread that Sandole was about ready to hang some of the younger crowd from his own camp because of their disruptions.

Mothers made sure to keep their young ones away from the marauders and under control. One young boy pretended to hang himself, and his father grabbed him up by the waist of his leggings and threw him into the nearby stream. The young marauders did not understand what the father said but did understand that the boy was in trouble for his actions. That helped them to feel a little safer.

Then Cytar angrily rode into camp, waving his arms around while speaking harshly. These actions set them to cowering again, although they understood a little better when he said something about Nickotian.

Eventually, Sandole helped the young marauders understand just how much everyone disliked marauders and what could happen to them when caught. He got them to understand that, although the children of his camp had behaved badly, the threat of hanging was real, and in fact, he had hung some marauders before, one being only fourteen. He reminded them of seeing eight of their number die as the result of one raid and how it felt to be abandoned when a raid had gone bad.

As Sandole now looked around at the youngsters, he saw shame, fear, and the desire to return home. As an example of how one should act, he sent for Oda. Sandole told of how brave Oda had been in doing his part to save his home. He explained how Oda's bravery differed from that of someone trying to steal what other people had worked so hard for. He told them of other marauders he had known, who had jumped at the chance to reform and begin useful lives when the opportunity had arisen.

Antana wanted to visit her home anyway, so Sandole sent her and Clartan along with Rolvalar and Declon to escort the youngsters home. He did tell them that if he ever caught them raiding again, he *would* hang them.

That night, the family said their good-byes to the four travelers. Cytar sent some jewelry with his brother to use for emergencies. The journey would lead them as straight as possible to the Gap Camp, where they would spend the winter. From there, word could be sent on ahead to Mountain Camp of their arrival.

9

Returning the Young Marauders to Their Homes

Antana had kept the party moving at a rugged pace, stopping only when Declon said the horses needed the rest. Rolvalar was beginning to show promising accuracy with his bow. Clartan taught him about tracking and hunting. Sometimes, after the evening stop, Clartan would have him track rodents for practice.

Declon continued Rolvalar's other training. The contrite youngsters were in a constant state of amazement at all the different types of combat Declon was teaching the little boy. Along with the combat lessons were other lessons, on how to get along with others and why it was important to do so. Declon was stressing these lessons for the benefit of the marauder youths, as much as he was for Rolvalar.

Rolvalar had decided he liked to be called Roly. No one knew for sure what had brought this about, but they humored him.

The entire party cheered the day Roly killed his first rabbit with his bow.

Snow had started to fall just as Declon led the traveling party into the Gap Camp. Voftonz was standing at the edge of camp, and Antana gave a screech of joy that brought others out to see what the excitement was all about. After seeing to the horses and hauling their gear inside, Voftonz welcomed everyone to the camp.

Clartan was welcomed like an old camp member, and Declon was almost revered. Roly, however, stole the day. The entire camp was taking pride in how well developed and mannerly he was. Many praises came to him when he showed his rabbit skin and told of how he had hunted it.

Finally, Antana introduced the young members of their party. She told how Nickotian was now recruiting children to be marauders, or marauders as they were called here. She told of his plan to use lions to wipe out Gondal, and forcing the children to drive the lions for a long distance by using firebrands. She mentioned his deranged anger toward the lions for their failure, and how he then sent the children to attack the camp, resulting in many being killed and more wounded. Then she explained about him losing all control because they were so unsuccessful in their attempted aggression against Gondal, even though it was his plan that failed. The narrative went on to describe how his insanity and cowardice drove him to abandon his badly wounded followers when they needed him most. She wanted all the peoples across the land to know what a sick, deranged person Nickotian was.

Barba told in detail how he ranted and raved at how stupid the lions were; when he found out they had not eaten everyone in the camp. She told of his plan to pass among the horse herd in the middle of the night, so they would not be seen as they tried to take the camp by surprise.

Uwe, the hunt leader, laughed and said that was without a doubt, the dumbest surprise attack plan he had ever heard.

Barba next told of how he would convince his recruits. "He would go into a camp where no one knew him and look for young people that were unhappy or dissatisfied with their life. He saw me having an argument with my mother about my not doing the work she had asked me to do.

"It was just a stupid little gripe from a very young and inexperienced woman, who had not yet learned what is truly important and what is not. Nevertheless, he used it to convince me to leave. He said I would live free from anyone ever telling me again, to do this or not to do that. Do you have any idea how much hard work is involved in driving a pride of lions over long distances with burning torches? That does not even take into account how scared you are the entire time that your torch will go out and the lions will turn back on you.

Barba continued, "We went to another camp where he found a young man that had just broken up with his love. Nickotian convinced him to come along and gain much wealth and importance. Then he could come back to his home camp so she could see what she had so stupidly thrown away. He died, crying from the pain of a terrible spear wound in his abdomen.

"One young woman was crying because she had had an argument with the man she was promised to. Nickotian found her crying and told her she was better than the man and deserved better. If she came with him, she would find any number of men that were better choices and much more appealing. It was a very small camp and the man was not worthy enough for the likes of her. She never returned to our camp after the raid on Gondal.

"These two little ones were promised a lot of excitement. Well, I guess they did get that, if you can call being wounded, abandoned, and threatened with hanging exciting." Barba finally broke down crying as she thought of all the young people who had not come back. Krontus jumped over beside her and held her in his arms, as she cried. A few tears could be seen leaking from his eyes as well."

Regaining her composure, Barba then told how Beezy and Alala had become extremely close. Both came from the same camp, and both had been wounded, Alala worse than Beezy, or anyone else that survived. She told how he had begun to get distraught when he thought she was going to die, and how, on this journey home, they were inseparable and held hands constantly.

The four from Mila had grown very close as well, into two very close-knit couples. Even though they had all been wounded, they had survived. Too many others had not.

Antana confided to Voftonz that she felt sure that these eight young people here would one day become the leadership of their communities.

A lull in the bad weather of early winter allowed Halgar to lead a large contingent of his Mountain Camp to Gap Camp to visit with Antana and her son. Braycon had stayed behind in charge of the ones that would guard the camp. They were all thrilled to see Declon, even though many only knew of him by reputation. With them came Apopus. When he heard the story of the young people, and that they were going to be taken home, he decided to travel with them. His company would be most welcome, as would his knowledge of trails through the areas they would be traveling. Being the trader that he was, he had brought all of his goods with him from Mountain Camp.

When Krontus stepped forward, Apopus saw him and gasped. He explained that Krontus was his sister's son, and just before he left on this latest trading mission, both Krontus and his best friend had gone missing. Apopus had started helping to look for them, until he heard they had been spending time with some man named Nickotian. When Apopus heard that name, he told everyone they had most likely been talked into joining a renegade band and told them everything he knew about Nickotian. More than ever, he would now see them home.

That night, Apopus told them of seeing Macelar in the Scytan River Camp. Macelar was having a fine time telling everyone about Cheeville. Macelar had left and was headed for Snow Camp when Apopus left to go to Meadow Camp where he saw

Galinia. She was now mated and happy. Meadow Camp was hoping Nickotian would return to visit them so they could give a party in his honor. Apopus laughed and said he was glad he was not the intended recipient of that particular honor.

Clartan began telling of all that had been done to build Cheeville and how the entire camp had taken on a new look. He described the building design, and proudly told how the idea had originally come from the Snow Camp complex. He had them laughing at his description of Sandole naming the Kychee Exchange and Cheeville, even including him and Antana as Kychee, as well as a large portion of the camp members of Gondal.

Voftonz told of how, last summer, Desya had been watching some of the children playing with some small clay figurines that they had formed. One boy had a clay bison. The boy had gotten into an argument with another child, and the clay bison had been thrown into the fire. The fire had later died out, and the next day, when Desya had begun to remove the ashes before starting a new fire, he found that the clay bison had turned to stone. Intrigued, he had worked with the clay until he learned how the fire had turned the clay into stone. Now Desya had a separate lodge dedicated to the making of the figurines. He agreed to give them a tour the next day.

Declon told of all the attacks on their camp and how they had gone to Simonia's Camp. There, they helped the camp members straighten out their lives and become as honest as any other merchants. Someone made a comment about the honesty of merchants, causing everyone to look at Apopus. They all started laughing, him included.

Clartan grinned and said, "When we helped Simonia's Camp, we returned the only man left alive after the failed raid. His name was Landar and had lost his right hand during the raid. Cytar convinced him to become a merchant. Then, we rode against Estavona's Camp and convinced the entire camp to reform. One of those men, Datura, had his right shoulder terribly injured and had only limited use after it healed.

"Landar talked him into joining the effort to run the trade center. While trying to figure out how to get traders to stop and trade in the camp, Landar and Datura came up with the idea of putting markers along the trail showing where the camp is. They seemed to be working very well."

"That is a marvelous idea," came a voice from the crowd.

"Say, I heard about those trail markers from some traders that I met," said Apopus.

Throughout the evening, Apopus had been watching Krontus and Barba. He started to dig through the items in his trade goods and pulled out a scarf. It was made of some type of strange material that had the appearance of hair.

"This is called a scarf and comes from Ur, a large camp out in the desert far south of Tonopus. They take the wool of a sheep and twist it into a string that can then be woven into cloth." Apopus smiled at Barba and handed the scarf to Krontus as he continued speaking, "You should give this to someone that means very much to you."

Krontus understood and smiled at Barba as he wrapped the scarf around her.

Barba began crying as she hugged both men, and Apopus received a kiss on the cheek.

Apopus carefully led the party south from Gap Camp to avoid all of the large holes in the area. Antana thought of the departure and leaving her mother and father. Once again, she had to tell them good-bye. Wemeta had hugged Roly and kissed on him until he ran and hid behind Halgar.

Halgar assured her that he would send a messenger to the Scytan with the latest news of Clartan and Marcina. Also, word would be spread to all the camps he knew, telling of Nickotian's recruiting of young adults and older children, either getting them killed or abandoning them to the judgments of angered, vengeful camps.

Once they were through the rugged area, travel became much easier. Apopus led them across wonderful grasslands, but also along the edge of a forest. Wood was plentiful here, as well as many herds of animals. This early in the season, the mammoths and wooly rhinos had not yet made the trip back south from the Great Ice Wall. There were, however, bison, aurochs, horses, red deer, saiga antelope, roe deer, reindeer, and megaceros, along with cave lions, wolves, hyenas, and many other animals.

Clartan started to name each of the different birds he saw, while trying not to name any more than once. Soon, all the younger members of the party were correcting him. Before long, even they could not keep up with all of the different types of birds.

Springs poured forth water from an uncountable number of sources. Vegetables of many varieties were sprouting everywhere. The temperatures were mild during this season, and by exercising proper caution, life on the trip through here was very enjoyable.

Declon brought the party to a halt near a large herd of bison. After close inspection, he motioned that there were hunters on the south side of the herd and for them to move west into the trees. After crossing a stream, he turned south again. Barba asked if the hunters could be her Bogdanan people. Declon told her it was, indeed, very possible. Still, it was not safe to be on the wrong side of the herd if it started to stampede.

At that moment, the sounds of something crashing through the brush reached them from the east. When the younger members saw the four adults raise their bows in readiness, they did likewise.

Part of the herd of bison charged out of the trees toward them. Once the herd had passed, Declon found a dead bull, two dead cows, and two dead calves. Scratching his head at all the meat they had just acquired, he chuckled and said to no one in particular, "Well, it looks like we eat well tonight."

Declon had Beezy and Alala stand guard with the two wolves, while the rest worked on the bison.

"Declon, Moon is growling," Alala announced softly.

Declon and Apopus came to the youngsters while Clartan moved off to the side. Four hunters came out of the trees and quickly assessed the situation. Apopus put away his bow and greeted the hunters. After a few words with them, he turned and called out Barba's name.

A naked, walking pile of bloody gore crawled out of one of the bison and approached. One of the hunters had jerked at hearing the name, but there was no way to recognize this thing coming at them.

"Wow, Barba, you look terrible," laughed Alala in Barba's language.

Barba looked down at herself and shrieked. "I will be right back," she said in her language as she spun on her heels and raced to the middle of the stream.

All hunters knew how nasty butchering large animals could be. Therefore, this group of hunters, even had they not understood her words, would have seen the humor in her situation.

Alala ran after her to help her.

A very clean and freshly dressed, Barba soon returned. The hunter, who had jerked at her name, was watching her closely as she returned.

"Barba, it is you," shouted the hunter.

"Father, oh am I glad to see you," exclaimed Barba as she ran into his outstretched arms. She then gave a very brief, shamed-faced explanation about why she was here.

Another of the hunters welcomed the party to the lands of the Bogdanans and said they would talk more after the meat was processed. He then turned to a very young hunter and told him to return to the main group and bring anyone that could be spared from that location. Turning back to look at the party, he laughed and said how amazed he was that so few could kill as many bison as his large hunting band had, especially with so many young people.

Barba's father advised her to stay clean until the others arrived. They would want to greet her also. She had been sorely missed.

Five more hunters returned with the young hunter, one being Barba's mother, and another her aunt. Of course, the young hunter had already described, in hilarious detail to the other hunting group, how Barba had first met the hunt leader.

After much hugging and crying, Barba's father intervened and had his daughter, her mother, and her aunt work on the meat, asking them to save any more talking for later.

Later on that evening, all the butchering had been done, and the meat was either cooking, or on racks being dried. As everyone sat eating, Barba told the Bogdanans all that had happened and how Nickotian had recruited them.

One man got her attention. "Is it just you? What about…?"

By then, Barba was sobbing and shaking her head no. His face fell at the news.

"I am sorry, but I am the only one from our people that survived. She went quickly and without too much pain. I truly do not think she had time to feel anything. Please do not ask me about the others."

Krontus put his arms around her and let her cry. Everyone could see how hard he was struggling not to cry. Barba's mother watched him protecting her and looked over at her sister. They nodded at the same time. Barba had found her man and he was taking care of her.

The travelers spent a quarter moon in Barba's home camp. They recounted all that had happened across the land, from the Far-Reaching Waters to the east all the way to the Far-Reaching Waters of the west. The people of the camp were in wonder at hearing so much news from so many different places. Antana invited the Bogdanans to visit the Dolnii. Clartan invited them to the lands of the Scytan, Apopus told them to be sure to visit Tonopus, and Declon invited them to both Gondal to the west and to his Kychee home far to the east. Even the four young Itals gave an invitation.

One morning, Apopus called everyone to listen as he said, "It is time for us to resume our travels. We will leave after the meal in the morning."

"I shall escort you to the camp of the Plains People, along with some of our people," the leader of Barba's old camp informed Apopus.

Barba had been very nervous since midday. Finally, she turned to her mother. "I love you and Father deeply, and I am so sorry for having hurt you the way I did. But there is one thing I have to tell you, and I want it to make you happy for me and not be hurt again."

"There is no problem, my child, your aunt and I have known ever since the first night in the hunting camp that you would be going to Tonopus with Krontus."

Barba stood there with her mouth open as her mother ran fingers through Barba's hair, smiling.

"But how…?"

"We have eyes, child, *and* we know how to use them. We saw how he comforted and protected you while you were telling us of what happened. He did it again here at home when you faced the entire camp with your misdeeds. He is a fine young man, and everyone here likes his uncle Apopus. Just make sure you and he stay on the correct path this time. No more evil."

Barba burst into tears and hugged her mother tightly. Her aunt moved up and wrapped her arms around them both.

Barba's father watched the women for a few minutes before turning to Apopus. "Will those two be welcomed completely in Tonopus? I understand there was another young man who also left with them. I know that even here, there are hard feelings toward them for surviving when our others did not."

"In all honesty, I cannot say. However, if they have trouble there, I will take them to the Scytan. I know that Snow Camp would welcome them with open arms. Clartan is from there, and Declon's brother was adopted there as brother to one of the men. Torena, Declon, and Cytar's sister is mated to the cousin of another Snow Camp man. I know that after I tell my sister that her son is alive, she will agree with the reason they should go there. She is well aware of how much I like the Scytan."

Clartan walked over and added, "I think it would be the best place for them."

"We should discuss their possible futures with them tonight."

Barba's mother and aunt joined in the discussions that night as well. A decision was finally reached. From Plains Camp, Apopus was to leave with the two and take them straight to the Scytan. Barba's camp gave the couple enough goods to load two horses for the couple to set up their new hearth.

A mating ceremony was held that night for them. Barba glowed with love as she looked at her new mate. Every time Krontus would look into her eyes, he would become speechless with emotion and pull her tight against him.

As the much larger party drew near the camp of the Plains people, Apopus told Declon about how Cytar and Macelar always sent someone ahead to warn the camp of their arrival to prevent trouble. One of the Bogdanans was known in the camp and said he would ride ahead to give the warning.

The campsite had just been set up when the rider returned. With him was a band of hunters from Plains Camp, which was led by the camp leader's Second. He told them that someone from the Plains Camp had spotted them, and his band had been formed to either met them or repel them as needed. When the messenger had ridden on ahead to meet them, the gesture was much appreciated.

Apopus knew the language spoken by the Plains Camp and invited them to eat, before they broke camp to move on to the Plains Camp. One of the Plains hunters was sent on into camp to announce the arrival of the travelers.

As Beezy and Alala greeted the hunters reservedly, it was evident that there was an undercurrent of latent hostility toward the two youngsters. Everyone in the traveling party became alert to any danger, which the two might face once inside the camp.

The camp was well within sight when a small group rode out to meet the approaching party. The parents of both Beezy and Alala were in the approaching group. The second introduced them to the camp leader.

"I understand you are returning Beezy and Alala. Why?" asked the camp leader.

Apopus gave a slight start, looked at Declon, and told him what the man had said.

Declon rose to his full height and stared hard at the camp leader before answering. He was speaking in Dolnii, because he knew Apopus knew the language well, along with the Bogdanans. Apopus translated as Declon began to speak.

"There is a great evil roaming among us by the name of Nickotian. He convinces children to run away from home, and he then gets them killed or captured. He abandoned these two children while they lay gravely wounded because he was too afraid of being captured himself to see that they received any healing after he coerced them to fall upon our camp in armed combat.

"It saddened our hearts when we learned we had killed a group of young people and wounded several more. We felt it our duty to make sure the ones we could heal were all returned safely to their homes. These two came from this camp, but if they are not welcome, *we* will make sure they are cared for elsewhere."

The camp leader quailed as he stared into the most powerful set of eyes he had ever seen. In desperation, he struggled to get a breath before speaking. Though he had meant to be forceful in his denunciation and banishment of the two young people, his voice came out weak and quavering. "If you wish to keep them, it is good, for we do not want the likes of them in our midst. You may camp here along the water tonight while their parents tell them a proper good-bye. We will provide food to you of course. We are not inhospitable, but we do not want them in our camp ever again. Our hunting group will stay with you tonight to insure your continued safety."

Declon made a point of snorting in deep disgust and simply turning away. He told Apopus they would make camp here and strode off. By doing so, he had shown that he felt the leader was no longer worthy of his attention.

"Who is he?" the leader asked Apopus.

"He now lives on the shore of the western Far-Reaching Waters, in the camp of Gondal, but he is the hereditary prince of the Kychee, on the far distant coast of the eastern Far-Reaching Waters. He hates marauders more than any man I have ever known. He has a fierce reputation for breaking them into pieces *with his bare hands*."

The leader turned very gray as the blood drained from his face. He now knew this was not a man to make angry and he had just done that very thing.

The parents of both Alala and Beezy helped set up the travelers' campsite to be near their children. The children were told how much they were loved and missed, and that their parents were much aggrieved by the way the camp leadership had reacted to the news of their return. Beezy informed them that he wanted the camp's spirit leader to come out and mate him to Alala.

While they waited for the Shaman to arrive, Apopus told of how he was taking the other two youths to the Scytan, and that Barba's camp had provided them with many items needed for their new hearth. Beezy's father said that his son would also be set up with goods by morning. Alala's father agreed to this at once.

For all of that evening and the next morning, Declon made it a point to be seen spending much time with the young couple and their families, while completely ignoring everyone else from Plains Camp.

As the traveling band mounted for their departure, the leader came out to see them off. Declon immediately rode out to the south, taking his group with him, leaving Apopus to speak with the leader.

"He was rather abrupt. Can he not even speak in leaving?"

Apopus was a master of putting on faces during his trades and now gave the leader a shocked look before answering. "If the families of either of these two ever need any help, all they have to do is let him know. As for the rest of you, well, he could care less what happens to you. I have traveled and lived with members of his family for several cycles of seasons now…and this is the first time I have ever seen…where not one of them gave out an invitation to anyone wishing to visit the Kychee Camp, far to the east. Declon went this far out of his way…to help your camp members return home safely…and you have now insulted him…terribly…by not receiving your own children back in a loving manner."

While the leader turned to look at the retreating back of Declon, Apopus turned his own horse and rode off to the east. The leader looked back to see Apopus riding away. Now, only the Bogdanans were left, preparing to leave to the west. He called out to their leader.

"I feel we have made a grave error in not accepting the two young people back home."

"Yes, you did. We would have welcomed Barba home, even though there were some who felt she cheated death, while their own children died. It is a natural emotion for those who have lost their children to feel, but your camp did not even lose anyone.

"Barba fell in love with Krontus and chose to leave with him, not because she was forced to, but because she did not wish her presence to cause further heartbreak to the other families. As for the man you insulted, he and his family have done more to destroy this plague of raiders than the rest of the people in these lands combined. Once Nickotian can be captured, most raiding will stop. That man's family is also teaching everyone who is interested how to defeat raiders, should any others come along. He has taught much to Beezy and Alala, but you will notice, he did not offer to teach anything to any of your people."

The camp leader fidgeted nervously and looked down at the ground, before looking back into the eyes of his old friend.

"You may not realize it yet, but you also insulted Apopus, and he was your lifetime friend. It will be a very long time before you see him again, if ever. Just whom do you think you will trade with now?

"We are also offended, but we will overlook the offense this time. You should spend some time thinking on the decisions of your camp, and then talk it over with them.

"By the way, I overheard the parents of those two speaking with Apopus, and he told them that they would also be welcomed into the Scytan. He will be speaking with the Scytan leaders, telling them to expect those two families before long. I suspect some others will soon become upset over this decision as well, once they think it over more thoroughly."

The enormity of his actions was becoming apparent to the Plains leader. Now he had to face his camp and tell them of the consequences.

Apopus saw the great mass of people and was glad he had remembered that the Scytan Summer Trades were being held at Valley Camp this cycle. It was the most southern of all the Scytan camps and the closest for him. The trip plan had worked well for him, as he had many new items, which he had not had when he was last here.

Inquiries quickly lead him to Tavous and Snow Camp. He was welcomed warmly, but when he said he had news of Clartan and Cytar, his arrival was greeted with rejoicing. That evening, he introduced his four young charges, which were welcomed with open arms just as he had predicted. Andonala declared that as her mate was the nearest kin to Cytar and his family; she was now the new aunt of all four of them. With such a determined look on her face, no one wanted to argue with her.

Lorailous, the mate of Marselac, told her that would be fine, but she would be their new *older cousin* and a friend as well. The two women laughed and hugged and then both hugged the young couples.

Apopus found Macelar getting ready to return to the west and asked him to travel to Tonopus with him. Macelar agreed to the trip, as it would take him on a route he had not traveled in many trading missions.

10

Leelee

Leelee was five full cycles of the seasons now. Spring brought many changes for her. Her mother told her that they were moving to her father's camp, where Zodar lived. Leelee liked Zodar.

Myling gave her father one last hug before turning to follow Pouwan to the camp of the Kychee. Leelee started the trip walking. She felt that she was a big girl now and being carried was for babies. Once Myling and Leelee were settled in the Kychee Camp, Pouwan would return to his home. Pouwan and Myling both carried new Kychee bows provided to them the last time Zodar had come for Leelee's lessons. Leelee carried her spear and a small bone sword was in a pouch on her belt. The weapons were very small and just her size, but she was very good with them. She also had a throwing stick on her belt.

Zodar had learned the throwing stick from the man from the south at the same time that Cytar had seen it. Zodar had spent time with the man and learned how to make and use them from him. Although he had not taught Cytar to use the throwing stick, he was teaching Leelee. As usual, she was a remarkable student.

"You and Leelee shall be missed in the village."

"I know. I would love to stay there for all my life. My heart cries to leave, but the spirits have spoken of how Leelee must be trained."

Pouwan laughed. "I started to teach her to hunt and track almost before she could walk. Did you know that when we went hunting a few days ago, she showed me how to find the trail twice when I lost it?"

"Pouwan, how could you possibly lose a trail? You are the best tracker my father has ever seen."

"It is true. I did lose the trail. The deer ran across solid rock and only left the tiniest scuff marks. I could barely see them, even with her showing me, but they stood out like a bright marker to her. I have never seen such ability in anyone. She can also spot the animals faster than I can. She was pointing to the deer while I was still trying to decipher where it had gone. The spirits are strong with her."

"Ssh, Pouwan, look," shushed Leelee as she pointed to a deer.

Pouwan grinned as he cast his spear. Now they would have meat tonight, and all because of a small child. It was embarrassing to be shown up by a small child but uplifting at the same time, for it spoke volumes about his training abilities.

Just as she always did, Leelee stood guard while Pouwan skinned and butchered the deer. He had taught her the importance of watching for predators while working on the animal to be eaten. At the same time, she also inspected his handiwork on butchering the deer. "You cut that piece too thick, Pouwan. It will take too long to dry."

"Yes, your highness," laughed Pouwan, pleased that she had passed his test.

"What is a highness?" asked Leelee.

"Someone that is too large for their leggings."

"Huh? If they are too large, that means they need new ones."

Pouwan sat back on his heels and shook his head and grinned as he looked at her.

"What did I do wrong this time?"

"Nothing, Leelee, he is just teasing you. 'Your highness' is what the daughter of a ruler is called, like the emperor that the Cheen People have."

"But you are the daughter of our leader," stated Leelee.

"Yes, but he is only the leader of our camp. The Cheen emperor rules over many camp leaders. If we had an emperor, he would rule over my father."

"I am glad we do not have an emperor. Grumpy-pa is smart enough not to need any help as leader."

Pouwan never failed to laugh at her favorite nickname for her grandfather. Langtou was anything but grumpy; however, the old man loved it when his granddaughter called him by that nickname. Woe to anyone else who dared call him grumpy though. It was indeed humorous to see such a strong man totally dominated by a little forth or fifth winter girl-child. It was as if she was the snake charmer and he was the snake, deadly to all except for her.

As he reflected on this truth, he realized his own daughter did the same with him, as did all daughters with their fathers and grandfathers.

A joyful procession escorted them into the Kychee camp. Truly, Leelee was like royalty here. Her mother was the daughter of one camp leader, and her father was the son of another camp leader. However, the Kychee were much more powerful in their area than their small camp size would have one believe. They were well known and respected, from the Island People far to the north, all the way south to the people along the coasts of the southern Far-Reaching Waters.

Fangthorn and Chonee stood in the center of the greeting party. As Myling stepped before them, Zodar introduced her to them. Chonee took Myling's hands and welcomed her to the camp of the Kychee. She then told Myling that, as the mother of their granddaughter, she was now considered their very own daughter and would be given the respect her status deserved.

Myling then motioned Leelee to come forward to meet her grandparents. Leelee stepped to her mother's side and looked at the two people in front of her. She put her hands together with her fingertips just touching her chin and bowed gracefully to them. "I am most honored and pleased to meet the parents of my father. I am your granddaughter, Leelee, of the Tyzeir People of my mother and the Kychee People of my father."

Chonee put her hands together with the fingertips touching her chin and bowed to Leelee. "You have wonderful manners, and we are most pleased and honored to meet our granddaughter. You are warmly welcomed to your new home."

Formalities over, Chonee then stepped forward and held out her arms to the young girl. Leelee instantly went into them and hugged her grandmother warmly. Leelee then hugged her grandfather and stopped to sniff his shoulder.

Fangthorn gave her a puzzled look to which she replied, "My humble apologies, it is just that you smell different than my Grumpy-pa, and I want to get to know you as well as I do him."

Fangthorn burst into a roaring laugh and held her tightly. "You have my permission to get to know me as well as you wish, my child. I truly hope you find much happiness here."

"I will, Grandfather. I have spent much time with so many people from here that I already feel as if I belong." She leaned back and looked into his eyes for a moment before continuing, "Do you mind if I find a favorite name to call you. I call my other grandfather Grumpy-pa, and I will feel much more comfortable with you once I find the right name for you."

Myling gave her daughter an exasperated look. Chonee laughed and told her that it appeared that Leelee had already read her new grandfather very well.

"Well, if anyone else dared call my father such a name, he would find it necessary to live up to the name and become very grumpy, indeed, at least toward them. But with Leelee, he finds great pleasure in the name."

"So it is with men and their granddaughters. Granddaughters can get away with many things that even daughters cannot. I can see that she is a very special person. I feel she even has my gift of seeing the true inner person inside of those she meets. It feels even stronger in her than in myself. This child is truly destined for greatness."

Chonee motioned to Fangthorn to pull his attention away from his new granddaughter and turned to present Leelee to the Kychee. A great cheer rose up because all here deeply loved Cytar, and if their Lady Chonee was happy with Leelee, they knew they would love her as much as her father.

Chonee started to lead the guests inside to eat, but Leelee turned to her and asked if she could speak to someone first. Puzzled, Chonee agreed.

Leelee walked over to a man in the crowd and held out her hands to him. Chonee smiled as she saw whom Leelee had approached.

As the man took hold of Leelee's hands, she looked deep into his eyes and said, "She still loves you and wants you not to be sad that she had to go to be with the creator. She is wrapped in the arms of the creator now and is very happy and well cared for. She asks that you live the rest of your life in honor of the creator so that you may someday join her there."

The man pulled her to him and hugged her as he cried. She kept her arms around his neck until he regained control of his emotions. "Thank you," he said as he released her.

Chonee turned to Myling and said, "His daughter died last moon of a fever that our healers could not cure. He has been very angry and hostile ever since she died. Maybe this will help him, or at least I hope it does. He has always been a very good man."

The man held her hand as he walked her back to her mother. "If she ever needs anything, just let me know." With that said, he turned and with a newfound dignity, walked back to his lodge.

Many tears could be seen throughout the crowd as he walked away. Leelee had just won the hearts of the crowd and become their new princess.

"I will miss the two of you," Pouwan told Myling and Leelee as he was preparing to return home.

Leelee threw her arms around his neck and kissed his cheek. "I will never forget what you have taught me, and I promise I will be polite when someone else tries to teach me to do things in a lesser way than you have taught me."

"Pouwan, give my father and your family my love and tell them how much I will be missing them. In fact, all of the Tyzeir Camp members are my people and I do not relish being unable to be there for them. Their needs are my responsibility. If I am ever needed, let me know. I think I have gained many helpful resources by coming here," Myling said from behind Leelee.

"Daughter of my leader, I will surely tell the camp how you feel toward them. They will be missing you as well."

Soon, Pouwan's back disappeared around a curve in the trail, as he headed back to his home and family.

Intense training began immediately for young Leelee. Although most of her instructors had made trips to her old home to give her some training, now she was here and the training was every day. Through the next several growing seasons, she would learn much and become a master of many skills.

Zodar taught her to fish out on the big waters and in the rivers. His favorite pastime was catching the fish. He had traveled extensively and taught her everything he knew of all the different cultures, customs, and languages he had learned. One cannot travel so much and survive without learning how to trade, so he taught her to become a master trader. Trading was always a gamble of sorts, so having a natural inclination and luck in gaming, he had learned and mastered the gambling games of many cultures. He now passed on that knowledge to her, including how to play and how to tell if someone tried to cheat. She became so adept at cheating; even he could no longer catch her when she did. Then, she would smile at him and show what she had just done. She learned to abhor the dishonesty of cheating, but she thoroughly learned the skills so that no one could cheat her.

Zestoan was the combat master of the spear, Atl Spear, "Flying Spears," and mounted lances. He also taught her the skills of riding her horse in all types of situations.

Kokarashi was the undisputed master of the bone sword, bow, and unarmed combat. He had spent more time with her in her old home than any of the others, except for Zodar. The two old men had developed a friendship closer than brothers and always traveled together. Kokarashi possessed another special talent. He was much stronger in psychic abilities than even Chonee. He would sit with Leelee, and they would stare into each other's eyes until they formed a mental link and could hear the thoughts of the other. Chonee would sometimes join with them in this exercise.

Soon, Leelee was able to receive mental images much easier than she had ever been able to before. One day, she saw the young daughter of the man she had helped on the first day in her mind. It came to her why the girl had died and how to cure the next person that contracted the illness. She gave this information to Kokarashi, Chonee, and the camp healers.

The entire camp met at dawn each day, for the "Shadow Dance Exercise" session before going about each one's own daily business. Late in the evening, they met again for a second session.

During the late cold season, while Leelee was in her ninth winter and doing her mental exercises with Kokarashi and Chonee, a new presence joined them. A shaman from far away said he was of the Kay People and had met Cytar when he traveled through there many summers before. He had experienced a vision about Leelee and her need of training from the Kay. He told them to expect visitors one day from the Kay.

As the grasses greened and the trees bloomed, a messenger came into camp and told of two strangers coming this way.

The next day, a man and woman rode into camp, leading several packhorses and one young, second-summer mare. They stopped just outside of the camp and dismounted while they waited for an invitation to proceed before entering camp. Chonee had them brought to her.

As the two walked toward her, Chonee could tell they were of the horse people. When they stopped, the woman stepped forward and greeted Chonee in broken Kychee.

"I am called Lazna, daughter of Boarza who is the Khan, or leader, of the famed Kay People. We are known in many places as masters of the horse and bow. We are peaceful people but will defend our lands with our lives. I am also the mate of Rafkar, and we are both friends of Cytar. He once told us we would always be welcomed here."

"You are most welcome friend of my son. I am Chonee and this is Fangthorn, our leader, my mate, and the father of Cytar."

"We have been sent to train a young one, the daughter of Cytar. We will teach her horsemanship, strategy, and fighting while on horseback using bows or lances. She will learn to survive on the steppes and in the deserts. Also, she will gain the knowledge and understanding of herding and caring for many different animals. We also have gifts for her and you as well."

Chonee smiled at Lazna as she made a slight motion of her hand. Leelee stepped up beside her grandmother. Chonee nodded to her and she said, "I am Leelee, daughter of Cytar and Myling. I greet you and welcome you to our camp. Tonight, we shall have a great feast in your honor and you can tell us of your trip here and of the time my father visited you."

Rafkar then led the young mare up and handed the reins to Leelee. "This is a very special horse. Her sire is our fastest messenger carrier and has won many races for us. Her dam is our most enduring horse. She can run longer than any other horse we have ever seen. This young horse is proving to have the best qualities of both her sire and dam. Lazna has been training her for you, but now will teach you how to finish her training."

"Thank you so much," answered Leelee with eyes shining toward the mare. The mare took a step forward and placed her head against Leelee and stood there waiting to be petted.

Lazna glanced at Rafkar with a shocked look in her eyes. "She has never responded to anyone like this before," she stated somewhat breathlessly.

"You will find that Leelee is special in many ways," responded Chonee, still smiling, though pride now shined through.

Rafkar had stepped back to one packhorse and brought two young wolf cubs to Leelee.

"Lazna remembered Cytar saying something one night about wanting some wolf cubs to raise and Train. Our shaman told us where these cubs would be found and that they were for you. The cubs are from different packs, one male and one female. The two wolves will be able to breed when they grow older. We arrived at the first den just as hyenas were killing the male's mother. We killed the hyenas and rescued the cub. The second one came from a flooded den. We were only able to save the little female. The mother and her other cubs drowned. The shaman said you would be in need of them when you travel to the west after your father."

Leelee fell to the ground playing with the new cubs while the horse held her nose close to the three playmates.

Lazna smiled and told Chonee, "We have other gifts for her as well, but I think she is lost to her new friends at the moment. However, we have these for you."

Two highly decorated belts and headbands were given to Chonee and Fangthorn. "We placed the symbol of the Kychee, as Cytar had described it, in the center next to the symbol of the Kay People. It is to tell any Kay you meet that you are considered to be of the ruling class of the Kay as well as the Kychee. All will show you the respect deserved of their leaders and will aid you if you are in need."

"We are honored beyond words. Come inside and rest now." Fangthorn motioned toward the doorway of his lodge. "Yontow, please put their gear in the guest lodge and care for the horses."

Over the meal, Lazna and Rafkar recounted the time when Cytar had visited their village.

"Before he came, we had one young man named Kailaf who was very boisterous and thought he was the best at everything. He made the mistake of insulting Cytar. He was going to kill Cytar and take his goods. Boarza, our Khan, rode up and became very angry with Kailaf for his lack of hospitality by threatening a traveler, rather than offering food and shelter. However, when Boarza took one look at Cytar, he told Cytar that if he so desired he could teach Kailaf proper manners but not to kill him. You would have had to see Kailaf's face when Boarza said that. Cytar laughed and gave Kailaf a lesson in manners that Kailaf has never forgotten. That was when Cytar helped me overcome my quiet shyness and made me realize I could outperform Kailaf in almost every endeavor, except for carving. Kailaf became a master carver after he found he was not the best fighter."

Rafkar held out a knife with an ivory grip, beautifully carved with the scene of a mother bear with cubs eating berries, and a pendant, with a hole at the top for a string. The pendant was carved into the form of a very pregnant she-bear. The carvings were very lifelike.

"Kailaf carved these for Leelee, after our shaman told us how she had appeared to him in a vision, as a mother bear defending her cubs. He said the cubs represented anyone that needed her protection."

Leelee took the pendant of the pregnant bear, looked at it, and then down to her own belly. "Well, it will be a while before this is me."

As she took the knife, she twirled it in an expert fashion before inspecting the carving. "It is a beautiful knife, both the carving and the quality of the knife. It has excellent balance showing the care used in making it."

Lazna was laughing. "I cannot wait to see his face when I tell him how you can twirl that knife. That should age him a bit to know a child of only five season cycles can handle it better than he can."

Lazna then pulled out a bow and handed it to Leelee. The same bowyer that had made the bow that Cytar had taken west with him made this one.

"It will be a little too strong for you right now, but will last long enough for you to outgrow it. I am to tell you that when you start your journey to the west, you are to stop at our camp, and he will have another one ready for you, that with proper care, should last for a long time."

The talk turned to children and Lazna's face fell. She still did not have any children, and it hurt her deeply because she wanted them so badly.

After watching Lazna for a few moments, Leelee went over and whispered into Chonee's ear. Chonee nodded and Leelee ran out of the room. Soon, she returned with a woman following her. The woman held an infant in her arms.

The woman handed the infant to Chonee. "This is why Leelee asked to leave the room. This baby girl has lost both of her parents in an accident. She has no other family left to care for her, and we have been looking for someone to adopt her. Her name is Pearl. Fangthorn and I have been thinking of adopting her, but we are so old now that it would not be fair to the child."

Tears came into Lazna's eyes as she thought of losing her own mother so many summers ago. Instinctively, she reached out for the small bundle. The small child looked up into Lazna's eyes and captured her heart.

Lazna looked at Rafkar and he smiled. "I guess I am a new father now, from what I am seeing here."

Lazna squealed with delight and nuzzled the baby.

Rafkar taught Leelee how the Kay fought from horseback, both with spears and the bow. She compared his techniques with those she had been learning from Zestoan and found the best of both methods. Both Zestoan and Rafkar also learned from her as a result.

Lazna began to teach her to make exceptional clothing, both in quality and design.

Her Uncle Delbeekar began teaching her to make tools and weapons.

Finally, Uncle Becarlon decided she was old enough to start learning what he knew. He was always inventing, or discovering new things, plus he had studied the fire mountain's iron for many seasons, and told Leelee that he marveled at how this iron never seemed to rust. He had gotten a piece of it off of the larger mass that was, more or less, in the shape of a triangle. It was as long as two of his fists and about as big around as his fists doubled together. One end was flat and the other came to a dull point. He mounted this onto a club and tried to use it as a hammer.

He liked the effect it had, but not that it kept slipping off the handle. After much effort, Uncle Becarlon used sand and a bow-drill with a hardwood spindle to drill a hole through the center of the lump. The hole was V-shaped and one opening was smaller than the other. He put the smaller opening down and put a wooden handle through it. A wooden wedge was driven from the top, down into the wooden handle to lock the lump onto the handle. Now, the way it worked as a hammer, pleased him.

Uncle Becarlon also had a very large lump with a flat surface on one side. He mounted this piece on a tree stump so that the flat top of the lump was about waist high.

He had also remembered from the fire mountain, that extreme heat caused the iron to become liquid. He found a type of clay that would become hard when exposed to extreme heat. It could then hold up under more heat than the iron without melting. Uncle Becarlon then made a clay mold in the shape of a knife, and a very thick-walled clay bucket to melt the iron in. After heat-treating the clay items, he melted a small amount of iron and poured the liquid iron into the mold. After it cooled, he found that it was porous and brittle. It broke apart when he hit it with the new hammer.

There was an open pouch nearby filled with powdered borax. He had once traded for it with some of the Desert People that lived to the west of the Cheen. He tossed the pieces of the knife into the hot fire he kept burning nearby, and as the pieces began to glow red, decided to try hitting them again with the hammer. The pieces had turned cherry red, and when he was taking them out of the fire, one slipped out of the wooden tongs he was using to hold them. It landed in the borax.

With much fussing, he took it out of the borax and saw some had stuck to the iron. Snorting with disgust, he laid the borax-covered piece on top of the other hot piece and hit the top one as hard as he could, with the intent of shattering both into tiny pieces. Instead, they stuck together and began to flatten out.

Leelee laughed at the expression on his face as he inspected the knife pieces. At first, he started to curse, but then remembered the young girl watching him. As he took time to think of her, he inspected the pieces and saw that they had become fused together.

He heated two more pieces, carefully put one on top of the other, without dropping them into the borax, and struck them with his hammer. Both flattened but did not fuse together.

"I think it was the borax that made the first two stick together, Uncle."

"I do believe you are right, Leelee."

He reheated these two pieces and coated one with the borax. Sure enough, when hit, they fused together. He reheated the two, now larger, pieces, coated one, and fused them together. Next, he heated them again and hammered the larger lump into a long flat bar. The metal formed easily enough under the hammer while glowing red, but he had made the width of the bar too wide, length too short, and the thickness too thin. To remedy this he heated the bar and folded it in half lengthwise, being careful to coat the inside of the fold with the borax. He began to notice that the more times he folded the metal over onto itself, the harder he had to work to shape the iron. He decided to fold it over several more times before roughly shaping it into the shape of a knife blade. Once he had the shape the best he could get with the hammer, he continued shaping it by using the sand. He then sharpened the cutting edge and polished the knife blade.

Uncle Becarlon felt that the blade was attractive but found that it was too soft to stay sharp. While lost in thought, he again sharpened the blade and laid it too close to the fire, allowing it to get too hot to hold. When he tried to pick it up, it burned his hand, and he dropped it. This time, the metal bounced to one side and fell into a bowl of water, vigorously steaming as it sizzled in the water.

Upon completing his *hot hand dance*, he retrieved the blade from the water and told Leelee that it was surely ruined this time. To his amazement, however, he found the knife to be well hardened, and it would now stay sharp for much longer.

Just to be sure that it would work every time, Uncle Becarlon dropped another piece of the metal into his fire and roughly shaped a small knife. He then heated it to a glowing red before dropping it into the water. Leelee got another laugh, when he pulled two pieces of the knife from the water. One piece shattered when he tapped it with the hammer. Many more experiments helped him learn the best method for tempering the metal in fish oil, rather than water, to just the right hardness.

During his studies of the iron, Uncle Becarlon had found a small deposit of copper and another of calamine. After forming the iron knife blade, he decided to try the copper. The copper also melted, though, at a lower temperature.

He decided that since he already had the copper melted, he would see what he could do with it and dropped in some of the calamine. A slag formed at the top of the liquid, and he scooped that off. Underneath the slag, he found that the copper had taken on a yellowish color.

Not being sure what to do with the molten metal, he looked around and found an impression in the sand, where he had earlier set the box of clay for the knife mold. One end of the impression had a deeper, narrower depression, caused by a board hanging down about the width of his thumb, along one end of the box.

Shrugging his shoulders, Uncle Becarlon poured the melted slag into the impression and let it cool. He figured that when he was ready to try to make something with it, he could reheat it and shape it the way he wanted.

After it had cooled, he picked it up and saw that a thin seashell had been at the edge of the deeper depression and, when removed, left a thin slit most of the way through the metal at that spot. He also noticed that the slit was just about the same length, as the width of the handle portion of the knife blade.

Finding that the yellow metal could be cut by a chisel that he had made out of a thick sliver from the original mass of iron, he used the hammer and cheisel to shear off the wide piece of metal and tried to slide the knife handle through the slit. After some sanding and careful shaving with the chisel, he got the yellow piece to slide over the iron. Leelee was watching very closely as he worked and told him that if it was shaped and polished, it would be pretty on the knife, against an ivory grip.

"Do you want to try to cut it into a shape?"

"Yes, Uncle. I think I can see the shape inside it already."

Uncle Becarlon had heard many artisans speak of seeing shapes in items before and understood what she had meant.

Taking a piece of sandstone, she began sanding off the edges and thinning the middle.

After working on the piece for a moon cycle, Leelee had made a polished, golden-yellow, finger guard, with little knobs on the ends, that curled away from the fingers for a prettier effect.

Uncle Becarlon helped her put the finger guard on the knife handle and then put an ivory grip onto it. This knife he gave to Leelee. It was very large for her now but would be of good fighting/butchering size for her once she was grown.

When she showed the knife to Rafkar, he told her that it was the most beautiful knife he had ever seen and when she came to the Kay Camp, to be sure and show it to Kailaf. He might be able to carve the grip for her as he had the on the flint-bladed knife. That would truly bring out the rest of the beauty it held.

A few days later, Uncle Becarlon came up to Leelee and handed her the large sheet of yellow metal, now mounted in a bamboo frame. She gave him a questioning look and then glanced at the sheet. Her eyes flew wide open as she saw her own reflection in the metal. Uncle Becarlon had polished the sheet until it reflected images wondrously.

Leelee threw her arms around his neck and told him how much this meant to her.

11

The Southern Route Going West

Declon traveled the route westward using the directions Apopus had given him. The trail ran close enough to the base of the mountains for water to be plentiful, and the temperature was warm. Occasionally, they would meet other travelers along this path. Declon decided to have them keep their spears at hand in the special spear boots hung on their horses but angled out of the way under the rider's left leg for ease in grasping, should a need arise. The spear boot was attached to the underside of the arrow quiver. A strung bow would also be stowed in a special boot attached to the top of the arrow quiver so it would also be close to hand if needed. The bows and arrows would be out of sight under a flap of leather, to help maintain a less stressful atmosphere when meeting strangers. When they dismounted, the entire quiver-boot would be slung from a shoulder and taken with them. A lot of thought had gone into making this arrangement function as easily as possible.

During the evenings, Declon made sure everyone practiced with the different weapons. However, when other travelers shared the campsite and watched, he only allowed them to practice throwing their spears at targets. He had no wish to show their unique combat moves to potential subversive attackers.

Declon was in hopes of finding Tycho in his home of Varnis, and that he could be persuaded to accompany them on to Mila. The trail they were following supposedly ran right through Varnis.

The four young people began to get excited as they recognized some of the landmarks within the Ital lands. The land elevation began sloping downward as they neared Varnis. The camp was situated on a very large island in the middle of a river.

An inquiry at the edge of the camp led them to Tycho's hut. Tycho was delighted to see his old friends, along with some new ones. He happily introduced Declon, Clartan, and Antana, along with the young people, to his family. Tycho explained that these were some of the people helping to make his travels safer. He invited them to stay with him while they were in Varnis. His hut was very large because he used it for storing his goods and as a trading post. His mate ran the trading post while he was on his trips.

During the evening meal, Declon explained their mission and asked Tycho if he would accompany them at least as far as Mila.

"It is interesting that you should show up here and ask that of me now, because my mate and I have been discussing the need for replenishing our stock here. I was just telling her this morning how I would like to go at least to Simonia's Camp and maybe even Gondal." Tycho looked at his mate, and she nodded.

"It is yes, then. I shall go with you, at least to Simonia's. Just give me a couple of days to prepare my travel stock for the trip."

The travelers were well pleased with the journey. So far, they had been able to see and travel with both Apopus and Tycho. The leader of Varnis Camp had assembled his camp together for the stories that the travelers had to tell. There were some people who just traveled around telling stories, and they were always in great demand. Most wore elaborate costumes to be easily recognized as storytellers. Many had bones, antlers, shells, or any number of other objects dangling from a staff, their packs or clothing that would make noise when shaken. Sometimes they would walk into a camp singing or reciting nonsense. All of this was done to attract the attention of the camp members. Most times, they were also traders.

By now, the adult travelers had told their stories so many times that they felt as though they were members of this strange group of storytelling traders. Even the young people were beginning to feel as if they were permanently on display.

Finally, it was all about to end for the last of the young marauders, as they entered their home camp of Mila. All of them were extremely anxious to see their families and hoped they would be welcomed back home. The thoughts of Beezy and Alala were still on their minds, and although, no one would admit it, they were full of anxiety. The four adults with them did their best to help the youths feel more secure.

Some of the camp children recognized the four and ran to tell everyone in camp that about the return of the runaways. Very quickly, a crowd began to form. Gina's mother came running, and Gina leapt from her horse to hug her. The other parents were soon hugging their own returned children.

Tycho acted as spokesperson for the four. He was well known here and one of their own people. After all of the camp elders arrived, Tycho gave them a quick explanation of the youths' situation. Declon had schooled him on how to stress that most of the fault was with Nickotian, but also that the camp elders were more responsible for the youths leaving with him than the youths were. They were young and had not yet developed better judgment; the elders were the ones who had allowed the Sarainian to hang around here, not the young people. Now the people of Gondal were trying to get the word out on Nickotian as far and wide as they possibly could.

A feast, and a much more in-depth story session, was held that night. Everyone was told about all that had happened to the youths during their journey, including how close they had come to dying from their wounds.

The next morning, a council was held to discuss the four runaways. After two days of council meetings, the camp chief came to Tycho and told him that although most of the camp wanted to welcome them home with open arms, there were a few who wanted to make trouble for them.

Declon told the chief that those few should make a more thorough inspection of their own actions in this matter. The chief told him that the camp elders would be looking at them much more closely, but the fact remained that the four would still have to contend with this. Even though it was decided they would be welcomed home by most, and the camp as a whole would do all they could to protect them, their safety might be in jeopardy from those few if they did stay. Gina and Bea had both broken down into tears. They simply could not understand why some of the people they had known all of their lives would be so cruel to them.

Declon gave them the same option that Apopus had given the other four. He would be happy to take them with him and find a place for them, even if it wound up being in Gondal. However, he felt sure they would be welcomed at Simonia's Camp. They had all heard the story of Simonia's Camp and knew they would not be looked down upon there.

Gina and Tamar decided to be mated, but Bea and Pino did not care for each other in that way, even though they were very close friends. They thought it best to wait until after they were settled and then see how things developed.

That evening, with their parents there to watch, Gina and Tamar were joined.

Tycho told the chief how the previous four had been set up with items to make a home, and the camp chief made sure these two were well taken care of. He also made sure that the other two were each given plenty of necessities. They would each need to have these items to make a home, whether or not they mated each other.

The band was set to go as soon as the youths said their good-byes. Directions to Simonia's Camp were given to the camp elders for anyone wishing to make the journey to visit.

As the band rode out of camp, Declon heard an angry murmur running through the crowd. Many were very angry that the young people had to leave. He felt that, once again, there would soon be others having to look for a new home. However, he was sure that this time it would be those troublesome few that would be looking for another home.

Tycho told them that the best way to go west was to first travel south to the coastal area and then follow a very good trail along the foot of the mountains. It would be much harder to go directly west through the mountains. There were trails, but the coast trail was substantially better and faster.

When they arrived at Geno, they met a man who owned a flat-bottomed sailing craft that could hold all of them and their horses. The man explained that he always sailed close to shore so he could land during bad weather. The flat bottom could travel through very shallow water, but did not take well to heavy weather. Carefully, the horses were loaded and they set sail. With the direction of the winds during this season, the trip to Marcel's Camp went much faster than if they had been on horseback. By traveling in this manner, the horses were rested and in fine shape upon their arrival in Marcel's Camp. At first, they had been very nervous at the heaving and bucking of the boat deck but had finally settled down and seemed to relax and rest.

During the trip, Declon told the master how he had grown up fishing from boats. Lines were promptly brought out, and Declon and Tycho fished for most of the trip. Roly wanted to fish but was told he was too young. These large fish would have caught him instead. They each gave the master a portion of their catches. A lot of the fish were eaten during the trip to help save food supplies.

Clartan did not fish at all. In fact, he almost had to crawl from the craft. He swore he would never again ride in anything that bounced and bobbed that much. He had been seasick the entire trip. A couple of the youths also looked happy to be on dry land again. The sailing master laughed and told them that this was a much smoother trip than usual. He started to weave and bob as he described how rough it could be.

Clartan looked at Declon and told him to get rid of this guy before he killed him. Declon chuckled and wrapped his arm around the sailing master's shoulders as he led him away and thanked him for the fast trip.

"There is one section I would like you to see." Tycho led them to the merchant's district. Old Marcel was there to meet them.

Tycho pointed to the tunics on the walls of their Merchant Centers and laughed. "Marcel, let me introduce you to some of those that started this practice of hanging out the tunics of marauders."

Tycho quickly made the introductions and explained how they had begun the tradition of hanging the tunics in plain sight.

Old Marcel spent the next hour with them discussing marauders and merchandising. That night, he supplied their beds and food.

Tycho spent the next two days trading. He sent a load back to Geno with the sailing master. From there, he had an arrangement with a man who had a string of horses and would pack-haul the load to Varnis for him. The man had several sons who always helped him.

Two fifth-summer boys decided that Rolvalar would make an easy target to pick on and started to call him Marauder Boy. Although he was young, Roly knew he did not like marauders and told them so.

"You are a marauder, and we are going to beat you and teach you a lesson."

"I am not a marauder. You leave me alone. I mean it!"

The two boys made a rush at Roly, but all the hours of training his parents and Uncle Dec had given him caused Roly to respond instinctively. One boy found himself under his friend and both had very sore ribs. They began to cry even before they got up to run away.

Old Marcel had seen what happened and caught them before they could get away. "You will stay right here until your mothers come for you," he told them.

Then he turned to Roly. "You are very quick, my young friend. You have been taught well. Do you wish for me to hang their tunics on that wall?"

Both of the local boys blanched at the thought of their tunics being on the wall.

"Nawh, just tell them I am not a marauder." Fire still glinted from Roly's eyes.

Marcel turned to the other two with a steely look. "This boy's family started the tradition of hanging marauder tunics on walls. They are first-rate marauder hunters, and he is being taught to carry on that family tradition. The next time you try to pick on him, *he* may just decide to hang your tunics up in order to *teach you* the lesson. I am very ashamed of both of you. You have disgraced our camp with this behavior. I think I shall have your mothers put you to cleaning out our Merchant Centers."

The boys groaned. This was not working out as they had planned. They hung their heads and began to silently cry as their mothers approached.

"They were very inhospitable and tried to beat up our young visitor. I think that if they have to clean out the Merchant Centers, they will remember to be more hospitable to visitors in the future."

"But why do you allow a larger boy to beat them and then punish them?" asked one of the mothers.

"First of all, we treat all visitors as friends and are hospitable toward them regardless of their size or age. We do not gang up on them two to one. In addition, the boy in question is only in his third summer and is standing right over there. Since when is it right for two fifth-cycle boys to pick on one third-cycle boy about anything?"

Both mothers turned to their offspring with stony looks and told them the age-old saying that must have first been used by mothers when all living creatures were still fish. "Just wait until I tell your father about this behavior, but for now, get busy as the chief said." With hands firmly gripping despondent shoulders, the mothers marched the boys to the first Merchant Center.

Antana approached Roly and told him that although he had done well this time, it would not be a wise idea to make a habit of beating up on other people, at least without good reason.

Marcel smiled and nodded his agreement with her.

The small band of travelers had finished their preparations for the journey and were giving their thanks to Marcel, when a young man came running into camp and told Marcel he had just seen a boat full of marauders unloading in a cove only a short distance away.

Instantly, Declon told his charges to prepare for the assault. Antana took the two wolves, Roly, and the two young women toward the tables. Clartan took the time to see Roly go under the covered table with his spear and the wolves and then took Pino across to the opposite side of the road. Declon and Tamar climbed onto the roof of the merchant place and behind the false wall at the front. The horses were tied next to the women. Tycho climbed to the roof across from Declon.

Marcel was still getting his own people in place when the marauders came racing into camp. At first, the marauders thought they had the advantage, until eight bows started spitting arrows at them, along with the spears thrown from the atlatls of the few camp members in place and ready. By the time Marcel got the last of his people in their places, over half of the marauders were already dead.

Some of the marauders ran for the horses tied next to the women. Before Antana and her group could kill all of them, Roly ruined the legs of three marauders that actually reached the horses.

Clartan and Tamar pulled their bone swords and began cutting down marauders in close quarter fighting. Antana grabbed her spear and, with it flying, met a second group charging the horses. The two young women behind her were able to continue with their bows, while Antana kept the marauders busy and away from them. Two managed to work their way to her side, only to have their legs ruined by Roly before Antana finished them.

One marauder climbed onto the roof and pulled his knife to fight with Declon. Declon simply slapped him and knocked him completely off of the roof. The marauder landed headfirst and never moved again.

As quickly as it started, the raid was ended. Fourteen of the marauders were captured alive, but with varying degrees of dangerous wounds. The other thirty-eight were dead.

The captured marauders were being heavily guarded while having their wounds treated. This was only after the healers finished treating the wounds of the camp members.

Once order was restored, Marcel met with his visitors to thank them for their help. He knew that without their rapid response, the marauders might have won.

"If you will gather the camp elders, I will give you a few tips before we leave," Declon said to him.

Declon quickly explained the importance of regular practice to keep the camp ready for this sort of attack. "Consider, also, that if word gets out about the continuous practice, marauders would be more likely to avoid this camp in the future."

"But how do we go about making these bows that you use so well?"

"I am leaving now and do not have the time to teach you. However, if you send someone to Gondal, I will be happy to teach that person how to build and use bows. You could also send them to Simonia's Camp. I am sure they would be willing to help you also. Just make sure that the next time you are attacked, your people are ready to meet the threat face-on.

"You should not have to take the time to place each person at the start of an attack as you did this time. The practice will insure that they know beforehand where to go on their own. Place each person according to their fighting skills to take the best advantage of each of your fighters. Those best at fighting with their hands go in front, those oldest or weakest at the rear along with a few good fighters just in case of a flanking attack against them. *Make very sure that those casting spears or firing arrows from the rear know not to hit your own front line people!* Those in the front will do you no good if *you* are killing *them*."

"I noticed that someone was under a table and spearing the legs of marauders that got too near," added one man.

"Yes, that was my little nephew. In my home camp far to the east, we learned that by teaching the young to use spears, we could put them under the tables and they could surprise those marauders that got too close to them."

"But what if some of the marauders decided to take him?"

"We stay very aware of the tables and what is happening around them. But we also teach them self-defense as well as fighting under tables."

Declon called to Roly to bring his spear. "Show these people how you would use your spear if marauders start after you."

"I put this in them," grinned Roly as he indicated the point of the spear.

Declon laughed along with the others then nodded for Roly to proceed.

There were regimented practice moves that Roly had to perform in making the spear fly correctly. He started slowly so that the elders could see *how* he made the spear twirl, and then suddenly, the spear became a blur as it sang through the air with a screaming song of death in the full-blown exercise. With the spear still whirring at full speed, it suddenly shot forward, stabbing an apple off the table in front of him. After removing it from the point, Roly started eating it.

The elders were amazed at the spear control that such a small child could have. They asked him if he had been afraid during the attack.

"Nawh, I had Moon and Mr. Duyi under the table with me. If any of the marauders came under there after me, they would have had to deal with more teeth than anyone would want to face. They are the wolves traveling with us," Roly finished with a grin.

Declon placed his hand on Roly's shoulder as he said, "In another three growing seasons, only a very highly skilled fighter would have a chance against him, as long as he is using his spear. We train all of our young people to fight in that manner. As they grow older, some continue with the spear while others pursue other forms of combat. However, even they will retain the knowledge of fighting with the spear. We make a habit of continuing this practice with all our learned combat skills, including combat without a weapon."

Declon explained that these skills could also be learned at Gondal. In fact, if they wanted to send a group to study all the techniques to Gondal, they would gladly be taught and housed until they each had fully learned whatever skills they found most appealing. Just make sure they understand that they should each learn a different skill to bring back with them to teach this camp.

Clartan had been riding ahead with Moon but now waited for the others to catch up with him.

"I smelled some smoke ahead. I believe that it is by that river near the old turnoff to Towsal's old camp. It sort of makes a fellow wonder if Towsal's has found a new batch of residents." Clartan grinned and Declon understood his meaning of the term *residents*.

Clartan led them to a place where they could just see over the crest of the hill without showing their full bodies. Declon and Clartan would ride on ahead and Declon would raise his left arm if he wanted the others to come help fight. He would raise his right arm if it were clear for them to come ahead safely.

As the two approached the river, they saw the camp. They called out a "hello" to warn the camp of their approach. There was no sense in causing undue alarm by surprising anyone. That was a good way to get a spear in the chest, even from friendly people.

Four people had been sitting at the fire, but now stood watching them approach. They held spears at the ready, though not threateningly. As they got close enough to clearly see the campers, a voice called out to them, "Hey, is that you, Declon? Where is that little bitty sister of yours?"

"Romaleo, is that you? I hope you are more friendly this time because Torena is not here, and I tend to be rougher than her."

Romaleo laughed. "I am always friendly these days. Come on into camp. I think you know these others also."

Declon saw Cartio, Bear, and Aria. Romaleo walked over to Aria and put his arm around her and grinned. "I am an old, mated man now."

Aria smiled up at him and put her arm around him as well before beaming her smile at the two old friends.

Declon and Clartan greeted everyone, and Declon told them the rest of his party was just behind the hill. He raised his right arm and soon the party rode over the hill.

Clartan recognized the campsite as the same one into which Estavona had led them when they came before to check out Towsal's Camp.

When Romaleo saw Antana and the wolves, he paled slightly, "I might have known you would have some of them with you." Then he laughed. "At least this time, I am on their side. You are all welcome to stay here with us tonight. This is the best place to camp around here."

"How is your hand?" asked Declon.

"I can hunt and track, and I can butcher the meat for a short while before it cramps up and I have to stop. I am good at guarding the meat cutters though, because it seems that I am more accurate with my throws now than I was before my hand was injured. All of that practice getting it back into shape may have something to do with that fact. It is not any good for hard work or delicate tasks like carving or weaving baskets though."

"Yes, I can just see you weaving baskets," laughed Antana.

"I am the basket weaver in the family, though by trade I am a master tool maker and an organizer," returned Aria.

"What do you do now, Bear?" asked Antana.

"I can find animals when no one else can."

"That is true," said Romaleo, laughing. "He has a gift for finding animals to hunt. I think it has something to do with his being able to smell meat roasting while it is still on the hoof."

"But I am a great trader as well. I am mated with Juna, the daughter of Petara. She is an even better trader than I am."

Declon explained how Tycho was a traveling trader while his mate ran the Merchant Center at their home camp. Bear grinned; he liked that idea and thought Juna would also. He would be speaking with this trader.

Antana noticed that Bea kept her sparkling eyes trained on Cartio. He was beginning to notice her as well. Grinning, Antana formally introduced them to each other. *After all*, she thought to herself, *it cannot hurt to help them along a little.*

Antana then explained to all that Bea was a master of weaving baskets. Then, while looking at Aria, she said, "Gina makes some of the finest clothing you have ever seen."

"And Tamar is quickly becoming a first rate hunter and tracker," interjected Clartan.

"I am a good wood shaper," added Pino.

Aria smiled at this news. Her tool making profession required her to work closely with wood shapers.

Sitting around the fire, Romaleo explained that they were on a hunting trip. Estavona had decided to open a trail along the river from the back of his old camp, all the way to the location of the old Towsal's Camp. Estavona and several men were there now working on the trail.

Clartan told of a herd of red deer he had seen to the south not very far from this campsite, although where they would be in the morning was anyone's guess. After a short discussion, it was decided that they would wait and find out in the morning.

Clartan found the tracks where he had seen the deer the day before. The herd had moved along a trail through some thin and scattered forest.

After following the tracks for a while, Cartio exclaimed, "I think I know where they are headed."

Declon turned to the young man.

"I once found a trail from Towsal's Camp running east to a really nice meadow at the head of a big valley. I think this is that valley."

"How hard is the trail into Towsal's to travel and how far?" asked Declon.

"Not all that far from the camp to the meadow, not more than two hands of the sun on horseback I would say. I am not sure how far it is from here to the meadow. I tried to tell Towsal about the trail once, but he just told me to mind my place and shut up."

"Towsal never was very bright," declared Aria.

"They really could be anywhere in here, so we should take our time and be watchful," stated Clartan.

As they rode, Declon looked around at the massive valley. He was sure there were more animals here than just the one herd for which they were searching. There was water here in abundance, along with plenty of feed, for all different types of animals. Some fed on grass, some on brush, and some preferred feeding on the trees. He was hoping the deer herd was headed for the meadow now, but he would keep this valley in mind for the future.

Clartan eventually found the deer in a small clearing near the edge of the trees. After placing everyone, Clartan took the two wolves and circled around to the other side to distract the deer. As their scent reached the deer, the herd began to move back toward the trees where the hidden hunters awaited.

Eight deer were quickly put on the ground. Fires were quickly built while the deer were skinned and butchered. By the time the first meat was ready to be hung and dried, racks were ready to take it. Enough wood was gathered to fuel many drying fires. Even as the daylight ended and was replaced by darkness, the firelight kept the clearing lit almost as bright as during the day. Clartan laughed and said that there would be very little trouble with predators this night.

Once the meat was properly dried, it was packed onto the horses that Romaleo had brought with him. Cartio's meadow was just ahead through the trees and he led them to the trail he had discovered. It was just a small game trail, made and used by the local animals, but it served the purpose well enough.

It was not long before they found themselves looking into the camp. Declon sent Romaleo ahead to let Estavona know how many were coming and from where.

Romaleo rode into what remained of the former camp and told Estavona that the Kychee were returning. He then stood out in the open and waved. Soon the party could be seen coming down into camp.

Declon decided that with a little work, Cartio's trail could cut a lot of time off of a trip to Marcel's Camp.

Work stopped, and everyone gathered as the party rode up in front of Estavona who then turned and shouted, "Stories tonight, my friends!"

A loud cheer showed camp approval of his declaration.

Estavona greeted his friends, including Tycho, and then looked down at Roly, "Now who might this young man be?"

Beaming with pride, Antana said, "This is my son. These days, we call him Roly."

"No, I remember your son, he was very little. This young man is half grown."

"I am too, Roly."

"Haw haw, so you are. My, how you have grown." Estavona held out his hands in greeting and Roly took them just as he had been shown and was looking very proud as he did so.

Declon then introduced him to the four young people he had with him. Quickly, Declon explained their situation.

"I see no problem here," said Estavona. "There is always room in our camp for such hard cases as these four. Welcome to the camp of reformed marauders." Estavona was grinning widely at them as he spoke.

"Estavona, would you show me around here, please?"

"Of course, Declon, but you saw it when we came here for the remains of Towsal's Camp."

"No, I did not come that time, Cytar and Clartan came. Ramoar and I stayed at Simonia's camp. This is my first time here, but I am getting an idea. I would like to look around and see if it might work."

Estavona led him out of the camp and toward the trail, which headed west along the north side of the mountains. It came to the narrow mouth of an old canyon. When Estavona and Declon passed through, it opened into a beautiful clearing. With purpose, Declon looked around and realized that the mountains to south, and a rock wall to the north formed the canyon. The wall curved toward the mountains at this end creating the mouth they had just passed through. As his eyes followed it, he saw that as it rose up; its top leaned inward, overhanging one side of the clearing. At the rear of the canyon on the western end, it narrowed down to just the trail and the river. His eyes traveled back to the clearing itself.

It was a very large and well-protected clearing that ran east to west with the river coursing through the middle. Declon could tell that even during spring floods, the river would not come up over its banks here.

"How is the trail back to your camp?"

"We are just finishing it up, so it is very good. It comes out into the clearing of my old camp and takes a little over a day and a half from here to there. We made a convenient and comfortable campsite about halfway, so traveling it is now quite easy."

"That knocks, what, close to half of a moon's travel off of the trip between the camps?"

"Yes, we are very happy with it. In addition, there is a very sweet blind-canyon just a short ways in that could hold a very large horse herd. It even has a small spring bubbling up in the back and flowing out to the river."

"Now I will tell you something of which you are probably not aware. The trail we just traveled over into camp, will take a lot more time off of the journey to Marcel's Camp. It needs a little work also, but its condition is not too bad. There are also great hunting grounds just a short distance from here," Declon was very happy telling Estavona about this.

Estavona grinned at this news.

"Why did you decide to open your road to begin with?"

"Declon, we are getting overcrowded at the camp, even with several families now living at my old camp. We have to double up the number of families in our living spaces and have been looking for some way to expand."

"I think this clearing is perfect for a new camp," said Declon, smiling. "There is plenty of good quality stone here to use for building. If you build similar to what we did at Gondal, this could be a first-rate camp."

"Yes, I see what you mean, but I have one very pressing problem. I will always need a top-notch Second, and Festuno fills that role perfectly. I do have two or three in mind who could also make a good Second here. Unfortunately, there is no one qualified to be the leader here, and I cannot run all three of the camps. I have no trouble with handling my old camp as a part of my main camp, but this is just too far away for me to be in charge."

Declon climbed up to the top of the wall and saw that, at one time, it had been a part of the mountain until the river had cut its way through. There was a natural notch at the top of the wall near its end where a shelter could be built for a permanent lookout. He gazed out over the entire area and liked what he saw.

"Estavona, I would be glad to be chief here. In Gondal, I am more or less a permanent visitor. Here, I could feel very much at home."

Estavona whooped loudly and took hold of Declon's shoulders. In his heart, he knew the problem was solved.

12

Chee Terrace

The four young people opted to stay and live at Declon's new camp. After spending so long together with him on the trail, they were very comfortable under his direction.

Clartan and his family said good-bye to Declon after failing to convince him to come home with them. Antana informed Declon of the attraction between Bea and Cartio. Declon was glad of this for now, he would also get Cartio and it only left Pino in need of a mate.

Tycho went with them along the new trail to Simonia's Camp. Estavona still insisted that the camp should keep that name.

They decided to stay at Simonia's Camp for a few days in order to do their trading and restock traveling supplies, before heading on to Gondal.

Both Declon and Estavona agreed that traders should be sent to Marcel's Camp and the Ghaunt Caves for supplies, as well as to spread the word about the new camp.

As the workers completed the trail, they were put to work building the new camp. Four strong bridges were constructed across the river to give plenty of access from one side of the camp to the other. Another bridge was built across the river, outside of the clearing, for better access to the future horse yard location.

Declon laid out the camp foundations close to the rock wall, leaving just enough room for children to play at the rear of the structures. Additional foundations were across the river, against the mountainside and under the overhang. The structures were constructed to his specifications and looked very similar to the ones in Gondal. There were four extra large structures, similar to Cheeville Center, at the east end of the camp. Two were erected on each side of the river, where visitors would pass them first. These would be used for trading and Declon began referring to them as Merchant Palaces. Together, they would make up his Merchant's Row.

At the far end of camp, coming off the mountain trail from Simonia's Camp, two more large structures would be used to comprise a Community Central. There were sixteen family lodges, with stone flooring, built in the same style as Cheeville. Each building had three lodges, three storage spaces, and a workshop. The two lodges next to the Merchant Palaces, one on each side, would be used to house visitors and traders. The spaces between the lodges were large enough for outdoor activities, but each could be enclosed to make an extra single lodge and storage space if needed. Declon made sure attachment points were built permanently into the structures for that very purpose. Stone-paved walkways, with overhead roofs, were put in between the lodges.

Cytar had described the horse shelter at Snow Camp to him, with the enclosed passageway and fire pits at each end. Before leaving, Clartan had also described it, while elaborating on how Cytar had spent so much time living in it with the two women one winter. Declon made sure to add the two fire pits and rock wall reflectors, along with rail dividers, to keep the horses out of the fires and from going into the lodges. The area where the feed was to be kept was also separated from the horses by rail dividers. The horse shelter was placed outside the camp clearing, around the east side of the rock wall, not too far to the north from the mouth of the canyon. Declon built the shelter using the rock wall as the west side and built walls of stone for the north and east sides.

The shelter was situated far enough back from the trail so that another lodge building could be placed between the trail and the horse yard fence. This lodge would house the horse wranglers. In front of the horse shelter was a fenced surround that could hold about forty horses. The horses could use the shelter; although forty could not fit inside of the shelter at one time. An enclosed walkway ran from the shelter to the wrangler's lodge. Another extended from the opposite side of the lodge, wrapping around the wall and connected to the entrance of the first Merchant Palace inside the camp.

A larger shelter was also built in the blind canyon, complete with a lodge for four wranglers and their families.

The horse wranglers would be solely responsible for the care and protection of the horses as well as making and repairing all tack used with the horses. It was also their responsibility to maintain the fences. Estavona said he had just the man to put in charge of the wranglers. His name was Boa; he was around forty seasons, as tough as rawhide and knew more about horses than anyone Estavona had ever met.

After spending a few days in Simonia's Camp visiting old friends and gathering goods to take with them, Clartan felt it was time to move on to Gondal. Tycho decided to travel on to Gondal with them. There were two other traders in camp, and when they heard that Clartan was heading for Gondal, they asked to go along. Clartan agreed after giving them directions to Declon's new camp. His party now included Antana, Roly, Tycho, and the two other traders. At the last minute, Landar asked if he and Dorazar could go along with them.

Romaleo asked Declon, "Would I be out of place here in your new camp? I mean with the history between us, well…"

"You are more than welcome here, Romaleo. What did you wish to do, work with the horses or hunt like you have been doing at the other camp or something else?"

"No…yes, what I mean is, I love to hunt and track, and I can do some things well when working with the horses, but not all. If Boa is willing to have me, that would be wonderful, or for me to hunt would be truly fine also."

"I am also good with the horses. I have helped Old Thomasa most of my life. I am getting to be a good hunter as well," said Cartio.

"How about you, Bear? Do you wish to stay at the other camp or move here?"

"I guess if you are willing to have Romaleo and those former young rabble-rousers, I would be welcome here also."

"If you are now living honestly and think you would be happy here, you will be welcome. I will not tolerate bad behavior, but I will treat all camp members according to how they behave and work to fit in here."

"I no longer cause trouble. I had that taken out of me by a great big giant of a man a few summers back," he grinned at Declon.

Declon clapped him on the back and welcomed him to his new home.

"To start with, I think all three of you will be my primary hunters. Which of you is the leader now?"

Both Cartio and Bear pointed at Romaleo.

"Fine, Romaleo, you are my new hunt leader. Find about four more hunters and take some packhorses back into that valley where we took the deer. Be sure to include Tamar and possibly Pino in the hunt. There should be plenty of herds there for you to hunt. We have to keep these workers fed. Aria, you did well on our last hunt. If you wish to go with them, that will be fine with me."

Aria beamed a smile at her new chief. "You will get twice as much meat back here if I supervise their butchering. But we should also take extra women to help with drying the meat."

"All right, Romaleo is hunt leader and you are my new lead meat cutter and tool maker. Work together and do what needs to be done. We need a lot of meat here as quickly as possible."

The hunters knew exactly whom they were taking and were out of camp in a very short while.

The old camp was dismantled, and everything usable was salvaged. If the new camp grew too large, the old site would be excellent for new expansion. For now, Declon would allow the old site to grow over and vegetables or grain would begin to grow, hopefully.

When the hunters returned, Declon stopped them and spoke with Aria. He felt that it would be less disruptive, if the meat was butchered and dried outside of the camp.

Looking around, Aria pointed to the area of the old campsite that had just been cleared and suggested that it would be a prime location for a permanent site. Later, perhaps, a cover could be put over the area to protect the meat handlers from bad weather. Declon agreed, and Aria got the meat started.

As soon as workers were available, a large paved and covered pavilion was built covering the new fire pits. The pits were complete with their own drying racks, so that meat could be dried even in wet weather. Leather walls that could be rolled up out of the way when not in use, or lowered to block a hot sun or bad weather, were hung on each side.

The roof had a high ridge in the center, slanting steeply down on both sides. The ridge was left open to allow smoke to escape even when the walls were closed. A raised, covered roof section, extended over and above the opening to block the rain or snow, while allowing free passage for the smoke. Even during a snowstorm, meat could be cut and dried here in comfort. With all of the drying fires lit, it would stay warm with the walls lowered completely down.

The Cheeville family was just sitting down to eat their evening meal, when one of the camp boys came running up and said that Clartan had just been sighted. Dinner was forgotten as everyone ran to meet the returning camp members.

Everyone greeted each returnee as they came into camp. Torena turned and looked at Cytar with concern showing in her eyes.

"Welcome back, Clartan," said Cytar as he looked along their back trail to see if Declon was coming in behind the rest.

"He stayed in Towsal's old camp," said Clartan, smiling. "He is rebuilding it and is going to take the leadership position there. And just wait until I tell you about the new trails."

Relief showed in the faces of both siblings. They both knew he had always been destined to be a camp leader. Now they would always know where he was.

That night after eating, everyone in camp gathered in the grassy area in front of the Cheeville Center to listen to the stories of their returning members.

As Declon strolled through the new camp, inspecting all the work and feeling proud of his new home, he saw Estavona riding in on the trail from Simonia's Camp. Together they walked up to the lookout point on the wall and were talking about the camp when they saw Romaleo's hunters, still far out on the trail, returning from their latest hunt loaded with meat and leading visitors. Quickly, Declon called down to some of the camp members to make sure the visitors' lodges were clean and ready for guests, while others prepared to handle the meat.

He and Estavona were just getting to the bottom of the lookout point, when Cartio rode in ahead, to inform him of the meat and visitors. He told Declon that they were from Marcel's Camp and were asking about training.

Declon grinned and sent Cartio back to bring them on in then turned to explain to Estavona about inviting Old Marcel to send some of his camp members to receive training.

Together, they met the incoming group. While the hunters took the meat to the butchering Pavilion, Romaleo presented the visitors to Declon and Estavona. After the introductions, Romaleo joined the meat cutters where Aria was directing the processing. Even here, a watch had to be kept for predators during the butchering.

There were six men and four women in the training party. The spokesman was called Aimeri.

"Marcel sent us to find the training that he was told about. We are to learn as much as we can, so that we can take these new skills back with us to teach others. Marcel also wishes us to give his greetings to those that train us."

"Yes, I am Declon, the one that offered to train Marcel's people. I am now the chief of this new camp and you are most welcome here. This is Estavona, leader of Simonia's Camp and a very good friend of mine."

Aimeri introduced the rest of his party to the two leaders. As Declon took the hands of one woman, Bibi, both gasped and jerked as if a bolt of lightning had just hit them, causing them to look into each other's eyes.

Estavona was watching and laughed. "You may not realize it yet, Aimeri, but this woman will not be going back with you. I think my enormous friend has just lost his heart."

Neither Declon nor Bibi heard Estavona or anything else, but the other women saw and understood what Estavona meant. With bright smiles, they readily agreed with him.

"But we are all supposed to go back, Marcel said so."

"Relax, Aimeri, I will explain it to Marcel, and he will understand. He is far wiser than you seem to realize," soothed Meg, another of the women.

Petara's mate, Maria, came up and said the lodge was ready for the visitors. Estavona looked to see if Declon was going to give a response, then chuckled and told the visitors to follow Maria to the lodge. He took it upon himself to herd Declon and Bibi toward the lodge. Meg helped him.

As the group came into view of the camp, the visitors gasped in wonder. Not one of them had ever seen or heard of anything like this camp. They marveled at the entrance and the accommodations inside.

Maria put the four women into the lodge next to the workshop and three of the men into each of the other two lodges. For now, their gear was taken into the lodges with them, but Maria showed them the storage spaces and said they were welcome to use them, if they wished.

They were by now standing in the workshop when Declon and Bibi came out of their little world of each other. Bibi made a small squeak when she saw that they were inside, causing the others to laugh.

Meg leaned over to Bibi and whispered loudly enough for everyone to hear "He is good-looking. I do not blame you at all."

Bibi responded by turning flame red.

Declon glanced over into the laughing eyes of Estavona who said, "It is about time someone caught you. It is not right for the leader to not be mated because that gives his camp the uncomfortable feeling that he will not stay around for very long." He held up one hand and continued, "No, do not deny it. I can see that you are hooked. And with her looks, I do not blame you at all."

Estavona turned to Maria and said, "A feast tonight! We will welcome the guests properly, and celebrate the future joining of your new chief with this beautiful young woman."

"I will take care of it, but the weather is beautiful so I think it should be held under the Pavilion tonight as there is still meat being dried, the hunters made a fine kill today. I think there will be plenty of room, but if it gets too crowded, some of us can stand out in the grass around the Pavilion," declared Maria.

"A marvelous suggestion, Maria, that will be a grand place for tonight's celebrating."

Declon and Bibi were both sputtering so Meg told Bibi how lucky she was to have found someone like him. The other two women joined in and the men started to congratulate Declon.

Declon and Bibi looked at each other, smiled, and decided things were as they should be.

The feast was a wonder of culinary delights. Nuts, seeds, onions, garlic, herbs, and tangy roots were mixed with crumbled loaves of baked grains. These were placed inside and around birds that had been rubbed with fat and salt before roasting. There were fresh bison roasts, stew made from dried meat, and vegetables from the storage. Fresh vegetables, both raw and cooked, accompanied the meat dishes. The tables were also adorned with special honey-sweetened loaves filled with berries. Some of the younger children had caught fresh fish that day, which were prepared simply and quickly seared on very hot flat rocks.

As everyone finished eating, Estavona stood and announced that Declon was going to be mated. Although most had already heard, a great cheer rose up at the announcement. Declon and Bibi were assisted to their feet as Estavona said it was time for them to meet their new head woman.

Declon laughed and held his hands out to get everyone's attention. "This is Bibi and she has come from Marcel's Camp to join us here at our new home. Now, I cannot bring my new woman to a camp that does not even have a name, so as of this moment, this camp will be known as Chee Terrace."

Another great roar lifted.

Declon allowed the crowd to assimilate the information before continuing. Holding out his hands again, he said, "There is other news. After much discussion with Estavona, I have decided to make Petara my Second and Boa will be head of the horse handlers. I am sure you have already guessed that Romaleo is lead hunter and Aria holds two positions, as both lead tool maker and lead meat handler."

Cheers came after each announcement. Now he looked at Maria, the mate of Petara, "Maria, you have done wonders organizing this feast tonight. Will you be my official Camp Hostess?"

Maria stood as her name was called and turned bright red at the praise. "It would be an honor for me to be in charge of all future feasts. One suggestion I have is that many of the celebrations be held right here under the Pavilion. Look how much room we have, even with all of our visiting friends. Of course, in severe weather, we have the two new community structures in which to hold our gatherings. It would be very crowded, though, to fit this many people into just one of them."

The suggestion was met with great enthusiasm. Declon allowed the cheers for a few moments before quieting them down and continuing.

"Estavona and I have been discussing the training needed for those of you from Marcel's Camp. In the morning, we will meet with you to help you decide what skills each of you wish to learn before starting the training. Some of you will stay here and some will go with Estavona to his camp for your training. I am not sure yet, but a few of you may even be sent to Gondal to train there. In this way, we can give each of you the best training possible. This way you will be receiving training from different sources, so you can then compare your training and take the best of it home with you."

Estavona stood back up and said, "In one moon cycle, I shall return with our shaman and Declon and Bibi will be joined. The shaman has a well-trained assistant who will accompany us to become your new shaman." Turning to Declon, he said, "I do believe this will make Chee Terrace a fully functional camp."

Unknown to Declon, Estavona had already sent a rider to let Gondal know of Declon's impending mating.

The resounding roar was deafening. The last of the work on the new camp had been finished that day, and those from Simonia's Camp would be going home in the morning with Estavona, some reluctantly. About half of Simonia's Camp had opted to move here to help get this camp started and give the older camp much-needed room.

Two more couples spoke with Estavona about moving to the new camp that night, and he agreed. Initially, there would only be one family in each lodge building, anyway, so there was plenty of room.

During the new camp's construction, Estavona had arranged for almost everyone from his camp to spend some time working here, in order to get a good idea of how this camp was built. Once everyone was back home, he would hold a camp meeting and reevaluate their camp to see if they could improve it. Thanks to Cytar, many of their lodges had already been rebuilt in a style similar to this, although the camp was not laid out nearly as well as Chee Terrace. In his camp, the new lodges had mostly been built over the older foundations, rather than placing the new structures in a more useful pattern. The interiors of those were also not as large as the ones here.

After going through all the different combat moves, it was decided that three women, Dina, Meg, and Cadice, would go to Gondal and train in unarmed combat, Flying Spears and children's training. If they learned quickly, they could also choose any of the other training they desired.

Estavona would take three men, Cyril, Looys, and Baya for training in bows, spear, lance, and mounted lance. They, too, could cross-train if they learned quickly.

Declon would keep Aimeri, Tan, and Fil, and of course, Bibi. They would receive training in bone sword combat, mounted archery, close quarters knife, and horned club combat. He would also be giving them training in combat strategy, which included prevention planning.

By breaking the groups up in this way, Declon felt sure that all of the trainees would take home the best training possible.

After studying the problem thoroughly, Declon decided to set up a practice field in Horse Canyon. He put a few camp members to work building targets and erecting a fence to keep the horses safely out of the practice field. There was currently plenty of room for a practice field that was large enough to even include the mounted training.

The horse herd would have to grow drastically before there would be any conflict with practice and pasture.

13

Declon Mates

Cytar was just finishing some repairs on the roof of one of the lodges, when he saw a rider rapidly approaching the camp. Before he came down from the roof, he called down to Sandole that a rider was coming fast, and it looked like Hertalo from Simonia's camp. He had just made it to the side of Sandole and Sabortay, when the rider reached them and jumped off his horse with a wide grin on his face.

"Well, from the way you were approaching, we feared terrible news, but that grin says otherwise," snorted Sandole.

"Estavona told me to get here double quick. I have very interesting news for Torena," answered the man breathlessly.

Torena was just coming up when she heard her name mentioned.

"I am here," she called as she ran the last few steps.

"It is about your brother, Declon. He is going to be mated."

"MATED?" Torena spun and grinned at Cytar. "Dec is getting mated."

"So I heard, but to whom is he getting mated?"

"Her name is Bibi, and she comes from Marcel's Camp. Marcel sent some of his young adults to be trained, and she was one of them. It seems that as soon as the two of them touched hands, they decided to get mated. At least that is the way I was told that it happened. Estavona told me just a little while later, to get my carcass down here and let you know."

Little feet could be heard running away and Cytar turned to see his daughter racing into the Merchant Center where her mother was. He grinned and looked at Torena. "I guess we do not need to tell Marcina about this."

"Why not?' she asked.

Just then, Marcina and Antana came running out of the center with Shalela and Roly right on their heels.

"What is this about Dec getting mated?"

"It is true. Estavona sent Hertalo to let us know."

"Yes, and Estavona said he will delay the mating ceremony for a few moon cycles, should any of you want to come."

Shortly after dawn, Estavona left with his camp members and the trainees who were not staying at Chee Terrace. Once they arrived at Simonia's Camp, he would send the three women to Gondal with some of his hunters as a protective escort and guides.

On returning to his home camp, he arrived just in time to meet Cytar and the mating party arriving from Gondal. There were also two traders and a storyteller wanting to go to Gondal. Estavona told them to talk to Cytar.

Cytar told the three that they would be most welcome in Gondal, but if they wanted to attend the ceremony for his brother in the new camp first, they could then travel to Gondal with his group.

Cytar also told the three trainees that they would be going to Gondal when he returned. For now, they would get to see their former camp-mate become the head woman of Declon's new camp.

Estavona looked at Cytar and the others. "Are you interested in what he has named his new camp?"

They all looked at each other and grinned before nodding for Estavona to continue.

"He has named his camp Chee Terrace. I think the name fits very well."

Romaleo rode back into camp with another man following him. The man was mounted and led a heavily loaded packhorse. As he rode up to Declon, he said, "He came along while I was putting up our new trail marker. He is a trader, so I told him we were a newly built camp, he decided to come and take a look at us."

"You are most welcome to Chee Terrace. I am called Declon, and I am the chief here. I heard the term *chief* used farther east and decided I liked it. Now I go by the title, Camp Chief."

The trader grinned at Declon's explanation and said, "I am thinking I have heard a similar term being used during my travels. I am Darsh. From far to the south, do I come, where it is being very hot, always."

"We have a friend that comes from farther south. His name is Apopus, and he comes from Tonopus."

"Ah yes, Tonopus. My travels have bringing me through there on my way north. I was travel to the north while riding on a camel for more than a full cycle of the seasons from my home before I am arriving in Tarsus, which is still being in much to the south of Tonopus."

"What is a camel?"

Darsh described a camel as best he could before continuing his tale.

"In my homeland, we begin to grow the barley for food now, and have grown the wheat for several seasons."

"You grow wheat and barley...on purpose? Can you tell me how?" Declon looked over to Bibi and saw that her eyes were shining with interest. She saw him look at her and nodded her encouragement.

"You are having the wheat or barley here?"

Bibi left at a hard run.

"We do. My future mate has gone to get some of each for you now."

Within a short while, Bibi had returned with two bowls, one filled with wheat and the other with barley. She handed the bowls to Declon. He saw that she was shivering with delight. Several other camp members had heard why she was getting the grains and followed her back.

Darsh walked out close to the Pavilion and selected two likely spots to scatter the grain.

"I will be needing bowls filled with dirt and water to spread over the grains."

"I am on it," called Romaleo as he turned away. He called out to some younger boys to help him.

"Maybe it is being too late in the season to plant for true, but we are doing it anyway so that I can be showing you *how* it is done."

Darsh indicated two areas for planting the grains, and Declon had some of the men mark a border along the edge of each with stones.

While this was done, and the water and dirt were gathered, Darsh used the butt end of his spear to cut shallow furrows along the ground. These were spaced apart at a distance of about three of his feet from one furrow to the next.

When Romaleo and his helpers reappeared with the dirt and water, Darsh continued his instructions.

"I am dropping the grain into the grooves which I cut into the ground. Very lightly, be covering the grain with a small amount of dirt, then take hand and shake water through fingers onto the grain seeds. Too much water will uncover the seeds."

Darsh put a few seeds into the furrows then dusted dirt lightly over them and sprinkled the water on top.

"Have young boys, all the time, to be chasing or killing any birds that try to get the seeds. Later, they will be having to keep the deer and other animals from out of the young grain."

Darsh handed the grain bowls to Romaleo. "Be spreading the wheat here and the barley into the other area. It is better separating the types of grains."

Bibi took one bowl and spread her grain in one plot, while Romaleo spread his in the other. One boy with dirt and another with water followed each. In a matter of minutes, both small plots were finished.

Darsh told the group as they finished planting to water every day, at first, to keep the seeds moist but not wet. If the weather allowed, and the season was not too late, the grain would soon be growing.

Declon showed Darsh to the lodge where he would stay and then introduced him to Juna, the camp's new master trader, and Bear, her mate.

Darsh was very impressed with the camp's setup. The lodge layout fascinated him. These were not the usual mud, skin, and brush huts. These lodges were built to last. The use of stone for building would be valuable information to the right person. He knew just the person to take it to, and he would go there on his way back to his home in the south.

Declon walked into the operating Merchant Palace, the only one open so far and found Juna negotiating with another trader. She looked up at Declon and gave him a brilliant smile. Declon had not even known this trader was in camp, and then he saw Darsh standing at a nearby table, looking through a pile of furs. Declon nodded to her before going back out.

"I guess we truly are open for business now," he chuckled to Bibi, as he glanced across at the trail from Marcels and pointed. Romaleo was leading two more new visitors into camp.

A broad smile crossed his face, as Romaleo got close enough for him to recognize Macelar and Apopus.

"Welcome, my old friends. Welcome to Chee Terrace," beamed Declon.

"I was a little worried when we first met this young rascal. The last time I saw him was after the raid where his hand was hurt. He told me he had reformed and that you were now his camp leader or chief."

"You see I did not lie to you. Here he is, just as I said he would be."

Declon laughed and gripped Macelar and then Apopus in mighty hugs.

"Romaleo, see to their horses and have their gear brought up to the Merchant Palace. Maria will see to their lodging."

"I am on it, Chief."

Macelar looked after Romaleo as he led the horses away. "He has sure changed."

"Yes, he was a little slow in making the change, but since he mated Aria, he has become a strong support for me. He is now my lead hunter, and she is my head meat handler and tool maker." Declon chuckled and continued, "I do believe he is getting to be as good at finding stray traders as he is at finding animals to eat."

Apopus laughed. "I would not think of that as a trait to complain about."

"Oh no, I am not complaining at all, at least so far. It will be when he brings in hundreds of traders every day that will start me to complaining."

Macelar and Apopus looked at each other. "Awh, to be so wealthy as to complain about getting more." Both men broke into laughter as Declon blushed.

"This, my dear friends, is my future mate, Bibi. You are just in time to see us mated."

"Mated? When?"

"As soon as Estavona gets back with the shaman. That should be in only a few more days."

Cytar and his little group had been drilling the new recruits on Estavona's training field, while waiting for him to ready everything for the trip to Chee Terrace. Sayta, Shalela, and Roly were used to help the trainees learn how to train and deploy children. All three children were very quick to inform them when they made a mistake. Antana told the trainees not to get upset when the children told them of their mistakes, because they learned faster when they knew someone was waiting to yell, "Wrong!"

The trainees continued to get a little upset until two of them told Roly to get under different tables. He got down on the ground between the two tables and put one foot under each table. After everyone stopped laughing, they all understood why getting things right was so important. All three trainees applauded Roly for his inventive way of demonstrating their error in a non-confrontational manner.

Estavona told everyone at the evening meal to gather at the *Old Camp* at first light, because they would leave from there for Chee Terrace. *Old Camp* was how they now referred to the section that once been known as Estavona's old camp.

Clartan grinned at Cytar and told him to just wait and see the new trail leading to the new camp.

The next morning, Estavona took the trail at the back of Old Camp, into the mountains, and then followed it as it led along near the river to the midway camp for the night. By the following midday, they were riding into Chee Terrace. Declon had been informed of their passage by a lookout that he kept watching the trails at all times.

Torena was the first one off her horse, and she leaped into his arms. After she held on for several heartbeats, he asked if anyone else wanted a neck weight for a while.

Bibi stood back and watched as three of the most beautiful women she had ever seen, *all* took turns hugging and kissing her man.

Declon saw her standing there and asked, "Would any of you like to meet my new woman?"

If any of the men answered, none were heard because of all the squealing from the women.

Declon held out his right hand to Bibi and grinned rather sheepishly. As she stepped forward and took his hand, he lifted it and twirled her across and into his left arm so that she stopped against him, facing the horde of relatives and friends.

"This is Bibi," he started before introducing her to everyone.

Shalela stepped up to her and took her hand. "I know we must seem very scary to you, but you are one of us now, so you get to be scary with us."

Everyone started laughing and Bibi told her, "I cannot think of any other way I could have been made to feel a part of this group as well as you just did."

Then all of the women were hugging each other and talking at once. Declon watched them briefly before motioning for the men to go up to the lookout station on the top of the wall. As the men passed by Maria, he asked her to let the women know where they were, when they finally thought about their men.

Cytar was amazed at how different it was here now. "There, where that pavilion is, wasn't that where the old camp was?"

"Yes, and look, you can see my hunters returning over the new trail which goes to Marcel's Camp." Looking down, he signaled to those below that the hunters were bringing in meat. "Now we can feast tonight. It appears they were very successful in their hunt." As he looked at Cytar, he beamed, "This place is unbelievably wealthy in food of all types."

Declon pointed toward the grain fields and told how it was done. They could see two large areas near the river down in the valley that were already being prepared for the grain planting next spring. They watched the hunters unloading the meat at the Pavilion, and he told of how well everyone in that area was organized to work on the meat. Declon explained that the horse yard could later be moved farther out into the meadow as the camp expanded.

Cytar watched his brother speaking of his new camp with so much pride and was delighted for him. Both he and Torena could now rest easy knowing Declon would never disappear on them.

At the evening meal, Estavona brought over a young man and introduced him to Declon and Bibi as Jocoa, their new shaman. He would be performing the mating ceremony, with the older shaman in the background to make sure everything went properly.

Declon and his new mate, Bibi, could hear the crowd waiting boisterously outside for the couple to emerge for the first time as mates from their lodge. The couple came out hand in hand to the deafening cheers of the camp and all of their visitors.

After the crowd finally quieted down, Torena went to Bibi and hugged her as she welcomed her to the family. Cytar told Bibi that she had his utmost sympathy in her choice for a mate and then laughed as he dodged his brother's grasping hand.

Maria then came forward and escorted the newly mated couple to the breakfast feast, held at the Pavilion, as it had officially now been named.

Cytar, and the group from Gondal, spent the next two days getting reacquainted with all of their old friends and meeting new ones.

Romaleo brought a very large bunch of colorful early fall flowers to Torena, which caused her to cry. After giving him a heartfelt hug, she told him, "I am so very happy and proud of what you have become, and how you have turned your life around."

"It is in large part because of you that I did so, Torena. That time in Gondal, when you walked up and again saw me as a troublemaker, I suddenly felt so ashamed of my life. When your family decided to give me one more chance, I decided then that you would never again have to look at me in that way."

"Oh, Romaleo, you make me so proud."

Romaleo held out his hand to Aria, and as she joined him, he rubbed her stomach and said to Torena, "I want you to be the first to know that Aria and I will soon have a new member of our family."

Torena squealed and threw her arms around Aria. Marcina and Antana joined them, and soon, the entire camp was crying and hugging the happy young couple; at least the women were crying.

As the noise died down, Torena held up her hands for attention. She took Ramoar's hand and turned to the waiting crowd, "I guess this is the time for wonderful news, so…" Torena then stuck out her stomach and rubbed it as she smiled coyly.

A new round of noise met the latest announcement. Declon picked up his little sister and hugged her. "I am so happy for you. I just hope it takes after its uncle and has my good looks."

"Hey!" shouted Ramoar before he grinned.

"Well, of course he'll have good looks if he takes after his Uncle Cytar." The crowd all turned to Cytar, who was grinning mischievously, and burst into laughter.

Bibi stepped over to Torena and whispered. Torena squealed yet again and threw her arms around Bibi.

Looking confused, Declon asked, "What?"

Marcina laughed and hugged Declon. "You are going to be a papa also."

"I...what...how...?"

"Surely you know *how* it happened," teased Antana as she watched the bewildered man.

Cytar reached into his pouch and pulled out three mother-of-pearl talismans, beautifully worked and carved with intricate swirls and spirals, and three very small ones. He placed the first around Torena's neck and handed her a second small necklace. When she saw what it was, she kissed him on the cheek and thanked him. She then stood with him, as he placed one around the neck of each of the two other new mothers and handed each a second, tiny necklace.

When they looked puzzled at the strangely shaped talismans, Torena told them, "It is believed by some that mother-of-pearl helps with motherhood and increases a mother's intuition. The small necklaces, with the tiny mother-of-pearl talismans, are for your babies. They will help protect the infants from any perils they will face in their new lives."

The rest of the day was one great party. Everyone would be starting for home the next morning. Cytar would take his charges back through Simonia's Camp with Estavona and then continue on to Gondal. It would be a race to make it back before the snow came.

Estavona insisted that they take extra clothing, shelter, and food for the horses, as well as for themselves. He had two of his extra horses packed with supplies for them. The horses could be returned the next spring.

Cytar had decided to spend the night in Traveler's Cave. Clartan killed a nice, fat red deer just before dark so there was fresh meat for the evening meal, which was now being cooked. Sayta and Shalela had insisted on doing the cooking. Torena allowed them to, but under the watchful eyes of their mothers.

"It has started to snow," Ramoar said as he returned with an armload of wood. Roly walked right behind him, also carrying some wood. Of course, his armload consisted of a few small pieces.

"I am now very glad we made sure to bring in so much extra wood. With what was already here when we arrived, we may not have to bring in much more before this storm lets up. Depending on the storm, we may have to wait until spring to completely restock the wood supply in here."

"Yes, but you could never have gotten so much wood without that helper of yours."

"Well, he gives orders very well. Every time he saw a limb he could not lift, he told me to get it." This brought a round of laughter along with cheers for Roly.

"I think we should all make one more trip before the snow gets too heavy," Cytar stated.

"Roly, you come help me," said Antana. Antana, Marcina, and Torena, along with Roly, hung a large leather ground cover across the cave opening. A permanent wooden doorframe had been installed at some earlier date for just this purpose.

With so many helping by going for just *one more load*, the cave was quickly packed full with wood. Only a short time later, the snow became a blizzard. It was nine days later before the weather warmed enough for the snow to melt sufficiently for the travelers to continue with their journey. The woodpile left in the cave was still larger than usual, so there would be no worries about someone arriving and not having enough wood in an emergency.

When Torena told the family she was expecting again, she found out that Edda was also.

There would be much for the camp to talk about this winter—the babies, Declon's mating, his new camp, and the promising grain fields. The traders staying for the winter each had stories to tell, as did the trainees from Marcel's Camp.

14

The Growth of Gondal

The winter seemed to go by rapidly. With all of the visitors and training, in addition to regular winter projects, no one had found time to get bored. As the snow began to melt, Gondal started their spring clean up and repair work. Sandole found two discarded piles of trash within the camp and called a camp meeting to make sure that no one left trash within the camp again. He had places set aside for trash away from camp, and he demanded those places be used. He told them that the camp would be kept clean even if he had to knock heads together to attain this goal.

Two new lodges were started, facing each other, on the east side of the camp. On the south end of Merchant Row, another group of fishing families, headed by Delac and Faleenia, began constructing their own lodges in a setup like Cheeville's. Two lodge buildings were erected on each side of the path, plus they built their own event center. This would put them closer to the boat docks on the south side, just as Cheeville put Ramoar and Locar closer on the north side. Sandole had not yet named their new area.

All the fishermen got together and decided to put a large merchant style building, behind the Merchant Row, facing west. It was between the Cheeville family section, and Delac's family section, to be used for cleaning and smoking the fish. Fresh fish could usually be found there, resulting in its being named the Fish House. A covered and paved path was built from each family section to the front of the new Fish House. Two paved paths ran down to the boat docks, and yet another path connected the docks.

Two moon cycles after the snow melted, a large group of traders arrived from the Ghaunt caves that included the trader, Darsh, who had wintered in one of their caves. In the group were two newly mated young couples wishing to move to Gondal.

Sandole interviewed the young couples. Darsh had been telling them about raising the grain, and they wanted to give it a try. After speaking with Darsh, the Gondal council became interested in trying to raise grain and decided to accept the two couples.

They were moved into one of the new eastside lodge buildings on the far north end of the camp, and plans were started for planting the grain out in a large meadow to the northeast of the camp.

Torena decided that if grain could be grown, so could vegetables. She planned to figure out how to go about it. Cytar laughed and said it would be just a matter of time before she had it figured out.

A half moon later, a young couple arrived from the south and wanted to live in Gondal. It turned out that he was the nephew of the twins, Fartez and Fontez, and his name was Miganos. They began training him to track and hunt. His mate, Elanza, was a very good carver.

Cytar was elated at how his holdings had grown. Not only did he manage his own animals, he also managed those of all of the family as well. The horse herd was again expanding, as soon, many of the mares would be giving birth. In addition, because of all the little cubs that were born, the size of the wolf pack was now almost beyond control. To top it all off, both Antana and Marcina had just announced that they would again be sharing pregnancies. He decided it was time to call a family meeting.

"I think that we should begin to train the young wolves and then trade them away. Traders should be a prime group to develop an interest in the wolves. It will be necessary for us to prove to them just how much help properly trained wolves can be, both for security and in assisting with hunting."

"I agree, Cytar. Of course, we will only have a few wolves to trade each summer, but that might make them more valuable."

"Oh, Papa, can Roly and I help train the little wolves?"

"Of course, Shalela."

"Cytar, Edda and I have been discussing how large our pack is getting, and we came up with similar conclusions. Although neither of us will be able to give our attention to the wolves full time, I think that with the help of the children, we can handle most of the training," said Antana.

"I will help you as much as I can, Antana. I do so enjoy the wolves."

"Thank you, Delphinia."

"Well, that takes care of the wolves, now for the horses. We need a similar plan for them. Most camps have some horses for trade, so we need to make our herd a little more desirable. We have always practiced selective breeding, so the best plan of action that I can think of to increase the value of each animal, is a lot of training. Some are only good as pack animals. Others are better for riding, and a few can handle both well. If we sort and train them accordingly, it will be easier to trade them later. I also think we need to take on more handlers. The two young men we have are great, but they are becoming very overworked."

"Cytar, I think each of them should have at least two younger helpers to train under them, possibly even three. There is an awful lot of work to do taking care of the herd."

"Maybe we should ask them how much help they could use."

"Good idea. Sayta, would you call Oda and Leban here, please?"

"Yes, Uncle Cytar. Can I help with the training? You know how much I love horses."

Everyone laughed, and Cytar nodded to her. Her love of horses was well known in the family.

Sayta ran around the lodge and a loud, shrill whistle was heard. Sayta came running back followed a short time later by the two young men.

Oda said he knew several boys and a few girls that might be interested and was told to find which ones he thought would be the most dependable, and for them to come for an interview. Sayta went to keep an eye on the horses while the two young men took off to find some helpers.

"Cytar?"

"Yes, Torena."

"We have helped everyone in camp that has needed anything and even given a lot to Simonia's Camp. Even with all of that, I have more now than I know what to do with. What are we going to do with all of this incredible increase in wealth?"

Suddenly, everyone in the family was looking at everyone else. This was a problem that not one of them had ever thought about having before. Everyone became speechless, until all suddenly broke into laughter at the same time.

The young man came walking into the camp from the north. He was intelligent-looking and appeared to have been well dressed at the start of his trip. Of course, he now looked rather well traveled.

"My name is Wayon, and I come from Bodus Camp. When I was younger, a man came to our camp, and I overheard him telling my father about Gondal. I must say, this is nothing like the Gondal he described."

Sandole swelled with pride before answering him, "We have made a few improvements. What was this man's name that you speak of?"

"I believe it was Dec-con, or something like that."

Sandole laughed and slapped the young man on the back before calling to Cytar.

"This young man is named Wayon. He comes from Bodus and said that your brother told them all about us when he was there." Turning to Wayon, Sandole introduced Cytar. "This is Cytar, brother of Declon. Unfortunately, Declon no longer lives here."

Though very young, Wayon was already an accomplished stone carver. When his parents suddenly died of a deadly fever, he decided to come here. He said he had news from the north and Sandole asked him to tell his stories that night at a camp feast.

After the meal that evening, Wayon told of how twelve had died of the fever during early spring, including his parents. Many others, including himself, had taken ill but had recovered.

He had also stopped at one of the Goyet caves and learned that they had defeated a raiding party. At first, there were some minor losses of stores and a couple of horses. Then Gillis, Kort, and Joord had decided to catch the thieves. It turned into a full-scale raid and the Goyets were more than a match for the marauders. Of the five marauders killed, three were young children.

Cytar and Clartan looked at each other and nodded. Cytar quietly slipped over to Sandole and told him that those marauders had to be Nickotian's again. Sandole agreed and said they would have a meeting in the morning to prepare.

"I would very much like to get that man." Sandole was pacing back and forth, as he talked. As he paced he saw Corb, now a young man of about eighteen cycles. Sandole watched him working with his new wolf, Shadow.

"Corb," called Sandole, "how well is your wolf trained?"

"He would sit, stay, and come at the time I traded for him. Now, he will also protect and find."

"How do you think he would do guarding this camp?"

"Well…" Cord hesitated, looking toward Cytar.

"The wolf is more than a cycle old now, Sandole, and wolves guard naturally. Cord also has a horse that was wild for the first two cycles of its life. As Long as Cord pays attention to both his horse and wolf, he will be aware of any and everything around the camp." Cytar turned to the young man. "Cord, stop every few minutes and give the animals a chance to nose around before moving to a different location. Be sure to watch them closely as you are traveling between stops because they will know, before you do, of any nearby threats. Try to keep out of sight as much as possible, the ones we are looking for are killers."

"Yes, Cytar."

"Also, do not take the same path, or stop at the same places, two times in a row. Do nothing to set a pattern. If you do, they *will* be waiting for you."

"Yes, Cytar."

For the next two moon cycles, Corb slowly meandered throughout the countryside. Occasionally he would, unexpectedly, show up in camp.

Oda had been exercising a horse, when he suddenly turned and rode up to Cytar. "Cytar, Corb is coming in. It looks as if he is bringing in someone who is hurt."

"Thank you, Oda."

Cytar hurried to the Merchant Row and saw Sandole also waiting for Corb to arrive. Faleenia, the camp healer, arrived just behind Cytar.

Cytar helped ease the man down.

When Sandole saw the man's face, he said, "This is Jock, a hunter from one of the Ghaunt caves."

"Got away…thought dead…fell…could not f-find me."

"Quiet, Jock, save your strength."

"Coming…many…"

"You two men, take him to Faleenia's healing lodge. Cytar, Sabortay, we need to talk."

"There's Clartan, you should have him talk with us."

"Clartan, over here."

"First, Corb, tell us about finding him."

"I was patrolling pretty far to the east, near Topknot Valley, when Shadow growled. When I saw where he was looking, I looked too. It only took a moment for me to see movement. It looked to be a man hurt and stumbling. I recognized him when I reached him. I finally got him up on my horse and brought him here. He mumbled all the way."

"Did he make any sense in his talk?"

"At first he did. It seems a large group of marauders ambushed his hunting party. He has no idea if any of the others were hurt, or if any survived."

"Anything else?"

"Yes, he overheard some of the marauders talking and understood enough to get the idea they were headed to Gondal."

"Corb, do not go back out alone. It is time for us to make up scout teams."

"Yes, Cytar."

"Sandole, I think he would do well with the twins and their nephew. The twins have developed a liking for wolves, and he has Shadow. I can take Sabortay and a couple of others along with Dac. Clartan has Moon and can take another team of his choosing. You can organize most of the camp here. Marcina, Antana, and Torena will be here with Midnight and the other wolves. Shalela and Roly have been training them to attack, among other things. I think a group of marauders coming into this camp will now be in for some very unpleasant surprises. Also, we have the three trainees still with us from Marcel's Camp, and this will be a very good lesson for them."

After making plans to meet at Topknot Valley, the three teams rode out in preplanned directions. Two days later, all three teams were together in the valley. The twins had found the location of the ambush and said it appeared that several hunters had escaped, but they had lost their horses.

The marauders had traveled northwest, and the twins determined that the marauders were planning on coming into Gondal from the north. Both men were convinced that the teams needed to get back to Gondal as quickly as possible.

Clartan joined the twins leading the combined team back by the most direct route possible. With those three, and Moon in the lead, Cytar knew no one would catch them in a trap. However, he took the precaution of having the rest of the group spread out to make a less concentrated target.

Shortly before Gondal came into sight, twenty Ghaunt hunters, also looking for the marauders, joined them. The hunters who had been attacked had made it home, and this band had set out to put an end to the marauders.

With the party now consisting of thirty-two people and three wolves, they adjusted their course to arrive at the north side of Gondal, to attempt to head off the marauders.

The combined force came out of the trees right behind the unsuspecting marauders and chased them straight into Gondal. The marauders were so intent on gaining the wealth of the camp, they were completely unaware of the large force behind them as they raced to the edge of the camp. They entered the camp with arrows flying at them, both from the front and from behind.

Only three marauders lived long enough to tell how Nickotian and Baytuk had stayed back in the edge of the trees and watched as the others had ridden ahead to destroy the camp.

Cytar looked back to the trees but knew that by now Nickotian was once again long gone. As much as he wanted to go after the Sarainian, he knew it would be futile. Carriage returned here.

"What an incredible coward!" snorted Sabortay. Everyone agreed with him.

Once again, the members of Gondal, along with the Ghaunt hunters, were subdued by the large percentage of *marauder* children killed in the attempted raid. All openly cried and vowed vengeance on the head of the Sarainian, as they put the children into the ground.

Word was sent to Simonia's Camp, and to the Goyet camps, of the raid. The Ghaunt party would take the story back with them. Soon, word was spreading throughout the continents of ancient Europe and Asia, by way of messengers, traders, and travelers. They told of the cowardice of the Sarainian and how he continued to lure children to their deaths.

In the manner of a true coward, Nickotian went into hiding. It would be a long time before he was heard from again. However, he vowed he *would* be back.

Torena was close to time for her baby as she sat watching Sayta, Shalela and Roly. Shalela was wearing a belt made from silk that Cytar had told her was given to him by someone long ago and far away. Shalela was to bring back the belt as soon as she had shown it to the others.

Shalela had taken off the belt and was watching it pass through her fingers, when she suddenly stopped and sat very still. Sayta and Roly both asked her what was wrong, but she did not respond to them. Sayta turned to her mother and asked what was wrong with Shalela.

Torena looked very closely at Shalela and told the other two children to be very quiet and not to touch her. Shalela began nodding slightly and mumbling. Sayta began to get scared, but Torena told her that Shalela had gone into a trance. She then told them that it was common for members of her family to have visions and asked Sayta to go and find her Uncle Cytar.

Sayta first went to Marcina and told her. Marcina sent her to Merchant Row to look for Cytar, saying that he would probably be in one of the Centers, then went to Shalela.

As Marcina entered Torena's lodge, Torena held her finger against her lips indicating for Marcina to be quiet. As Marcina sat next to Torena, Torena smiled at her and patted her hand, then turned back to watch Shalela.

Cytar soon arrived with Sayta, and Torena indicated for him to sit quietly also.

After Shalela had been in the trance for about a half of a hand of the sun, she came out of it and saw everyone watching her. She smiled at them and turned to her father. "My sister, Leelee asked me to tell you *hello*. She and her mother are now staying with your mother and father. She is being trained to fight and to heal. She said she will see you some day, and for you to be looking for her."

Cytar's mouth dropped open. Marcina looked at Cytar, and Torena patted him on the hand and laughed.

Shalela held up the belt. "Leelee told me that this once belonged to her mother. I could see her mother and she is very pretty. So is Leelee."

Shalela waited for her father to answer her before continuing.

Cytar slowly smiled and told Shalela, "Her mother's name is Myling, daughter of Langtou, leader of the Tyzeir People. Zodar once saved his life."

"Zodar! That is the name she said! He is one of the people training Leelee. Another one was Careechee? No, that is not right."

"Kokarashi?"

"Yes, that was it, Kokarashi."

Torena squealed, "Oh, I miss those two old men so much. Mother and Father also."

"I told Leelee about Sayta and that you were expecting again. She said she would tell Chonee."

"Oh, thank you, Shalela. Chonee is our mother."

"Wait, Father, I am supposed to talk with her again in a few moments. She is going to get Chonee and Kokarashi. They will join with us this time. They wanted to see both of you. They also wanted to see Uncle Dec, but I told her he has his own camp and mate now, and that they are expecting a baby also."

Torena told Marcina that if she held hands with her and Cytar, she might be included in the link. Sayta was to hold Torena's other hand and Roly's hand, and he held Shalela's hand. Shalela would also hold Cytar's other hand, completing the circle.

Torena told them to go ahead and join hands. Perhaps they could reach Declon while they waited for Leelee.

A full hand's span of sun later, everyone was in a wonderful mood. Declon had, indeed, been reached and joined them when Leelee returned with Kokarashi and Chonee. Leelee had been very excited at meeting her father and finding out that she and Sayta were almost exactly the same age. Sayta was just as excited about being in a mind link with so many people, some of whom she had never met. She knew it was real because of her Uncle Dec.

Torena groaned then smiled at Sayta and asked her to go and get Faleenia and tell her the baby was coming. Marcina immediately ushered everyone out and instructed Roly to ask his mother to come and help. She then sent Shalela for Delphinia and her sister.

While everyone was waiting, the fishing fleet came in. Ramoar bathed and waited with the other Cheeville men. At every little sound from anywhere around the camp, Ramoar would jump up and look toward his lodge. He was not even able to tell of the day's fishing until Delac came by to see how Torena was doing.

It was well after dark when Torena had her son. She named him Sair.

Cytar and Marcina sat with Torena as she fed Sair. Marcina was still astounded at having participated in the mental linkage led by her daughter. She knew of only a few shamans powerful enough to do such a thing, and they had just communicated between two of the Scytan camps. The effort was so stressful for them that they would only attempt it under the direst situations.

Yet not only did it not seem to tire Shalela, she had done it a second time a short while later, taking the entire family along with her. Even more surprising to her was when Declon had been reached to also join in the link.

"Torena, how did my daughter connect with her sister so far away?"

"Our family has always had the ability to link with each other and with others."

"Yes, but, I have only known of a few with enough power to reach others, and it always drained them in the process."

"That is because they did not do it correctly. If you strain yourself to make a connection, it will drain you. What you have to do is to allow your mind to flow through the natural channels. That way, you are not drained."

Marcina sat looking at Torena wondering what she was talking about.

Torena laughed when Marcina's expression reflected her thoughts. "There are natural channels that one who is gifted can use, if they know how. My mother and Kokarashi, both very gifted, have taught Leelee. That, and her own ability, is why she was able to reach this far, though even I am amazed at the extent of her abilities."

Marcina sat spellbound as she listened to Torena. Cytar joined them in time to listen as well.

"Now, I can see that Shalela has the same level of abilities as Leelee does. I do not know of anyone who has ever achieved the reach that these two have. I could feel that Declon was as amazed as I. Mother and Kokarashi did not seem surprised, but they have been working with Leelee for a long time. However, I could feel their excitement at being able to see all of us."

"Mother, do I have that ability also?"

"Yes, Sayta, but your level is about the same as my own. Neither you nor I could reach my mother without help, although we could reach Declon if we had to. We do not use the ability all the time because, well, if I called to you every few minutes, you would soon get upset with me." Torena gave her daughter a big smile.

"Mother, why did Leelee not let us see her mother?"

Torena glanced at Marcina and laughed. "She did not want to cause Marcina to become uncomfortable."

Sayta turned to Marcina, "Why would you be uncomfortable if she had shown us her mother?"

It was Marcina's turn to break into laughter. "One day when you are older, you will understand the answer to that question."

"But if I am too young to know, how did Leelee know?"

"Maybe my mother or her own told her not to when she asked."

"Oh. Can I try to contact Uncle Dec now?" asked Sayta.

Cytar roared with laughter and hugged Sayta. "You listen about as well as Shalela does."

"Huh?"

Cytar kissed the girl's forehead and stood up. Holding out his hand to Marcina to assist her as she stood, he said, "It is time for us to go."

15

Trainees Return Home

The time finally arrived when Cytar and Clartan would be returning the trainees back to Chee Terrace. Marcina, Antana and their two children would go with them, along with the wolves: Dac, Moon, Midnight, Blackie, and Sorrowful Jo. Shalela had named her wolf Sorrowful Jo because of how she always looked so forlorn, when she was being trained to *stay* while she was still just a cub.

Cytar had wanted to leave sooner, but Marcina told him that they needed to wait until after Edda's baby was born. Eight days after Torena had Sair, Edda had her son, Narlo. Cytar led the party out the following morning.

Cytar decided to travel south along the coast trail and turn east at the river trail. Everyone began to make jokes and laugh as they passed the trail marker telling them to turn east onto the trail. At this point, the trail followed a wide meadow-like clearing that ran between the river on the south side of them and the woodlands to their north. More woodland could be seen on the opposite shore of the river, which grew all the way to the side of the mountains even farther south.

As the northern treeline began to swing in close to the river, the horses and wolves began to show indications of something lurking inside the trees. Cytar had everyone prepare for danger and by watching the animals, he was soon sure it was humans that waited.

As his bow barely came within range of the trees at that point, but not close enough for anyone within the trees to take a shot at them, Cytar called a halt and sat watching for the person or people to come out into the open.

Before long, it became evident to those concealed, as to why Cytar had stopped, and that he was not going to come any closer until he knew who was waiting. A group of twelve men rode just out of the trees and halted. Clartan grinned at Cytar and rode about a third of the way to meet them.

One man rode out about the same distance and called out to Clartan. His command of the Ghaunt language was poor but understandable. "You are trespassing on our land and now you must pay our toll."

"Just how much is your toll?"

"We may decide to let you leave, alive."

Clartan laughed and raised his left arm. Two arrows rapidly left Cytar's bow and both buried into a tree behind the most distant marauders. When the arrows hit, the marauders nearby gave startled yells and looked back at the tree, then called to the man talking with Clartan.

"Now, I will tell you what you will do," said Clartan in a stern voice. "You will drop your weapons and have your men do the same. There is no way you can get to me or the trees before I kill you, so do not even consider such an action. Now!"

The man looked back at the tree and then at Clartan, who now held a drawn arrow pointed right at him. The man was smart enough to realize the situation he was in. Neither he, nor any of his men, would have a chance against someone using such weapons as these. With a curse in Espanz, he threw down his spear, and then he turned and called for his men to also throw their spears down.

Clartan had the men dismount and gather away from the weapons before Cytar brought the rest of the party closer. The leader watched Cytar closely as he approached. Never had he seen a weapon that could strike from so far away. Maybe the stories he had heard about the people this side of the mountains had been true, after all. Nevertheless, if he could get just one of those weapons, he would be the top outlaw leader in all these lands.

One man had tried to make an escape, only to find himself suddenly surrounded by a pack of snarling wolves. He was completely perplexed, wondering how to go about fighting well-armed people and ferocious wolves at the same time. Clartan securely tied the hands of each of the marauders behind their backs with no more trouble, while the rest of his party sat on their horses with bows ready.

All the thieves' horses were tied together so none of them could try to make another escape attempt. At first, the marauders thought that rest stops might offer a chance to get away. However, the wolves quickly quelled such hopes, as the marauders saw that they sat watching them while licking their chops. It was chillingly obvious to them that the travelers wanted one of them to try to get away so the wolves could be fed.

At the entrance to the valley, a party of twelve Ghaunt hunters led by Gautier met the travelers at the trail marker showing the turnoff to Simonia's Camp. Word had reached the Ghaunt caves of the band of marauders, and they had come looking for the thugs. Cytar asked them to assist in getting the marauders to Simonia's Camp and asked if Gautier could send a messenger on ahead, to let Estavona know that they were coming. Two days later, Festuno and four other men met them and they rode back into camp together. Festuno told Cytar that Estavona had also sent a messenger to Declon about the marauders.

Declon and two of his men rode into camp shortly after midday two days later. Accompanying him were two traders that had just crossed over the mountain from Alba De Casa, and both were familiar with the atrocities committed by this particular band of marauders. They agreed to speak against the marauders, telling everything they knew or had heard. They would also take word back to the other side of the mountains concerning the fate of this band.

Estavona spoke with Cytar, Declon, and Gautier. Together, they decided that, as the four major areas affected by these marauders were now represented, they would hold a council and interview each rogue separately and judge them accordingly. However, it was agreed that Meg would also sit with them to represent Marcel's Camp.

Estavona spoke to the marauding group, introducing the five judges, and explaining which area each was representing. The two men from Alba De Casa were introduced next. All the marauders would now understand that this hearing would be a regional decision, not just a local one. Aside from those actively guarding the prisoners, everyone else in camp was to observe the proceedings and would be allowed to make statements, as long as they were respectful and not disruptive.

There were three very young people in the group, a female and two males, who were able to convince the judges that they wanted to go straight. It was decided that the female would go to Gautier's Cave, one man to Chee Terrace, and the other would stay with Estavona.

As for the rest of the marauders, they were each declared a continuing danger and hanged. The traders from over the mountain were both very impressed at how fairly the problem had been handled and had agreed with the judgments given.

The next morning, Gautier took his people home, along with some of the marauders' tunics, while Cytar decided that his party would continue to Chee Terrace with Declon. Especially so after Marcina reminded him that Torena had said not to come back without word of Bibi's and Aria's babies. The trainees that had stayed in Simonia's Camp would travel with Declon also.

The ride back to Chee Terrace was made in the beautiful, summer splendor, found only on the side of a lovely mountain. The weather was much nicer here than even at the Ghaunt caves, as close as they were to the north. Along this northern side of the mountains, it was warmer in the winter and cooler in the summer. South of these mountains, it was most unpleasant because it was so arid and very hot.

At the overnight camp, Shalela came and sat with her Uncle. Declon smiled at her and questioned her about Leelee and the mind link.

"I must tell you that I was most impressed when you contacted me to join in the link. Did you have trouble reaching me?"

"No, Auntie Torena did most of the link to you, she said she knew you better and how to reach you."

"Well, maybe so, but she was not leading us anymore once you made the contact with Leelee. I think my mother and Kokarashi were impressed by you also." Declon looked at Cytar and said, "You should be proud of that little Leelee, as well, baby brother, she is a precious doll."

Cytar seemed to glow. "Yes, she sure is something. That contact was the first I knew of her existence, but now I can hardly wait until I can give her a hug."

"Papa, I need more training. Leelee said everyone there has been giving her training since she was born, so she will be able to handle a terrible problem some day. She said there was even a woman, Lazna, who had come with her mate, Rafkar, from the Kay People to help her. Why would strangers come from so far away?"

"I met Lazna and Rafkar when I was on my journey west. She trained Dancer and Whirlwind, and I traded with her for them, and I taught some fighting moves to Rafkar and others in their camp. Now they are returning the favor. It is always good to make friends wherever you go, because you never know when you might need their help."

"Teach me something right now."

Cytar grinned at Declon and picked up a small stone. He held it in the crook of his left finger and shot it away with his right finger just as he had done when he showed the Dolnii how to do it. The small stone made a whirring sound until it hit a much larger stone and then whined away into the distance. He then helped her learn to shoot rocks that way while Declon showed Roly. The women from Marcel's Camp sat open-mouthed as they watched the rocks being shot, singing as they ricocheted off of other, targeted rocks.

"The first time I saw him do that, he killed a rabbit," reminisced Antana.

Soon, rocks were flying in every direction. Declon and Cytar sat back and had a hearty laugh at how everyone in camp was now sending off the little rocks, in hopes of learning a new way to kill rabbits.

Shalela started to giggle. "Now I have something that I can show Leelee the next time we link."

"Tell her Kokarashi was the one that taught us."

"Yes, Uncle Dec."

"Bedtime, children."

"Yes, Mother."

"Bibi, he is so good looking."

"Thank you, Marcina, I bet Torena's son is, also."

Bibi had named her son Abe, and Aria had a new daughter named Rose. Marcina and Antana continued to gush and fawn over the two new babies, along with Meg, Cadice, and Dina. Meg promised to tell Bibi's mother all about Abe and Declon.

The men quickly grew tired of how the women were carrying on and left to find some refreshment.

For the next five days, the trainees all met together and exchanged notes. Cytar and Declon supervised and helped them whenever they needed it.

At last, the team from Marcel's Camp was ready to go home. No longer could the young people be referred to as trainees, because each one was proficient in at least one type of combat and was qualified to teach it to others. Working as a team, the collective teachings of many people were being taken back to Marcel's camp for all to learn.

Romaleo and Bear were saying good-bye to Aimeri when Romaleo started to laugh. "I am so glad I gave up the life of a marauder. Within the next two summers, your camp will be as deadly to marauders as we are now. Who knows, what we have started here just might bring about the end of all marauding, everywhere.

Declon heard him and retorted, "Do not ever count on that because there will always be someone who thinks he is special and smarter than everyone else. It is usually because they are too dimwitted to know better, although, there will occasionally be some very smart ones that are just rotten inside, so watch out for those."

Everyone in the camp was gathered to see the guests off and said that it felt as if they were losing family. Romaleo was taking his hunters out anyway and invited the newly trained group to travel along until each party split to travel different paths.

Cytar and his party said their good-byes and rode out taking the old valley trail to travel directly home without going through Simonia's Camp.

When traveling for any long distance, experienced travelers knew to keep to existing trails. The trails were usually first made by wild animals and led around dead ends and areas that were harder to traverse. Animals knew where mountain passes were and where rivers could be forded, as well as how to avoid impassable rivers, ridges, and canyons.

For this reason, the traveling party was following the well-established traders' trail that ran east to west north of the mountains. As they came upon the trail marker that pointed north to the Ghaunt caves, they decided to visit Gautier's cave. Several of them had come close while chasing marauders, yet none of them had visited any of the Ghaunt caves, even though knowing many of the people there. This time, though, Gautier had given them directions to his cave and invited them to stop in on their way home.

Following the trail north, the woodlands became very dense before finally thinning out again. The travelers relied on the foodstuffs that they carried with them while passing through the densest portion of the woodlands, for there were few animals to be seen. The trail was wide enough that, by slowing or stopping occasionally, the horses were able to graze. Once the trees thinned out again, Cytar and Clartan were readily able to supply fresh meat, and though young, the children were becoming very good hunters and trackers as well.

After crossing a river that ran west, they were soon spotted, met, and escorted to Gautier's cave, located on another river that ran to the south. The cave was close to the river and many of the cave members could be seen at the river fishing, while others were processing the meat from that morning's hunt.

Gautier was delighted that they had accepted his invitation, and after explaining that there were a few other caves close by, sent messengers to them with word of the visitors and that there would be a big celebration feast in two days. As soon as the horses were unpacked and the party settled in, Marcina, Antana, and Clartan began helping with the meat, while Cytar took Shalela and Roly down to fish in the river.

Although the cave members were using nets and traps to get the fish, Cytar found a quiet spot where some brush hung out into the water and gave each of the children a string with a gorge tied to one end, which was used for catching smaller fish. The gorge was a short stick, pointed on both ends, with a string tied in the middle. It was small enough for the fish to swallow. When swallowed, it would turn sideways, and because of the pointed ends, it would stick into the fish and become lodged. The harder the fish would try to dislodge it, the deeper it would embed, and become even harder to dislodge. The string would be used to pull the fish out of the water.

Cytar showed the children how to catch insects and then how to put them onto the gorge to use as bait. As the children caught their small fish, Cytar would clean them. By the evening mealtime, there was a large mess of fish ready for cooking. Cytar looked at his hands and at the two filthy children. Grabbing his daughter, he threw her into the shallow water. Roly jumped in, laughing before Cytar could reach him. Cytar then jumped in and all three were bathing when Marcina came down to see where they were. Seeing them in the water, she decided to join them and made sure all three received a thorough scrubbing.

The next morning, several people of the surrounding caves had already arrived and Gautier had them all join that morning's hunt. He was proud of his hunters and the area where his camp hunted. Scouts had reported a herd of red deer and he wanted to get as many as he could for the feast.

Charz was hunt leader for Gautier and was in charge of the hunt. After talking with the scouts to determine the best place to wait for the deer, Charz led the hunters out and placed them where he wanted them. The scouts would get behind the deer herd and drive it toward the hunters.

Shalela waited in place with Marcina, and Roly was with Antana, when the herd passed by. To the surprise of the Ghaunts, the two children, both now well passed their sixth cycle of seasons, killed two yearling deer, each with a single arrow.

Charz and Gautier came by while everyone was field dressing the deer and were amazed that two such young children could each kill a deer while using such little bows. The two deer were close together, and Shalela looked at Roly and just rolled her eyes.

Roly was not so quiet. "My bow may be short enough for me to use easily, but that does not mean it is too weak for hunting. What good would it do me to have such a weak bow? I want to be ready to fight marauders, not sparrows."

Antana popped him on the back of his head with her fingertips, but Gautier just laughed. "I think you have a good point there, young man."

"They have both worked very hard to build enough strength to use these bows, although, the bows are not so strong that they would ruin their bodies using them," explained Marcina.

Roly handed the bow to Gautier with an arrow. "Sorry, but this arrow is as long as this bow will handle."

Gautier tried the bow and was surprised at how light the draw was and glanced at Marcina. He had expected it to be much stronger because of the deer that Roly had shot with it.

"You will notice that the two deer are very small and young, and also, we were very close when they were shot. The bows will also hit much harder than you would think possible, when up close, and could kill a man as easily as those deer. Do not miss the fact of where both deer were hit by the arrows. Many hunters do not worry enough about how accurate they are with their weapons when they hunt. All too often, they are under the impression that bigger spears, or any other weapon, means that even a hit in the tail should be enough to take down the animal, no matter how big and strong it is."

"Well, I have to agree with you on that point," agreed Charz. "That is one of my strongest gripes when training inexperienced hunters. Would you mind if I say a few words at the feast about that subject and bring these two children up with me as examples?"

"You will find that these two are very used to training others and stressing such points because they have been doing it all of their lives."

"Yes, just ask Marcel how I showed his council how to use a spear."

"Roly, do not be a showoff."

"Yes, mother."

"Now go and finish your deer."

"Oh, all right."

The two men chuckled as the two children went back to their two deer.

As the two got to their deer, Shalela stuck out her tongue at Roly and tore into her deer with a passion, all the while giggling very hard. Roly took his small ax and deftly split the chest cavity of his. It was a draw as, having finished cleaning the deer; they spun to each other and yelled, "Done."

All too soon, the travelers were back on the trail again. If leisurely traveling on horseback and camping out in the open, through country so devastatingly beautiful, it took your breath away; hunting and gathering meat, grains, and vegetables for meals, and depending on your horses and wolves to help spot such dangers as marauders, and extremely large predators, can be called uneventful, then the trip back to Gondal was uneventful.

Sandole held a great feast upon the return of the travelers. After eating, Sandole had them come forward and tell *all* of the latest news. Marcina, Antana, and Shalela told *all* about the new babies and how all the women were doing and what they wore. The stories covered the group's travels from Marcel's Camp, the marauding band that tried to hold them up, the trial with all the people involved, and the visit to Gautier's Cave.

It was a party atmosphere, which meant a very long night for the camp, because no one wanted to go to bed and miss any of the stories. When the travelers finished relating the adventures during their excursion, some of the others wanted to bring the travelers up to date on what had been happening around Gondal while they had been gone.

The first snow was still on the ground when Marcina found Shalela sitting on the bed platform in her sleeping alcove crying.

"Oh, Mother, Leelee was so scared about a vision she had about something bad happening here. She did not know what it would be, just that she saw me crying very hard because of it. She said I was older than now, but she did not know how much so."

"Maybe we should go and see your Aunt Torena."

"Yes, come on, and hurry."

Marcina led her daughter to the next lodge and called out to Torena, who immediately invited them inside.

"That is all she said she saw, Aunt Torena."

"Torena, why can she not see more detail?"

"Marcina, visions are usually more suggestive in nature. Most times, when one has a vision, they have to sit and meditate on it in an attempt to gain insight to the true meaning of the vision."

"Wonderful, you have a vision and decide bad things are in the future. There is no telling what the bad things are, or when they will happen, just that they will, maybe, happen sometime. Then you are left all upset and start to worry over the vision and what may happen someday, or maybe not at all. I do believe that if I were subjected to having visions, they would make me go insane."

"It is all right, Mother. Aunt Torena, Sayta, and I will handle the visions, so you do not have to."

"That is very comforting, sweetheart, now all I have to do is handle the information I get when one of you has a vision." Marcina shook her head and made a face at Shalela, causing both Shalela and Sayta to giggle.

Torena watched the two young girls for a few minutes before saying, "I think it is time for us to start the next phase of mental training. Normally, I would wait for two or three more summers, but with Leelee at the level she is, and the constant contact between the two of you, we need to do it now."

A few moon cycles later, Marcina contracted a high fever, and although she recovered, she miscarried her baby. A half-moon later, Antana also miscarried. For the next few moons, both women were very depressed.

Torena finally told Sayta and Shalela that they were going to do a mind link and reach out to remove the depression from the two women. Soon, everyone was back in high spirits, and totally unaware of what Torena and the two girls had done.

For the next three cycles of seasons, life was good. No attacks had been reported anywhere, Gondal had prospered and grown, and everyone was happy. Torena had even managed to get a few vegetables to grow in her garden, mostly the ones with larger seeds like beans, melons, and squash. She had found seed on some carrots, but they were so small that they were hard to collect. After much effort, she managed to get some of them to grow.

Shalela seemed driven to train in combat and sparred constantly with both Sayta and Roly so that all three were becoming exceptional in their abilities. Roly was now included in the mental training as well. Under the guidance of Torena, Cytar, and Leelee, all three youngsters soon reached a high level of proficiency, and Shalela actually managed to reach the same level as Leelee. Sayta became nearly as good. Roly was also very good, but also very inconsistent.

Here are some exciting scenes from the first chapter of book 3:

1

Tragedy

Sayta was now in her tenth summer while Shalela and Roly were in their ninth. Sair and Narlo had both just gone into their third summer.

Fields of wheat and barley were waving in the breeze, a large herd of very high-quality horses, all trained for various tasks, trotted and played in the two camp enclosures. Several enormously large wolves circled the herds with their human companions guarding the horses.

Stone-paved paths, with covered protection and hanging lamps to light the way at night, ran through every part of the camp. No longer did anyone have to slop through mud and water when it rained.

Gondal had become renowned as a fabulous trade and cultural center, drawing more people to move to Gondal every summer. The result of such growth was that many more lodges, workshops, and Merchant Centers had been built. Even the practice fields had to be expanded to accommodate the ever increasing numbers.

Pavilions were located in various areas of the camp, where craftsmen sat and worked on projects such as tools, leather treating and leather goods, fish and meat processing, and various other projects. There were carvers, wood shapers, and jewelry makers. Smelly projects, such as leather tanning and fish oil processing were located at the very edges of the camp, to help keep the smell down inside of the camp.

A steady stream of traders passed through Gondal from all across the land. A very large dock was built because some traders even came by way of the water, in larger boats built to handle open water sailing. Traders had found that, where sailing was an option, much more could be carried in the boats than overland with horses.

"Papa!" cried Shalela as she raced to her father.

"What is it Shalela?"

"Leelee has just yelled at me to look out because danger is coming."

"What were you doing at the time?"

"Training one of the wolf cubs, but there was no danger around me there."

"Go and tell your Aunt Torena to alert everyone here and I will go alert Sandole."

Cytar grabbed his bow and quiver of arrows, before running to where Sandole could always be found while overseeing his camp.

The camp was soon armed and ready, even though they did not know why. The horses and field workers were brought in for protection. Sandole called up to the guard in the lookout tower, which had been built the summer before, and asked if she could see anything.

At first, she saw nothing, but as she turned to scan the water, she yelled and pointed to the shore in the south. "A large boat is unloading a lot of people that look to be heavily armed. They are turning this way. Sandole, there are a *lot* of people in that boat!"

Sandole sent three more archers up into the tower. From that location, they could hit targets anywhere around the camp.

Part of the practice that each person went through was where to go during a raid and when the alarm was given, the positions were quickly filled. Though the numbers were not exact, there were about two hundred adults over the age of fourteen, two hundred children from four through fourteen and one hundred children three and younger.

The age separations were based on the fighting ability of each age group. Everyone was judged individually and placed within the group that fit the person's own abilities. If a full-grown man moved to Gondal who had no training at all, he could find himself placed under a table, or even hidden away with the smallest children, until he reached combat proficiency.

Standing platforms had been built above the roofs of the buildings, so that archers could be placed on them without damage to either the roof or the person. A few of the other fighters were also placed on the platforms to help protect the archers, in the event that any marauders gained the top of a roof or platform. In addition, the archers in the tower and on any one platform could give added support to any other platform if needed.

Cytar and Sabortay led the cavalry with each taking a unit of twenty. Although a unit was primarily armed as mounted cavalry, every member also carried a lance and knife, plus either a bone sword or horned club.

The close quarter fighters using lance, spear, sword or club, were dispersed among the tables in front of the Merchant Row. A few of the camp members even preferred such weapons as fishnets or axes.

Clartan and Antana led those using the bone swords while Marcina and Torena led those with flying spears. Sayta was up on a roof with her bow while Shalela and Roly were still in the group under tables, at least until the fighting started. Both of the little ones then crawled out and fought between Marcina and Torena.

Two hundred and seventy eight well-armed marauders, a few even armed with bows, swarmed over the camp and into a virtual hive of stinging weaponry. Although the invaders had been trained to fight, none of them had ever seen anyone fight like these Gondalians did. As a result, they were cut down like the grain in the fields.

Twenty-seven members from Gondal were killed and seventy-one wounded, while 251 of the marauders lay dead and twenty-seven wounded were captured. All but fourteen eventually died from their wounds.

As the marauders were being checked, someone yelled a warning, and all turned to see that the boat was sailing close, past their fishing docks. Even as they turned, an arrow hit Marcina in her arm. Cytar saw Nickotian standing on the boat and heard him yell, "I got you, bitch," before ducking out of sight before Cytar could get an arrow to him. The boat then turned into the wind and rapidly gained speed as it sailed away.

Do not miss book three:
Home Is the Back of a Horse
In the epic saga of

The Carved Knives

CPSIA information can be obtained
at www.ICGtesting.com
Printed in the USA
FFOW01n0646280916
28028FF